BEAR

THE WILL SLATER SERIES BOOK THREE

MATT ROGERS

Cover design by Onur Aksoy.
www.liongraphica.com

Join the Reader's Group and get a free 200-page book by Matt Rogers!

Sign up for a free copy of '**HARD IMPACT**'.
Meet Jason King — another member of Black Force, the shadowy organisation that Slater dedicated his career to.

Experience King's most dangerous mission — action-packed insanity in the heart of the Amazon Rainforest.

No spam guaranteed.

Just click here.

BOOKS BY MATT ROGERS

THE JASON KING SERIES

Isolated (Book 1)

Imprisoned (Book 2)

Reloaded (Book 3)

Betrayed (Book 4)

Corrupted (Book 5)

Hunted (Book 6)

THE JASON KING FILES

Cartel (Book 1)

Warrior (Book 2)

Savages (Book 3)

THE WILL SLATER SERIES

Wolf (Book 1)

Lion (Book 2)

Bear (Book 3)

BLACK FORCE SHORTS

The Victor (Book 1)

The Chimera (Book 2)

The Tribe (Book 3)

The Hidden (Book 4)

The Coast (Book 5)

The Storm (Book 6)

The Wicked (Book 7)

The King (Book 8)

The Joker (Book 9)

1

Khabarovsk
Russia

Of all the dark and traumatic memories Will Slater had collected over the course of his life, none sent more chills down his spine than the recollection of an all-out war in the depths of an abandoned gold mine on the Kamchatka Peninsula.

The Russian Far East hadn't broken him, but it came close. He couldn't remember a time he'd experienced such unbelievable panic — standing in that freezing elevator as it ascended from the bowels of the earth, his stomach tumbling over and over, dwelling on the ballistic missile bearing down from above.

He'd sworn off ever returning.

Some experiences stick with you, no matter how tough you are.

And now, here you are...

The city of Khabarovsk rested at the tip of a narrow stretch of the Russian Far East, flanked on either side by the vast landmass of China and the Sea of Japan. In fact, the ground underfoot rested only a couple of dozen miles from China's border.

If he wanted to, he could abandon everything he'd come to the region to accomplish and disappear into the wilderness — given his skill set and experience, it wouldn't be hard to cross the border undetected.

Then he could vanish.

Like the ghost he was.

It hadn't been easy to return to Russia.

Wryly, he noted the cinematic nature of his stance. He stood atop a precipice looking out over the Amur River, in a small unpopulated courtyard resting a few miles from the train he'd arrived on. The wind howled icily against his frame, battering the heavy overcoat draped over his shoulders. He hunched a little lower and adjusted the rusting payphone receiver in his hand, sliding a gloved finger around it to prevent it being blown away in the gale.

He shielded his mouth with the other hand to prevent interference.

'Not long to go,' he said. 'Almost the end of the line.'

'Okay.' The deep voice on the other end crackled in his ear.

'You don't seem interested.'

'I'm not.'

'I'm here to put my demons to rest.'

'Be careful. Russia's not a kind place.'

'I haven't spent much of my life in kind places. Consider what we discussed.'

'I'm not interested.'

'Sit on it. I'll be in touch.'

'I'd prefer you didn't call me again.'

'Sit on it,' Slater repeated. 'Take care.'

He slammed the receiver back into its cradle and set off through the dreary streets of Khabarovsk, retracing his footsteps back to the unimpressive railway station they'd arrived at only a couple of hours earlier. It hadn't been recommended that they venture far out into the city — Khabarovsk, he'd been told, had an unsurprising lack of tourist appeal, and there wasn't much at all to see or do.

But that suited Slater just find.

He didn't want to see or do anything.

He just wanted to think.

The freezing winter air chilled his bare scalp, and he caught a series of suspicious glances from locals surprised to see an African-American in these parts. It mirrored the same reactions he'd received on his initial trek to the Amur River.

The Trans-Siberian Railway attracted tourists of all kinds, but Slater assumed none of them chose to stray far from the railway station at this particular destination, which probably made the locals curious whenever a bold soul decided to venture out into the cold.

There was nothing remarkable about the city, but Slater wasn't paying attention to it in any case. He trudged through narrow streets, dwarfed on either side by nondescript blocks of grey residential apartments, as if giant indistinguishable slabs had been tossed into a 3D printer and distributed throughout the city at random. There was no particular order to things — not that Slater cared, anyway.

His mind was consumed by memories of the Russian Far East, and what he expected to find at the end of the line.

Truth was, he didn't know. He'd never received counselling or therapy of any kind — he figured if he'd achieved the feats of the past on his own, he could deal with them on his own, too.

Besides, he didn't want to talk about his problems.

Not to a soul.

He wasn't sure if he was legally allowed to anyway.

Any therapist up to the task of tackling the mind of Will Slater would need all sorts of high-level clearances to even make an attempt.

But, contrary to his natural tendencies, the journey across Russia had been entirely without incident. He'd lost count of the days — they'd all blurred together as he withdrew into himself over the course of the train trip, taking a much-needed break from life, not bothering to interact with any of the other passengers on board.

He would have all the time in the world to socialise later.

All things considered, he was a young man.

But it sure didn't feel that way.

Physically, he was as good as new. A solo career in black operations of the highest importance had all manner of downsides, but the one positive benefit it instilled was the self-discipline to simply do whatever one put their mind to.

That had never left.

Slater didn't think it ever would.

So, despite the fact that his mind had been through enough struggle and pain and unrest and stress for over a decade to mentally ruin a weaker man, he'd kept himself in the condition of an Olympic athlete. By this point it came naturally to him — he didn't see it as an option. He simply pushed his body to its limits in any way he could — powerlifting, running, periodic visits to mixed martial arts gyms around the world.

His exterior was unblemished. Good genetics must have favoured his bone structure, because all the injuries he'd sustained over his career had never resulted in permanent disability. He'd always healed, always returned to full health given enough time.

The inside of him was what he'd come to Russia to tackle...

He made it back to the railway station with eight minutes to spare, barely paying any attention to his drab surroundings. He shuffled through a cold dull terminal and scanned the same ticket he'd used all the way along the Trans-Siberian Railway. Then it was back on board the luxury private train he'd spent the past week of his life on.

He stepped into the familiar air-conditioned communal passenger carriage he'd chosen as his favourite only a few short hours into the trip, and slotted straight back into the same four seat booth on the left-hand side of the carriage. Right now the view was dismal. The giant spotless windows faced a railway platform that looked like its caretakers had abandoned it a decade ago.

Sharp contrast to where you're sitting, he thought.

But that was another aspect of Slater's new life — he'd come into the possession of hundreds of millions of dollars a few months earlier. An explosive stint in Macau had changed his life in several ways, namely the digits in his bank account and the revelation that he was no longer being hunted by the United States government. The new information relaxed him somewhat, but he'd never been checking over his shoulder in the first place.

Even when he was being hunted, he'd never expected them to catch him.

And he'd already been rich. A successful career at the highest level of secret military operations paid beyond well, so money had never been a significant factor in his life. He'd always had enough of it to do anything he wanted.

So really, nothing had changed.

Back to the road.

Back to solitude.

Back to observing the world.

Then, as the train pulled away from Khabarovsk's railway station and set off on the first steps of its final leg to the port city of Vladivostok, Slater began paying attention to the passengers around him, including a couple of fresh faces he hadn't seen before.

And suddenly everything changed.

2

Slater had spent most of his life in situations that people preferred to avoid, which meant he knew exactly how to pick up on the subtle cues that meant someone was scared for their life.

Across the aisle, seated in the other four-person booth, was a party of three men. Slater wouldn't have paid them any attention had he not made brief eye contact with the guy furthest away from him, a guy he'd never seen before, which drew his attention for the couple of seconds necessary to deduce that all was not well.

The guy was dressed in an expensive business suit tailored perfectly to his frame — nothing out of the ordinary on this train. Slater's deluxe suite for the journey across Russia had cost him the equivalent of twenty thousand U.S. dollars to acquire, so the fact that the man was obviously wealthy did little to surprise him.

But it was hard not to linger on the sight of the blood draining from the man's cheeks. His eyes were wide and unblinking. He was doing everything in his power not to appear terrified — and Slater had to admit the man was a good actor. If he'd made eye contact for a second less he might have shrugged it off as nothing and turned his gaze back to the city of Khabarovsk passing them by.

But he realised the underlying tension at play, and from that point onward everything became clear.

The other two men in the booth — seated opposite each other on the aisle seats — were dressed in identical attire and sported identical demeanours. They wore cheap suits, not tailored, workmanlike and utilitarian. They both sported pronounced jawlines and the same shaved heads. It was as if they were deliberately trying to look like twins.

Slater recognised the cruelness in their faces, even though they were doing nothing but sitting rigid in their seats. He didn't spend long glancing across at the party, but a few seconds was all it took to understand what was going on.

The man in the expensive suit was there against his will.

As soon as the dynamic became apparent, Slater honed in on the finer details. There were a couple of wet spots dotted along the guy's collar, which ordinarily he would have chalked up as nothing but now recognised as nervous perspiration. The guy was trying a little too hard to seem nonchalant. Anyone who studied him for any significant amount of time would see the rigidity of his posture before long.

The men in the cheap suits were hired muscle, positioned across from each other to form an imperceptible barricade. They were there to ensure the guy in the expensive suit didn't try anything funny, like making a break for it or calling for help. The fact that Slater hadn't seen them before raised questions — had these men been on the train since Moscow, or were they fresh arrivals?

Slater hadn't bothered to check whether the train

accepted new passengers or not. He'd assumed the stopovers at various cities and towns were simple pit stops.

Now that he thought about it, he seemed to recall people showing up who hadn't been there before. He hadn't paid attention to it at the time. Usually his situational awareness was unparalleled, but he'd allowed himself to slip on the luxury train.

He'd considered it a safe haven.

He shouldn't have.

The guy in the expensive suit glanced across the aisle again, and Slater made eye contact with him for a second time.

As soon as the man recognised Slater's glare he averted his gaze, staring sheepishly at his feet.

So you don't want to be helped, either, Slater thought.

Slater couldn't put it together. Not yet. In all likelihood the man in the expensive suit was being forced along this journey — whether a loved one was being held hostage or his finances were at risk, it didn't make a difference.

Slater began to sort through a wide range of reasons, compiling a mental list, but then a fresh sight tore his attention away from everything he'd just seen.

He caught a glimpse of another passenger further along the carriage. The man had a booth all to himself. He wore dirty tan khakis and an oversized blue jumper that hung strangely over his frame. He was skinny, but Slater could tell from the veins and knots in his hands that there was strength in his physique. He was wiry, but athletic. His hair was jet black, but despite the fact it had lost none of its colour it was receding all the same, creeping back across his scalp to inevitable doom. He looked to be in his forties.

And he was sweating like hell.

Slater couldn't believe what he was seeing. The new guy

was just as jumpy as the suit-clad man, but positioned a couple of booths down the carriage. Slater had only managed the briefest of glances — to get a proper look, he would need to lean into the aisle and reveal the fact that he was interested.

Slater had seen none of the four suspicious men before, which set off a long list of possibilities in his mind.

Now firing on all cylinders, he rattled through some reasons.

They could all be connected, having spent most of the last seven days holed up in their private cabins to prevent suspicion. Now that the luxury train was on the last leg of its journey, they might have decided to take a risk and spend some time in one of the shared commuter carriages. But the positioning was odd. Slater would have put one of the hired brutes in each of the booths, to prevent anyone causing a scene.

So maybe this new guy had nothing to do with the other three.

Slater figured there was no point shying away from what could be a potentially disastrous situation, so he leant across the empty aisle seat beside him, as nonchalant as possible. All the warning signs fired away, hinting that all was not as it seemed.

He stared straight into the eyes of the man with the receding hairline, and the guy visibly reacted, shrinking away from the sudden scrutiny, wiping a bead of sweat from the side of his forehead despite the chill in the air.

Then the man shot to his feet and hustled for the other end of the carriage, moving with enough restraint to minimise attention, but hurrying all the same.

Slater ignored the three men across the aisle, and slid quietly out of his seat to follow.

3

Positioned at one end of the train carriage, tucked away in the furthest corner, shielded from prying eyes, Misha Bessonov noticed the two men hurry past him.

He reached for the MP-443 Grach pistol in the leather holster at his waist.

He'd been working for the Federal Security Service of the Russian Federation for the last five years, each of which he had spent as a highly devoted and respected employee. Most of his time had been spent in the field, adapting the old-school methods of the Russian military to the new world. There had been plenty of opportunities to demonstrate his counter-terrorism skills over the years, one of which was presenting themselves right now.

Because there was some shady shit going down in Vladivostok.

And this train seemed to be a hotspot for undesirables.

He'd been keeping tabs on Viktor Gribkov for the seven days he'd spent on the train. According to all the intelligence files he'd been able to gather, the man was forty-three years old and had been working at a shipbuilding plant in Vladivostok for the better part of three years now.

What couldn't be explained were his reasons for fleeing to Moscow two weeks earlier, abandoning his position in the plant with enough haste to draw attention. The Federal Security Service had noticed the ruckus Viktor had stirred, and instructed Bessonov to keep tabs on the man in Moscow to see what he did next.

Then it had all changed.

Almost as quickly as he'd hurried away from the shipbuilding plant, Viktor suddenly felt the need to return. He'd booked a last minute ticket on board this private train and made the journey across the Trans-Siberian Railway, heading straight back as if nothing had happened at all.

But Bessonov had been silently observing the port worker for the entire duration of the trip — civilians weren't very good at noticing surveillance — and had concluded that the man was terrified for his life.

And then there was the matter of the businessman and the two thugs...

Bessonov had only noticed that party a couple of days earlier, but it hadn't been his main priority. His attention was consumed by Viktor, and the other three could wait, but Bessonov certainly suspected they were up to something.

What is it about Vladivostok that attracts scum?

And now, a whole new realm of possibilities had opened up, because of the African-American man trailing a couple of feet behind Viktor with intent in his stride.

Who the hell is this new guy?

Bessonov didn't know. But, judging by the tension crackling in the air, confrontation was about to occur. And he couldn't sit back and let that take place without making a move himself. He needed more detail. It had been a painful seven days of quietly observing patterns in behaviour, wondering just what the hell Viktor's intentions were and speculating as to whether the train was about to go up in a raging fireball.

For all Bessonov knew, Viktor might be conspiring with the black man to set off a bomb. For the entire duration of the journey Viktor's choice of attire had been odd — everything was one size too large, and none of it fit right, or looked appealing in any way.

What's he hiding?

Bessonov wasn't about to wait to find out.

For all he knew, he might be the only thing resting between the innocent passengers and a thunderous fireball.

He checked briefly down the aisle as the two men hurried straight past him and ducked into the narrow corridor at the end of the carriage, but no-one was watching.

Good.

Bessonov thumbed the safety off the Grach pistol and waited for the proper opportunity to shuffle after the two-man crew.

He would get answers.

Whatever it took.

4

The man with the receding hairline didn't realise Slater was on his tail until it was far too late.

The guy slipped into a corridor connecting the carriage with the booths to the dining car. Slater was familiar with the next car — he had spent much of the past week gorging on potatoes and dumplings and all manner of traditional Russian cuisine.

He didn't like to admit he had a drinking problem, but he hadn't been able to resist the vodka and cognac on offer. Today, though, he was sober.

Which helped with what came next.

A quick look over the man's shoulder revealed the dining car packed with passengers, all of them hunched over heaped plates of food from the buffet. It was the peak of the lunch hour, and if they made it through to the dining car Slater would have no chance of effectively confronting the guy. It had to be here, in this narrow, dimly lit passageway, the entire thing rattling and shaking as the tracks underneath it shuddered.

They were leaving Khabarovsk's outer limits.

Entering the desolate no man's land of rural Siberia.

Now.

Slater closed the gap — only a few feet by this point — and surged into range. The man noticed, jolting on the spot as he sensed movement only a few inches behind him. He began to twist on the spot, a reactionary impulse move, and Slater wrapped one hand around his thick tuft of dark hair and yanked hard to the left.

Nerve endings fired atop the guy's scalp and he naturally stumbled in the direction Slater threw him.

Straight through one of the restroom doors.

They burst into the bathroom, Slater following straight after the man. The space they entered was tight and claustrophobic, even more so than the adjacent corridor. It was a space designed for one person. He reached back with one of his winter boots and thundered the door closed behind him. The door rattled in its frame, but that was the only noise the altercation caused.

Otherwise, no-one made a sound.

Slater didn't think a slamming door would draw much attention.

He had a few minutes.

The guy had started sweating even harder, his eyes bulging in his sockets, his lips flapping. Slater sensed something palpable in the air — some kind of horrified reaction to the confrontation. This man hadn't wanted to be disturbed. He had certainly been planning something.

The hairs on the back of Slater's neck rose, and he bundled the guy into the opposite wall, crushing an elbow against the soft tissue of his throat to cause as much discomfort as possible.

He needed the guy in a panicked state.

He needed answers.

'You speak English?' he hissed.

When a couple of seconds elapsed without a response, Slater squashed his elbow tighter into the guy's neck.

The man spluttered and wheezed and went red.

'English?' Slater said again.

'Not much,' the guy grunted.

'But some?'

'Yes. Some.'

'Who are you?'

'What?'

'What's your name?'

'Viktor.'

'If I let you go, will you answer my questions?'

'Yes. Yes. Please ... keep quiet.'

Slater hesitated — it was an odd request. He'd assumed Viktor would scream for help at the first available opportunity, but instead the guy seemed terrified of that exact situation.

He didn't want to be discovered.

Slater let go of Viktor's collar and backed off a step. He didn't want to come off as entirely clueless — which he was — because it would make Viktor clam up. He wanted details, but he wasn't quite sure how to get them. He made up his mind in the space of a half-second, chose an avenue of approach, and got to work.

'Who's after you?'

'I'm sorry?' Viktor said.

'Don't play dumb. Your English is fine. You can understand me. Why are you hiding?'

'Who are you?' Viktor said.

'I might be able to help.'

'No. You cannot help.'

'How do you know?'

'You are not Russian. You are a foreigner. What is your business here? This is not your world.'

'Who's after you?' Slater repeated.

'No-one.'

'Don't lie to me.'

'Why? You know nothing. You want me to give you information. Why do you want this? You get involved with this and you get killed.'

'Maybe.'

'You should not be confident.'

'I get involved with things for a living. I haven't been killed yet.'

'Not like this. Leave.'

'What if I don't want to?'

'I am not going to help you.'

'I never asked you to.'

'So what do you want from me?'

'Information.'

'I already told you. Do not get involved. How do you not understand this?'

Viktor's eyes lit up with intensity, piercing into Slater for the first time. Since stumbling into the narrow bathroom the man had maintained a steady drooping gaze, refusing to make eye contact. But now he lifted his head and stared directly at Slater, as if urging him to follow his requests.

Slater couldn't remember the last time he'd been pressured into doing anything.

He stood his ground.

'The three men in the booth,' Slater said. 'You know them?'

'What?'

'The three guys in suits. One of them looks nervous, like

he's being guarded, or held against his will. What do you know about that?'

Viktor continued staring, flabbergasted. 'You need to mind your own business, my friend.'

'So you do know—'

Viktor held up a hand. 'I know nothing. I don't know what you are talking about. But you need to mind your own business all the same. What are you expecting?'

'Huh?'

'You push me in here and want answers. You want to know about three men in suits. Why do you want to know all this?'

'I'm curious.'

'Russia is not kind to people who are curious.'

'You know that from experience?'

'Sort of.'

'You going to Vladivostok?'

Viktor waved a hand in a broad sweeping gesture, addressing their surroundings. 'Only place to go on this train.'

'You got business there?'

'I am not telling you anything.'

'Is anyone on this train in danger?'

'No.'

Slater said nothing, shooting daggers across the tight space. 'You'd better be telling the truth.'

'I am the only one in danger on this train. And it won't happen here. It will happen in Vladivostok.'

Something shifted in the air, and Slater sensed a breakthrough. He'd positioned himself between Viktor and the door, and with thirty pounds more muscle and three times the strength the man hadn't even attempted to make a break for it. Now he was cracking under pressure, beginning to leak details...

But Slater didn't get to finish his line of enquiry, because the door to the bathroom thundered inward and hit him in the small of his back, taking him entirely by surprise and sending him stumbling forward — not very far, but enough to create the slightest gap for a body to force their way in.

The next second, someone charged straight into the room, and Slater's brain went haywire as he picked up the glint of gunmetal in his peripheral vision.

5

Shut down the threat.

Slater didn't even take the time to get a glimpse of who his attacker was. With three men now crammed into such a tiny space, there was little room to breathe, let alone move. He only saw the gun, and suddenly cortisol flooded his senses, activating an instinctive reaction to the newcomer.

He got his feet under him and powered straight back across the space as soon as the new arrival — a man roughly the same height as him — forced his way into the room through the gap in the doorway. Their frames collided, both of them moving at an equal speed in the confined space, but Slater had built up his fast-twitch muscle fibres over a decade of combat.

He seized the upper hand.

He won the collision.

The tide shifted, and the newcomer fell straight back into the half-open door, slamming it closed. Slater breathed a sigh of relief — the fight would be muffled from the rest of the passengers in the carriage, sitting peacefully just a dozen feet from their location. He bundled the new guy into the door and made a lunge for the weapon, bringing his forearm down in a clubbing motion across the guy's wrist.

The gun was an MP-443 Grach — Slater hadn't made out any of the features of the guy who was attacking him, but a single glance in the direction of the sidearm confirmed its make. He battered down on the man's wrist and the guy let out a grunt of frustration.

But he held tight.

Slater smashed his right shoulder into the guy's chest, hurling him back against the door again. It rattled on its hinges, and he swung at the gun with his bare knuckles, throwing caution to the wind.

Fuck it.

Break your hand if necessary.

Just strip him of that weapon.

His punch snapped one of the guy's fingers — the bone break made an audible noise in the confined space. The man grunted again, but kept a vice-like hold on the MP-443.

Shit.

Now the guy had a chance to launch some offence — Slater had spent vital seconds fixated on the gun, leaving himself exposed to a punch. He heard the bare knuckles whistling through the air toward the side of his head and recoiled in horror, recognising the incoming strike as accurate enough to shut his lights out. It was blindingly fast, too — another half-second of hesitation and he would have caught the sweeping left hook in the soft tissue above his ear.

But his reflexes pulled through at the right moment, and the punch grazed off the side of his head, firing nerve endings across his temple but causing no significant neurological damage.

Then the gun began an upward trajectory toward Slater's unprotected face.

Go.

Slater hadn't realised it, but he'd been holding back. In the chaos and confusion he hadn't been able to discern any of the man's features — the guy could be anyone. He didn't want to put all his power into the brawl in case he did something he would regret. But the sight of the Grach's barrel moving directly toward his face triggered the primal portion of his brain, recognising the confrontation as potentially fatal.

As soon as his mind said *Go,* Slater went.

He clenched his teeth and his face turned to stone as he battered the gun away as effortlessly as swatting away a fly. His forearm broke a couple more of the guy's fingers and the newcomer released his grip on the weapon, but Slater hadn't noticed he'd disarmed the man until he'd thrown a slicing uppercut like a piston, detonating it off the soft tissue of the guy's throat. He felt muscle tear under the force of his maximum effort and the newcomer collapsed, sliding down the wooden door and slumping into a crumpled heap on the tiled floor.

All went still.

Slater grimaced as silence fell over the tiny room. The Grach came to rest in one corner of the bathroom, spinning slowly on its side. The man he'd struck down was unconscious — the bad kind of unconscious. Slater could visibly see his throat closing in as he struggled to breathe, and he stifled a curse as he realised the damage was irreversible.

Ten seconds later, the guy was dead.

His airways had collapsed.

'Jesus Christ,' Slater muttered.

He replayed the entire ordeal in his mind, analysing

each impact and noise to guess whether anyone in either of the two nearby carriages had heard.

Probably not, he concluded.

Not a single word had been uttered, and although the incident had sent Slater's brain into an adrenalin-spiked whirlwind, he realised all hope hadn't been lost yet. All things considered, the brawl had unfolded relatively quietly. All he had to do was stay low in the bathroom and hope no-one came rushing in after the newcomer.

Finally, Slater had the chance to get a proper look at the man.

The guy was dressed in regular black suit pants and a plain white shirt, with a puffy windbreaker draped over his frame. The jacket hadn't been zipped up and now it spilled open on either side, revealing a small identification card poking out of the lip of the inside pocket. His guts twisting, Slater bent down and plucked the card free.

He recognised neither the symbol on the upper left hand corner nor the Russian characters running in lines across the face of the card.

He turned and handed the card to Viktor, who had pressed himself as far back across the narrow room as he could. The man's face had turned white as a sheet. It took him a few moments to work up the common sense to take the card and scrutinise it.

'He's fucking dead,' Viktor muttered.

'I know that. I did it.'

'You didn't have to kill him.'

'Are you blind? He was a second away from blowing my brains across the room. What do you think he would have done to you?'

Viktor twirled the identification card in his fingers, but his brain didn't seem to connect the dots. He stared down at the writing with a vacant expression, his eyes glazed over.

'Viktor,' Slater said.

He knew the news would not be good — only a certain subsection of society carried identification cards in the first place — but the revelation was suitably grim regardless.

Viktor looked up, swallowing hard. 'He's with the Federal Security Service.'

'Counter-terrorism?'

'Yes.'

Slater closed his eyes momentarily, composing himself. For once, he might have bitten off more than he could chew.

'Viktor, you'd better start telling me what you're involved in,' he said. 'Because that guy sure as hell wasn't here for me.'

6

Ten minutes had elapsed since the vicious, no-holds-barred fight to the death, and no-one had materialised on the other side of the door to ask what the hell was going on in the bathroom.

So far, their cover hadn't been blown.

Slater and Viktor were just ordinary guys to the rest of the carriages.

So far...

None of the colour had returned to Viktor's face. It seemed a human life taken in such close proximity had turned him into a nervous, bumbling wreck. Slater couldn't help wondering if there simply had been a giant misunderstanding.

'I swear,' Viktor said, his eyes wide. 'I do not know those other three.'

'There's some shady shit going on here.'

'I know. But I cannot tell you anything. If I do, I die.'

'I might kill you myself.'

'No,' Viktor said, shaking and sweating but holding his

nerve. 'If you were going to do that you would have done it already. You are a good man.'

'I just killed a law enforcement officer.'

'Like you said. He pull gun.'

It seemed that as the tension increased in the air, Viktor's English became more broken.

'You don't know anything about me,' Slater said. 'You sure you want to test your luck?'

'You going to beat it out of me? You not that type of guy.'

'Like I said ... you don't know.'

'You are still talking. You are not hurting me. That is the answer.'

Slater bowed his head. 'Look, if I'm being honest I don't want to make you panic any more than you already are. You look like you're losing your mind. I just want to help.'

'That is my problem to deal with.'

'I'm making it mine.'

'I told you not to.'

'Well, now there's blood on my hands. That guy—' Slater pointed back at the corpse, '—was making it his problem too. Everyone in that goddamn carriage seems like a nervous wreck and I want to know why.'

Viktor visibly shuddered as his eyes drifted to the dead man. Slater paused, momentarily confused, before realising that he'd been around death for so much of his life that it had become a relatively normal thing to witness. To the common folk, the previous ten minutes would have been a life-changing experience.

'Sorry,' he said. 'Try not to focus on him.'

'It is hard when you point right at him.'

'Forget he's there.'

'Okay.'

Viktor gulped back a ball of apprehension.

Slater sighed. 'Who are the three men in the carriage?'

'We went over this already.'

'I'm asking you again. Because it's too much of a coincidence that one of them seems just as nervous as you.'

'I am telling you the truth. Look into my eyes. I do not know them. But maybe they have something to do with my business in Vladivostok.'

'Viktor,' Slater hissed. 'Tell me. What the hell is going on in Vladivostok? What's your business there?'

'Maybe you know. I cannot tell you.'

'What do you mean I know?'

'You might be connected. Why are you headed to Vladivostok?'

'I've been on this train for a week. I'm following it to the end of the line.'

'Why?'

'No particular reason.'

'This is also a coincidence,' Viktor mused.

And how many coincidences could there possibly be?

Slater remembered his last two adventures — if you could call them that. Yemen, followed swiftly by the carnage in Macau. That wasn't even taking into account the decade of madness preceding those isolated incidents — they, however, were more notable because of their randomness.

His career had involved being surgically implanted into the toughest war zones on the planet, sent to wreak havoc as a one-man wrecking ball.

But he'd got out of the game.

And still the madness had followed, hanging over him like a cloud.

He remembered his conversations with a fellow operative, the solo freight train named Jason King. His comrade hadn't been able to escape the carnage either. It attracted both of them like flies to shit — it was about time Slater accepted that. He didn't know whether he was deliberately seeking out chaos, or whether some subliminal node in his brain was forcing him into the fray without him realising.

But his life had devolved into a seemingly endless list of coincidences, each of which culminated in devastation.

Slater looked back at the dead Federal Security Service officer at his feet and couldn't help but realise that the confrontation was another spark, another moment of ignition that no doubt would spiral into something uncontrollable.

'Viktor,' he said slowly. 'You might not understand what I mean by this, but I can't avoid getting involved now. I can't walk away from this, now that I've killed this man. It's not who I am — it'd be going against my DNA. I'm going to see this through to the end. Now, for God's sakes, tell me what you're involved in.'

'I am going back to Vladivostok to die,' Viktor said.

7

The words hung in the air, poignant enough for Slater to take a moment to pause and consider their weight. Viktor wasn't joking — Slater could see the raw fear in his eyes, the acceptance that he would soon meet his maker. That's why he had been scared out of his mind. He was grappling with the notion that he wouldn't be on this earth for much longer.

And it seemed inevitable.

Slater understood, finally.

There was no-one accompanying Viktor. He was acting on his own accord, complying with whoever had ordered him to Vladivostok.

Slater imagined there was an understanding in play.

The knowledge that if Viktor didn't do as instructed he would end up in unimaginable pain.

Or his family would die.

Slater had years of experience with those kinds of situations. It was unfathomable what someone would do to protect their loved ones.

'What do you need to do in Vladivostok?' Slater said.

'Nothing.'

'Just die?'

'I will return to my place of employment.'

Slater's eyes widened. 'You're going *back*? You're originally from the city?'

'Yes. I live there.'

'You're being awfully uncooperative, Viktor.'

'There is only so much I can tell you.'

'Why?'

'Because you seem like the kind of man to go and crawl around places you are not welcome. And once I am dead ... if it comes out that I told you what I am involved in ... I can only imagine the consequences.'

'You have a family?'

'Yes.'

'Have they been promised safety if you return?'

'Yes.'

'I see.'

'So, you see, I cannot tell you. Because if you go investigate — which I know you will — and you fail, my wife and children will be tortured and executed.'

'I never fail.'

'You will fail,' Viktor said, with the kind of unbridled certainty that Slater knew didn't come around often.

The man was absolutely sure.

'You think those three guys I'm fixated on have something to do with it?'

'Maybe. Not my business.'

'You don't care, do you?'

Viktor sighed. 'It is hard to care about anything when you know you are going to die.'

'Why did you run?'

Viktor said nothing.

'How did they get in touch with you? To tell you to come back.'

Viktor said nothing.

'Where are your wife and children?'

Viktor said nothing.

Slater grimaced — he sensed that he'd reached the end of the line. Adrenalin and panic had kept Viktor talking but now the man was regaining common sense, clamming up as he realised he'd already said too much.

'What stops me following you when we arrive in Vladivostok?' Slater said finally.

'If you do that, then you are a cruel man,' Viktor said. 'You will be sentencing my family to death.'

'You seem to think failure is inevitable.'

'You cannot stop what is happening.'

'You sure about that?'

'Yes.'

Slater sighed. 'It's twelve hours from Khabarovsk to Vladivostok. You really don't think I could come up with something if you work with me? I want to help you.'

'Thank you for the offer, but I must decline.'

'You saw what I just did. I can do it to the men holding your balls in a vice.'

'No, you cannot.'

'What if I told you who I really am?' Slater said. 'Would you work with me then? You don't know anything about me.'

'I do not wish to know anything about you. Please, sir, if you want to help me ... leave me be. I have accepted my fate. Do not make it worse for me and my family.'

Slater didn't respond for what felt like an eternity. He needed time to think, time to process what had unfolded — less than half an hour ago he'd been without a worry in the world, and now he was embroiled in a situation he knew nothing about, fighting to worm an explanation out of a man who wanted nothing to do with him.

Perhaps Viktor was right.

Perhaps it wasn't his place to decide to get involved.

But he was involved. He sensed the presence of the dead man behind him and felt a stab of guilt, despite the fact that the officer had pulled a gun on him with every intention of using it.

Counter-terrorism.

What the hell are you up to, Viktor?

But the man was horrified around death, which meant this wasn't his fault. He had no motivation to bring Slater on board — he was resigned to his fate.

Slater made up his mind, and begrudgingly shrugged his shoulders.

'Fine,' he said. 'I'll respect your wishes. I hope you're content with your decision.'

'I am.'

'Then goodbye, Viktor.'

'What are you going to do with...?'

'The dead guy? No point pretending he's not there.'

'You kill so ... casually.'

'I didn't intend to kill him.'

'You hit him so hard...'

'That's how I hit people. Sometimes I can't restrain myself if there's a Grach heading for my face.'

'A what?'

'It's a type of—' Slater said, then stopped in his tracks. 'You know what — forget it. This isn't my problem. You said as much yourself.'

'You never told me what you're going to do with him.'

'Leave him in here.'

'You sure that's a good idea?'

'I'll handle it. Go back to your seat, Viktor. And if your decision changes, you've got eleven hours to approach me. I'll be in the same seat. If you want to talk, don't be shy. I'm not going to force you into anything.'

'Thank you,' Viktor said, 'but I made my decision long ago.'

'I can see that.'

Slater stepped aside — it took every ounce of effort to do so. He turned his eyes away from Viktor as the man shuffled past, stepping tentatively over the corpse on his way out. Viktor creaked the door open a crack and checked the coast was clear before slipping out into the corridor. He shut it quietly behind him.

Slater was left alone with a dead Federal Security Service officer, and his thoughts.

You're letting a man die.

A man who might not deserve it.

He shook the thought off and set to work hiding the body as best he could.

8

The plaster ceiling tiles didn't budge, no matter how much effort Slater put into shifting them. After retrieving the MP-443 Grach and shoving it into his waistband, he balanced on the cistern for as long as he deemed prudent, then abandoned his efforts and simply stuffed the body into one corner of the room.

There was nowhere to hide it, so he exited the bathroom just a couple of minutes after Viktor and ducked into a neighbouring supply closet, making sure none of the train's staff caught him in the act. He found a yellow *caution* sign gathering dust on an otherwise empty metal shelf and peeled the sticky backing off as he crossed back to the bathroom door. He slapped the sticker on the wood and shuffled back to his seat, accepting that it was unlikely to prevent anyone checking but hoping it would suffice to get him through the next eleven hours.

Even if the corpse was discovered, the staff wouldn't want mass panic to break out. They would keep it contained until they arrived at Vladivostok. If they opted to keep all the passengers on the train until the police arrived, Slater would force his way out.

Until then...

He took up the same position in the empty booth, staring out at the undulating landscape. The terrain varied from craggy rock formations towering over everything in sight to endless fields of snow disappearing into the horizon. Slater let his mind go blank, aware that if he dwelled on what had occurred he would find it hard to resist getting involved.

Because that's what you do for a living.

You get involved.

The sheer isolation of the region captured his attention for several hours. He sensed Viktor's presence across the carriage but positioned himself in the window seat, cutting off his view of the rest of the passengers. Apart from the three men opposite. They, however, seemed to pay him no attention at all. He guessed they had their own problems to dwell on. The one in the expensive suit certainly did — every time Slater threw a glance in that direction the guy was still nervously sweating.

Whatever the hell was going down in Vladivostok, he couldn't imagine a scenario where he wouldn't stumble across it in due course. It seemed to be a combination of fate and sheer dumb luck, but he couldn't go for months without running into something horrific.

In Yemen he had thwarted plans to release a weaponised strain of the Marburg virus across the streets of London, and in Macau he had intervened in the kidnapping of a nine-year-old girl embroiled in a dark world he would much rather forget.

Shien.

He wondered where she was now.

Thinking of the dead man in the bathroom, he realised he had made the right call by leaving Shien in the hands of an old friend. He couldn't stay with her. He couldn't stay with anyone, or form an attachment to them.

He attracted disaster.

But, on the other hand, he fixed problems, too.

So maybe he was destined to be alone until his body broke down and he became useless to the crusade of vigilante justice he'd been taking part in ever since he left the ranks of the United States government.

Hours passed, but it felt like minutes. Slater had been through so much over the course of his life, and the times where he could sink into the depths of his own mind flew past. His life had been one of pain and suffering and constant discomfort, but in these moments where he could analyse what he'd done he found himself realising that he wouldn't trade his experiences for anything else. He thought of the havoc he'd prevented, both during his time in the service of the government and outside of it.

That led him down a tough mental path.

He couldn't sit back and let Viktor die.

The man was terrified, and he wasn't thinking straight. He didn't know who Slater was. He had accepted his death, but he didn't need to. There was hope. He simply couldn't see it.

Slater had never willingly let a man or woman die when he explicitly wanted the opposite. He had come up short many times — often it was impossible to prevent — but he had always given his all to protect those he determined were in need.

And he wasn't about to let this be the first time.

So, Viktor's opinion be damned, Slater would go hunting when they arrived in Vladivostok.

He remembered the last time he'd visited the Russian Far East — it seemed to be all he thought about when his mind settled into tranquility and took on a life of its own. That experience had spiralled into madness — Jason King had called, and Slater had answered. He couldn't let his comrade down. King had been trapped in a mine skewered into the bowels of the Kamchatka Peninsula, beat to shit and on the verge of death. Slater had been attempting retirement in Antigua, but he hadn't been content. Upon receiving the call he'd forcibly commandeered a private jet and thrown himself out of the aircraft over the most desolate stretch of Russia, using an emergency parachute to make a hasty landing in the wasteland. From there a relentless barrage of destruction followed in his wake.

That trip had proved what he could do.

With the knowledge that somewhere deep inside him was an unstoppable freight train of potential, he found it impossible to waste away on an island resort. He was worth hundreds of millions of dollars, but none of that mattered.

Pushing himself mattered.

Utilising the talents he'd spent his life compiling mattered.

Helping Viktor mattered.

Then, when he had all but decided to force his way into the fray, regardless of what the parties involved thought of it, he caught movement in his peripheral vision. It happened fast, and for a moment he thought he'd made a grave mistake by not staying on his guard.

He realised that if anyone had chosen that moment to rush his booth and fire a shot through the side of his head, no amount of lightning fast reflexes would save him.

But it wasn't a hostile.

It was Viktor.

The pale man dropped into the seat opposite Slater, directly facing him across the small table in the centre of the booth. Slater stared, waiting for Viktor to utter the first words. He didn't want to push him into saying anything he didn't want to say.

Viktor had to *want* Slater to help.

'I work for the Medved Shipbuilding Plant,' Viktor finally said. 'Or, at least, I did. I stumbled onto something I should not have seen, and I ran. They ordered me back when they realised what had happened. But if I go willingly to my death, then I'll be letting things unfold exactly how my employers want them to. And I cannot do that. I need to try and stop it. So I'd like to work with you. I'd like to take your offer. I've had time to think.'

'Medved,' Slater said. 'That means—'

'Bear.'

Slater glanced across the aisle of the carriage and realised both of the muscly henchmen in the cheap suits were staring directly at the pair of them, their gazes fixed on Viktor.

Oh, that's not good.

9

Viktor started to elaborate, but Slater cut him off with a single look, his eyes dark and broiling with intensity. Viktor understood and shut up immediately, the blood already beginning to drain from his face again. He sensed the gravity of what was taking place — he didn't know exactly what was going on, but he latched onto the sudden tension in the air and froze on the spot.

Slater stared back at the two henchmen — they hadn't budged.

Medved Shipbuilding Plant.

They'd overheard.

It was all connected. Somehow. Some way.

And these men had lethal intentions in their eyes.

The businessman hadn't noticed. He was deep in his own head, staring out the window and shifting nervously in place with no knowledge of the silent standoff taking place just a foot to his right.

Slater reached down slowly and slid the MP-443 Grach out of his waistband, bringing it inch by inch into full view of the two guys in the cheap suits. One of them nodded, a wry smile spreading across his face. He lifted up his jacket to reveal a fearsome-looking sidearm resting in a holster attached to his belt. From the brief glance Slater got of the weapon, it looked like a Desert Eagle.

There would be hell to pay if a firefight broke out.

All three of them recognised that. An all-out gunfight would cause untold civilian casualties — there were at least twenty other passengers in the carriage. Slater didn't think either of the pair cared about that, but then the train would stop in its tracks as pandemonium broke out and they wouldn't make it to Vladivostok.

They had business to attend to in the port city.

Business that no doubt involved the shipbuilding plant.

An uneasy stalemate settled over the aisle — no-one knew what the correct course of proceedings should be. Anyone unaccustomed to tense situations would have averted their gaze, but Slater kept his eyes locked on the two men, studying their subtle mannerisms, trying to find an opening or a chance to act. At the same time his mind raced, trying to figure out exactly how the pieces of the puzzle fit together, contemplating the connection.

It all led to Vladivostok.

But there were hours of the trip left, and the situation needed to be dealt with. Slater kept staring and noticed the hesitation in both men — they were unsure. They knew Viktor was a threat, but they were puzzled. They didn't know why.

Viktor had been telling the truth. The two parties weren't connected.

The two bodyguards didn't know who Viktor was.

But they knew about the shipbuilding plant.

And they knew Slater meant business.

Slater jabbed a finger toward the other end of the carriage and raised an eyebrow inquisitively. Both men continued staring. Neither budged. But neither showed signs of hostility, either.

Slater opened and closed the four fingers on his right hand against his thumb, making a *let's talk* gesture, and once again jabbed his finger in the direction of the carriage's end. He was pointing to the rear of the carriage, in the opposite direction of the bathroom with the dead man. The other way led straight into the dining car, and Slater had no intention of talking to the two men with witnesses around. Only a couple of days into the train's journey he'd seen a door at the very front of the train leading into a carriage reserved for staff.

Hopefully, with only a few hours left on their journey, the carriage would be deserted.

Otherwise things could get messy.

He was under no illusions as to what the bodyguards wanted to do with him. He was armed, and didn't shy away from confrontation. He seemed to be conspiring with someone who knew a great deal about the shipbuilding plant. All of these aspects combined into a serious threat, one that needed to be eliminated before they arrived in Vladivostok, even if the men knew nothing about Slater or who he worked for.

Getting rid of him was the safest option, by far.

There seemed to be a great deal on the line, even though Slater had no idea what it involved.

But the pair of bodyguards must have thought he was a moron, because the hint of a smug grin spread across one of their faces and they nodded in unison, accepting the silent proposal. To reinforce his supposed idiocy, Slater shoved the Grach back into his waistband and turned both palms out, each hand facing the men across the aisle.

I don't want to fight.

They certainly did, but they feigned their own innocence by following suit, draping their jackets over the holsters at their waists so that the weapons disappeared from sight. One of them swept his hand in the same direction Slater had pointed.

After you.

They must have thought they'd struck gold. Here was a significant threat that could pose serious problems to them once they arrived in Vladivostok, but he seemed to be walking willingly to his death, completely unaware of what their intentions were. Slater knew exactly what they were thinking, but he played the role of the bumbling dipshit by nodding and smiling politely.

He got to his feet, leaving Viktor sitting alone in the booth, pale as a ghost and visibly shaking.

'No,' Viktor whispered, barely audible.

Slater heard, though.

His brain was firing on all cylinders, attuned to the slightest twitches and the softest sounds. He heard Viktor's quiet protest and ignored it — Viktor must think he was an idiot too. He realised no-one in the carriage knew his background — sure, Viktor had watched him kill a man without much effort, but anyone could get lucky with a single punch.

Slater stepped out into the aisle as the train rattled on the tracks, and paused momentarily to get his balance. When he righted himself, he walked straight past the three men on the other side — by now, the man in the expensive suit had noticed what was going on.

Slater strode purposefully down the length of the carriage and moved through to the next one.

Silently, the two bodyguards left their booth and trailed behind him.

10

He didn't dare look back — he had a role to play, and it meant pretending that he trusted the two men completely. So he stared straight ahead as he moved through carriages packed with passengers, politely skirting around plump men and women reaching for their luggage on the shelves overhead or heading for the restrooms at the end of each carriage.

One of the train's staff smiled at him as he moved past, and he returned the gesture. She was moving in the opposite direction, which meant she would pass by the bodyguards a few seconds after she passed him. Slater listened closely and heard both men softly step aside, only a couple of feet behind him. They were keeping close on his heels.

The strange procession made their way through the train, probably seeming perfectly ordinary to any onlookers. Slater, however, hadn't been on edge like this in quite some time. He knew conflict was inevitable, in the same way he knew the sun would rise each day. That was just the nature of the beast. He had spent enough time in these kinds of situations to recognise the electricity in the atmosphere.

Right now, everything pointed to death.

Either him, or the two guys behind him.

They wanted him out of the equation, because they didn't know what his business with the shipbuilding plant involved.

Slater passed another pair of staff serving drinks and traditional Russian snacks in the frontmost passenger carriage. He nodded to them, and they nodded back. On the last few hours of the journey, Slater couldn't imagine any of the staff loitering in their quarters. There were jobs to be undertaken.

He would have complete privacy if he forced his way in — he was sure of it.

Then the three-man unit crossed into carriages containing the sleeping quarters — Slater passed the door to his deluxe suite without a second look. The whole time his mind roared, running through all the potential ways the encounter could unfold.

He couldn't talk to the pair, or pry information out of them. Any attempt to subdue them wouldn't work — he could tell they were trained, otherwise they wouldn't have been assigned the role of protecting the man in the expensive suit. So to try and beat them down without giving the fight his all would only result in disaster. It would only take a narrow window of opportunity to capitalise on one of Slater's mistakes, and then the fight would be over. Two on one — especially against men who were expecting it and ready for it — had to be over in a matter of seconds.

He couldn't hesitate, or he would die.

They passed through the final carriage open to passengers, skirting around a group of civilians heading back to their sleeping quarters — probably to pack their things in anticipation of arriving in Vladivostok. Then Slater came to the familiar wood-panelled door, labelled *Staff Only* in a number of different languages.

He turned back ever so slightly, showing no trace of hostility in his mannerisms. He caught a glimpse of the two bodyguards hovering behind him, only a few feet away, standing side by side across the narrow aisle in case he felt the need to flee. They were boxing him in, their hands crossed together in front of their bodies so they could wrench their weapons free in an instant if the situation required it.

They're going to kill me.

Without a doubt.

Slater didn't make direct eye contact, instead raising a palm to silently tell them to be patient. Then he turned back to the door and rapped on it once, slamming his knuckles against the wood with enough force to draw the attention of anyone inside. He waited three seconds, then rapped again.

Nothing.

No-one home.

Nodding satisfactorily, he checked once more behind the bodyguards for any sign of witnesses. Finding nothing but an empty corridor, he bent at the knees, lowering his bodyweight a few inches. Then he slammed his shoulder against the right-hand side of the door, putting enough forward momentum into the charge to snap the lock. Any other door would have left him looking like an idiot, but this train was archaic. It had been renovated and decorated and made to look luxurious, but the foundations were old and suffering from all manner of wear and tear.

Slater burst into the staff quarters, which consisted of nothing more than a few shiny plastic booths and a kitchenette taking up the far third of the carriage. He assumed the staff's sleeping area was in another carriage.

'Shut the door,' he said.

He doubted either of the men spoke English, but they understood all the same. The man on the right — a little taller and a little heavier than his partner — reached back and wedged the broken lock back in place as best he could.

It held.

They were alone.

11

Slater raised both eyebrows at the same time and leant forward imperceptibly, drawing both men in a little closer. They paused — one of them had already started reaching for his gun, but the gesture was strange enough to make them hesitate.

Perhaps Slater had important information...

Before they even realised what was happening Slater reared his head back and lashed out with the underside of his heavy winter boot, slamming the sole into the solar plexus of the guy on the left. For some reason the breaking ribs made no noise, but Slater felt the sickening crunch underfoot and knew the injuries would be horrific.

That was enough to give him comfort.

Before the guy had even started to collapse, Slater jerked forward at the waist and slammed his forehead into the delicate cartilage of the other guy's nose. The second man hadn't had the chance to recoil, so his septum cracked and blood spurted from both nostrils at once. He made to let out a howl but Slater clamped the guy's jaw shut with a whistling uppercut, twisting his hips to transfer all the natural momentum of his body into the punch. The man's teeth smashed together and he stumbled back a couple of steps.

Then Slater's mind went haywire as he noticed the guy on the left reaching for his Desert Eagle.

It seemed that the man hadn't gone down like Slater anticipated, instead riding out the pain of his broken ribs and making a lunge for his weapon all the same.

Slater twisted back in the other direction and launched a turning side kick, aiming for the guy's jaw with as much accuracy as he could muster. If he connected, it would be lights out.

But he missed.

The smaller guy with the broken ribs darted out of range and ripped the Desert Eagle from his holster. In one smooth motion he thumbed the safety off and brought the massive firearm up to aim at Slater's throat.

His pulse racing, his senses reeling, Slater finished turning a full revolution to ride out the inertia of the missed kick. He'd put his all into it, and now he found himself on the back step.

He would die.

But, thankfully, the guy on the right — his nose broken and a handful of teeth falling out of his mouth — came lunging into range with a panicked burst of adrenalin. He wasn't paying attention to his surroundings — he was in pain, and had chosen to take all the rage he was feeling and direct it toward Slater.

If he'd stayed put, Slater would have died.

But instead he charged into range, making the other guy hesitate — a Desert Eagle round would put a crater in both of them, and the smaller man didn't seem to want to gun down his comrade just to incapacitate Slater. At the same time a wave of unavoidable pain creased his features — the agony of the broken ribs had finally caught up with him.

He'd been able to keep it at bay for a couple of seconds, but the window of opportunity to move without hindrance was rapidly closing.

Slater absorbed a wild, looping haymaker to the side of his skull — it hurt, but didn't slow him down one bit. With that out of the way, he snatched two handfuls of the taller guy's jacket and hurled him straight into his friend, pinning the gun between their bodies. Both of them went down in an ungainly heap and Slater followed them to the floor.

He knew if the Desert Eagle resurfaced, his life would be over. He picked the taller guy up with one hand and delivered one of the hardest punches he'd ever thrown in his life, breaking a cluster of bones in his cheek and sending him straight back onto the tiled floor, unconscious. The guy with the broken ribs began to worm his way to his feet and Slater stomped down on his chest, driving him back into the floor with enough ferocity to send the Desert Eagle spinning away.

The guy squeezed his eyes shut and curled into the foetal position, in so much pain that he found it hard to move.

Slater glanced at the Desert Eagle resting in the corner of the room and shook his head. A gunshot from such a fearsome pistol would sound like a bomb going off in this confined space. It would attract the attention of everyone on the train.

This would have to be done silently.

Uncomfortable about what had to be done, Slater hardened his features, turning his face to stone. He bent down, rolled the guy with the broken ribs onto his front, and silently looped a forearm around his throat.

He started to squeeze.

12

A steady murmuring arose in the carriage Slater had spent most of the journey in. Not for any notable reason — he guessed it was simply because they were approaching their final destination. Everyone was restless, eager to depart and either explore the port city or make the long winding journey back to Moscow.

Sensing eyes in the back of his head, Slater lowered his gaze toward the floor and slumped his shoulders, making himself as small as possible in an attempt to avoid attention. He dropped back into the seat opposite Viktor, who hadn't budged since he'd left. He sensed the man in the expensive suit staring at him, in disbelief as to what had occurred. He might not know yet that his two companions were dead, but he would soon come to that conclusion.

Until then, Slater had to make Viktor understand certain things.

'Where are they?' Viktor said, this time having the common sense to keep his voice low.

'They joined the other guy.'

'What other guy?'

'The bathroom guy.'

'Oh... oh no.'

'I didn't have a choice, Viktor.'

'Who are you?'

'I offered to tell you. You didn't seem interested.'

'I thought it was luck. Now I am interested.'

'There's plenty of time for that later. Right now, we need to get a few things straight.'

'Such as?'

'You need to do exactly what I say. The guy across from us — *don't* look — can't hear us, but any second now he's going to wander over and ask what happened to the men he was with. He saw them follow me. He's looking at us right now.'

'What happens when he comes over?'

'You'll see. But if I even look in your direction you need to do everything I tell you to, as soon as I tell you to do it. Got it?'

'Yes.'

'I don't take this lightly. I understand your family's at risk, but I can help you. Quick question.'

'Uh-huh?'

'You think the guy across from us speaks English?'

'How am I supposed to know?'

'I don't know what it's like in Russia. Many of you speak English?'

'Roughly a third of us. Most have some kind of grasp on it. We need to in this day and age.'

'Okay. Perfect.'

'Why do you need to know?'

'I need to catch him off guard. And I need him to understand.'

'He's coming.'

Slater noticed movement out of the corner of his eye and spotted the guy in the expensive suit slinking slowly out of his seat. He was cautious and hesitant and in no way comfortable with approaching, but Slater could tell the guy didn't have any other choices. Without his two friends he seemed lost. Nervous and uncomfortable and out of his element.

Suddenly, Slater realised the dynamic wasn't what he originally thought. He thought the guy in the expensive suit might have been held against his will by the two henchmen, but they hadn't been sitting across the aisle seats to prevent him from leaving.

They'd been protecting him.

Not keeping him in.

Keeping other people out.

'Sit the fuck down,' Slater hissed before the man even had the chance to open the conversation.

It took the guy entirely by surprise, and he flapped his lips like a dying fish, trying to formulate a response.

Before he could, Slater yanked one of the dead men's Desert Eagles out of his jacket pocket and waved it in the direction of the man. 'Three seconds before I blow your brains over the far wall. I'm not afraid to.'

The guy sat down next to Viktor, never taking his eyes off Slater for a second. He didn't blink, didn't breathe, didn't move. Slater realised the fear he'd seen in the man's eyes hadn't been because he was being held hostage.

It was because he was scared to reveal something.

He was implicit in all of this.

Somehow.

'English?' Slater said.

'Yes,' the guy said, with less of an accent than Viktor.

'You someone important?'

'You going to kill me?'

'Answer the question.'

'Sort of important,' the guy said.

'You're a businessman?'

'Something like that.'

'What's your name?'

'I would rather you kill me than tarnish my reputation.'

'Who said anyone's reputation is being tarnished?' Slater said.

'Why else would you be here?'

'What are you involved in?'

'Like I said ... I would rather you kill me.'

He was sweating and shaking and pale, but he seemed sincere enough. Slater tucked the Desert Eagle under his jacket as a staff member strolled past their aisle, offering a warm smile as she glanced into the four-seat booth. Slater smiled back, and she continued on her journey down the carriage. Breathing a sigh of relief, he poked the barrel of the pistol against the inside of his jacket material, letting the businessman know he could kill him with a simple pump of the trigger.

'What do you want?' the businessman said.

'You ever seen this guy before?' Slater said, motioning to Viktor with the gun barrel.

The businessman glanced across. 'No.'

'What's your name?' Slater said again.

'I told you, I'm not—'

'You really ready to die?' Slater said.

'Iosif.'

It meant nothing to Slater. 'What business do you have in Vladivostok, Iosif?'

'Where are my friends?'

'Those were your friends?'

'My business associates.'

'I thought they were holding you hostage. You seemed awfully scared.'

'I'm not scared.'

'You look terrified.'

'Well, I am now. You're pointing a gun at me.'

'You looked pretty scared before guns were in the equation.'

'I'm a nervous guy, I guess.'

'Your English is quite good,' Slater noted.

Iosif shrugged. 'You want to be anyone in this country, you learn English. Helps with international trade.'

'Is that what you do?'

'Sort of.'

'You going back home too?'

'What?'

'Never mind. You been to Vladivostok before?'

'A couple of times. It's not my favourite place on earth.'

'So why are you headed there now?'

'Business.'

'What kind of business?'

'Contract work.'

'Stop bullshitting, Iosif. Tell me about the Medved Shipbuilding Plant.'

Iosif tried acting nonchalant, but it was difficult with a barrel aimed at his face through a jacket. The blood started to drain from his cheeks, turning them white. 'I don't know what you're talking about.'

'Your business associates did. They tried to kill me because they overheard myself and my friend Viktor here talking about the plant. What do *you* know about it?'

'My business is there, that's all.'

'You'd better start being clearer, and you'd better start

filling me in, or I'll blast a hole through your chest. I'm not joking. I killed your two friends just five minutes ago. If you think I'm bluffing, try me.'

'I don't think you're bluffing.'

'Then start talking. Start giving me information, or this is going to get painful.'

Iosif sighed and bowed his head. 'Look, I'm going to Vladivostok for personal reasons. I'm visiting friends. They're doing something ... illegal. Unsavoury. I don't want to talk about it.'

'You'd better start talking about it, or—'

Commotion flooded the carriage, causing an outpouring of protest. Slater masked the sight of the Desert Eagle poking against the inside of his jacket but kept the weapon trained in the direction of Iosif. At the same time he flashed a glance in either direction down the aisle, leaning across to get a better look. It sounded like all hell was breaking loose — in neighbouring carriages he heard literal cries of distress.

Shit, he thought.

He'd shoved both of the bodyguards' corpses into a supply closet connected to the staff's quarters, but it had been a rudimentary job only intended to get him safely through to Vladivostok. It seemed that either the Federal Security Service officer in the bathroom had been discovered, or the supply closet had been opened.

Either way, the carriage suddenly came alive with nervous energy.

Three plainclothes officers rushed into the aisle — one of them shouted a long string of Russian to the passengers in the cabin, then handed it over to a second man who repeated the spiel in English.

'Ladies and gentlemen,' he said. 'There has been a critical incident onboard this train. I would like to ask you to remain in your seats until we arrive in Vladivostok, for your own safety. Once we arrive we will arrange transportation to the nearest Primorsky Krai police station for questioning. If I could ask you all to make no sudden movements and stay where you are seated, we will get to work securing this train. Thank you for your patience. I must ask you all not to panic. This situation is under control.'

Shit, Slater thought.

They knew there was a murderer onboard. Anyone jumping to their feet in an attempt to flee would be swarmed by every security officer on the train. Slater saw the glint of gunmetal out of the corner of his eye and realised one of the officers had drawn their weapon. He had it aimed at the floor, but he was scouring each booth for any suspicious activity.

The tension ran thick in the air.

Slater knew he had no choice but to stay where he was seated.

If he killed Iosif, he would need to mow down every officer on the train.

For now, he was trapped.

13

They made an odd trio — Slater, Viktor, and Iosif. Neither of them had any connection to the other, apart from the Medved Shipbuilding Plant linking Viktor and Iosif. Perhaps they came from different sections of the plant; perhaps their business was in no way connected. But Slater couldn't know for sure, because his line of interrogation had ceased with the sudden presence of the officers. Slater scrutinised their clothing but couldn't make out whether they were undercover members of the Federal Security Service, or members of a different faction.

He doubted they were connected to the man he had killed in the bathroom.

That man had been after Viktor.

Investigating him.

Following him.

These men seemed more like officers of the peace, stationed on the train to prevent any kind of disruption, there to respond hastily in the event of an emergency like the one they were dealing with right now.

Slater found it odd how many policemen had flooded

the train's aisles — if there were three in this carriage, it meant there had to be at least ten or fifteen spread across the entire train. But, then again, desperate times called for desperate measures.

And these were desperate times.

Slater had been keeping a close eye on the news ever since he'd made it out of active duty. His mission to rescue Jason King had elevated tensions between the United States and Russia to heights unseen since the Cold War. That had happened months ago, but the world had changed regardless.

King had been sent into Russia to investigate the disappearance of aid workers on the Kamchatka Peninsula, and the havoc he'd caused had seized the attention of the political elite in Moscow. Slater's involvement had only escalated tensions, until the shadowy elite had deemed it necessary to destroy a great swathe of the peninsula with a ballistic missile to preserve their dark secrets.

It had then become public knowledge that a black operations soldier working for the U.S. government had infiltrated Russian soil. Since then, the respective governments had been embroiled in political conflict. Each side knew the gravity of what they were doing — an escalation to actual war would wipe both countries out, so efforts were being made to calm things down. Slater had watched the political battle unfold from the sidelines, holding the knowledge that he was partially responsible. If he'd never gone to Russia to help King, the man would have died deep underground, carrying his secrets to his grave.

Instead, they'd escaped, and Black Force collapsed in the aftermath of the failure in Russia. Slater and King had been cast out into the world and hunted for their wrongdoings. Only recently in Macau had Slater discovered he was no longer a topic of interest to America. They weren't searching for his head anymore. They had their own problems to deal with, and ultimately they'd concluded that he'd done the right thing in the Russian Far East.

He was, in all respects, forgotten.

And that suited him just fine.

It left him free to wander the globe.

But Russia was still volatile, with most of its citizens reeling from the news that America had inserted an agent into their country who had killed a vast swathe of their people, no matter how corrupt they were. Tensions were still at an all time high. People were angry.

And, it seemed, the Trans-Siberian Railway had become a hotspot for potential terrorist activity.

So the three plainclothes officers kept watch over the carriage as the train screamed toward Vladivostok, its pace increasing as the drivers recognised the need to arrive in a hurry. The more time they spent on the move, the more chances the murderer had to devise a plan of escape.

Slater couldn't imagine the police presence that would be waiting for them in Vladivostok.

He needed to think. Frustration boiled inside him, mostly due to the fact that he'd uncovered almost nothing about either Viktor or Iosif's intentions. Both were stubborn bastards who needed to be poked and prodded and coerced into revealing the slightest details. And there was no way to force anything more out of them whilst three police officers patrolled the aisle directly alongside them. Complete silence had fallen over the carriage — the kind of terrified silence that began when ordinary folks were scared for their lives.

They didn't know what was going on.

Slater did.

When the officers made it to the other end of the carriage, Slater threw caution to the wind and jabbed the barrel of the Desert Eagle against his jacket, displaying it to Iosif. The man deliberately ignored it, pretending not to see. He stared out the opposite window.

'Hey,' Slater hissed under his breath. 'Start talking or I'll kill you right now.'

Moving painfully slowly — which Slater knew was deliberate — Iosif craned his neck to meet his gaze.

'No, you won't,' he muttered.

And he was right.

Slater clenched his teeth to stop himself reacting.

He couldn't do a thing.

His threats fell on deaf ears, because Iosif knew Slater would have to shoot his way through an army of police officers if he decided to fire the weapon. Iosif thought Slater was scared of failure, but Slater knew it wouldn't be a problem.

The truth was, he'd killed enough officers of the law today.

There was a Federal Security Service officer lying dead in a small bathroom just a few dozen feet from his seat, who in all likelihood hadn't deserved it. He'd tried to shoot Slater, but, all the same, Slater found himself wracked with guilt. The guy had been pursuing Viktor, who — as far as Slater knew — was probably knee deep in some kind of horrific shit himself. Perhaps he should have stepped back and let Viktor get arrested.

But there hadn't been any time for that. He'd found himself sandwiched between two parties and forced to act.

That kind of situation seemed to present itself rather frequently in his life.

He let the Desert Eagle fall back against his hip and sent

a piercing glare across the booth, letting his rage brim to the surface for a brief moment.

There would be hell to pay if he made it off this train at Vladivostok without incident.

There would be chaos when the passengers departed, and in all likelihood Iosif would take the opportunity to disappear. Chaos didn't favour someone trying to keep tabs on two men, one of whom wanted nothing to do with him.

But Slater realised, in a fleeting flash of colour, that Iosif wasn't his main priority. Viktor wanted to cooperate with him, and all roads led to the Medved Shipbuilding Plant. Even if Slater lost Iosif, he would get all the information he needed out of Viktor. Just because he didn't know anything right this second, it didn't mean all hope was lost.

Viktor wanted to help.

The tense silence reached a fever pitch as some of the passengers noticed Vladivostok approaching out the window. Slater craned his neck to see out the glass pane beside him after he realised there was no point trying to keep watch over Iosif. The man wasn't going anywhere for the foreseeable future. Even if he tried to run, the officers would have him in handcuffs before he could make it out of the carriage.

All bets were off when they arrived.

Slater caught a glimpse of the approaching port city, which seemed to carry with it a shift in atmosphere. They were no longer travelling through the desolate, inhospitable stretches of the Russian Far East — instead, civilisation approached. It brought with it a sense of safety, of community. They raced toward the city with the subtle understanding that Vladivostok had infrastructure and resources — they wouldn't be abandoned in the Siberian wilderness if they broke down, as shelter and food and drink were only a few miles away now.

Even from this distance Slater could sense the activity taking place within the city limits — he saw flashes of snow-covered roads clogged with vehicles, and looked out across a sea of residential buildings crammed side by side, awfully similar to Khabarovsk.

As they approached, Slater swallowed a ball of anxiety. Those kind of sensations didn't come to him often, but he didn't like anything about this situation.

He'd been thrust into a labyrinth of mystery.

It was a grim day, the air thick with drizzle and the sky overhead swirling with storm clouds. Snow covered the buildings, and misery dripped in the air. The tension made the artificial air-conditioning inside the carriage seem sterile, not at all comfortable. Slater swallowed again.

The train rocketed toward the train station in downtown Vladivostok.

He had never been more uncertain.

14

Frozen in place on the tracks, surrounded on either side by empty concrete platforms, Slater quickly understood that he would have to try something drastic if he wanted any hope of making it out of sight of the authorities with Viktor and Iosif in tow.

They had been stopped at the train station for nigh on thirty minutes now. Everyone had been ordered to remain in their seats until the platform was secure, at which point the civilians would be ushered out into the cold carriage by carriage, to be screened and processed and shipped off to the nearest police station for questioning.

Slater had no interest in taking part in any of that.

But he simply couldn't find a window of opportunity. Viktor and Iosif sat side by side across from him, still as statues, neither of them going anywhere in a hurry. The three plainclothes officers continued to patrol, every now and then throwing odd glances into Slater's booth, but never growing suspicious enough to vocalise any of their concerns.

Slater grimaced. He had to get off this train. And going

about it in an orderly, cooperative fashion wouldn't get him anywhere. He noticed the three officers growing lackadaisical in their patrols. They were still keeping disciplined by sectioning off three portions of the carriage and checking the booths for any sign of trouble, but Slater started to sense minute-long windows where none of the three looked at him.

The mechanical hiss of doors opening rang through the carriage. Ever so slowly, trying to minimise the attention on him, Slater looked over his shoulder and felt a blast of cool air on his face, washing in from the far end of the carriage, coming in through an opening just out of sight.

Natural air.

Not artificial climate control.

They'd opened the doors in anticipation of herding the passengers off the train, and Slater glanced out the frosted window. A cluster of armed policemen milled about on the platform, slowly creating formations to funnel the civilians through to the station's main building.

The building itself was enormous, a great slab of straw-coloured stone with two connecting facades attached to each side of the main structure. All the foot traffic arriving along the Trans-Siberian Railway were funnelled through the colossal building on their way out into downtown Vladivostok, but Slater guessed the delay had been caused by emptying out the station for the logistical nightmare that would soon follow.

But they weren't ready just yet.

Cordons were still being created. Policemen were congesting in groups across the platform, muttering to each other as the sleet battered their all-weather uniforms.

Slater sensed the last opening he would get to instigate chaos.

And he seemed to have a particular knack for that.

Fuck it.

Now.

He wrenched the Desert Eagle out from under his jacket as soon as he realised the three plainclothes officers were clustered down the other end of the carriage.

'Run!' he roared at the top of his lungs, a word so common in pop culture that it would be understood by ninety-five percent of the people on the train whether they spoke English or not. '*Run!*'

Then he pumped the trigger over and over again, emptying the rest of the Desert Eagle's magazine into the roof of the carriage.

15

Those generally unaccustomed to unsuppressed gunfire would liken a shot from a Desert Eagle to a nuclear bomb going off in their ears.

The seven consecutive blasts roared like thunder in the enclosed space, tearing giant holes in the flimsy metal roof of the carriage, exposing the interior to the snow and the elements.

But no-one noticed the wind howling in through the cluster of holes in the roof, because by that point everyone in the carriage had let out guttural screams. They were fearing for their lives, and when people feared for their lives all order and reason was hurled out the window.

Slater hadn't known whether the Desert Eagle was chambered with .357 Magnum rounds, .44 Magnum rounds or .50 Action Express rounds. As the gunshots ruined his hearing and the high-pitched whine of tinnitus filtered into his eardrums, he realised it was the latter.

0.50 caliber rounds were the largest caliber legally allowed in a handgun in America, mostly because they caused enough noise to deafen all the occupants of a regular suburban street. In a confined train carriage, it sounded like the world was ending.

Moving faster than almost anyone on board the carriage, Slater dropped the empty pistol, wrapped a hand around the collars of both men opposite him and hauled them out into the aisle.

'Exit,' he demanded, even though he couldn't hear himself speak — and he doubted either of them could hear his words either. '*The exit! Move!*'

There was no chance of the plainclothes officers getting a beat on who had fired the gunshots. They were in the midst of a panicked crush of terrified passengers, all throwing their personal safety aside to get off the train as quickly as possible. With everyone in the vicinity seized by mortal fear, Slater used it to his own advantage.

As possibly the only person aboard who didn't think they were about to die, he shoved and pushed and hurried Viktor and Iosif through the throng of terrified civilians.

They burst out onto the platform at the same time as all the passengers running along the entire length of the train.

Pandemonium broke out.

Slater seized the nearest officer, who looked as if he'd been caught in the middle of a war zone, and pointed a shaking finger back at the train. With eyes wide, he screamed, 'Murderer! Help! Gun!'

The guy seemed to understand, and although he didn't burst off the mark to throw himself into the line of fire his attention turned imperceptibly to the body of the train itself.

Slater followed the dozens of passengers sprinting for the train station's giant exit building. They'd reached the apex of chaos — the policemen had lost their one opportunity to form a rudimentary barricade around the fleeing passengers, and instead several streams of sprinting civilians opened up, hurrying straight past the officials who were focused on the train itself.

No-one knew who was in charge.

No-one knew how to react in the heat of the moment.

And no-one knew exactly where the threat was coming from.

That suited Slater perfectly.

He put all his strength into keeping as tight a grip on Iosif's collar as he could — that was the most volatile aspect of the entire ordeal. At any point the guy could break away and disappear into the streets of Vladivostok, and then Slater's best avenue of enquiry would be lost.

He paid less attention to Viktor — the man had already pledged his allegiance to Slater before things had gone awry, and Slater imagined the man would continue to stick with him.

The three-man unit, joined by Slater's vice-like grip, hurried straight into the giant train terminal. The building's domed ceiling stretched far overhead, an impressive sight in any other circumstance, but Slater wasn't interested in the architecture. He barely paid the giant stone walls and colossal interior any attention, instead focusing on every shadowy corner for signs of law enforcement.

It seemed the policemen's actions had ended up being their biggest hindrance. The terminal was completely empty. Staff had been evacuated, passengers told to disperse. Slater couldn't see a single soul standing in their way. Even if there had been, there were dozens of other people all around Slater, sprinting for the road outside Vladivostok's downtown train station with the verve that only materialised when they thought they were at risk of being shot.

Slater forced Viktor and Iosif across the shiny floor of the terminal and smashed open a pair of giant wooden entrance doors. The building opened out onto a wide road covered in a thin layer of snow, almost entirely devoid of vehicles at this time of day. It was mid-morning, and the streets seemed quieter than usual — the early morning's commuter rush had subsided.

Slater took a moment to catch his breath — even though he'd been the one to cause the carnage, the adrenalin spike had materialised all the same. A giant cloud of fog steamed out from between his lips as he exhaled, keeping Viktor and Iosif in a tight grip. A sweeping set of concrete stairs fanned outward from the entrance to the station, leading onto a wide footpath.

Across the street, a row of residential apartment complexes hovered ominously.

'Where to?' Viktor panted.

Slater saw terror in the man's eyes. Viktor didn't want to be in Vladivostok. He wanted to be hundreds of miles away, in relative safety, but he had been called back to face his fate. Stepping out of the relative comfort of the train station had been a significant checkpoint, a realisation that he was here, in the place he had fled from just days earlier, a place that could only spell trouble.

'Relax, Viktor,' Slater said, still panting. 'We'll sort this out.'

The hint of a reassured smile began to creep across Viktor's lips, and he took a pause to gather his senses. Passengers from the train were fleeing into the streets all around them.

'We'll sort this out,' Viktor repeated.

He seemed to enjoy how the words sounded.

Then a warm burst of liquid hit Slater in the face, and a

half-second later he felt a horrendous tugging sensation against his fingers clutching Viktor's collar, and a half-second after that the deafening crack of a long-distance gunshot resonated across the road.

It took Slater far longer than it should have to understand that Viktor's head had exploded.

16

Now, he wasn't causing chaos.

He was right in its midst.

Reeling, thrown to the wolves, his mind raced as he instinctively ducked at the knees, minimising his target area. The burst of weight against his fingers had been him taking Viktor's entire deadweight in his grip — the man had become a corpse in the blink of an eye as the top half of his skull disintegrated, showering Slater in a fine mist of gore. He let go of the dead man, recognising a lost cause when he saw it, and started piecing together what the hell had happened.

Sniper rifle, or a long-range assault rifle, fired from across the street.

He thought he'd caught the slightest hint of a muzzle flare out of the corner of his eye before Viktor had died. That left him completely exposed to a follow-up shot, and he scrabbled across the freezing concrete in an attempt to throw off the gunman.

Which meant he lost Iosif in the carnage.

If he'd thought the civilians all around him had been

panicking before, he was entirely unprepared for what came next.

Rabid screaming broke out everywhere at once — at least a dozen people had seen Viktor die. A body slammed into him from the side — a heavyset man running full-pelt toward the stairs — and he lost purchase on the slick stairwell. He slid out, crunching into one of the steps and taking another civilian off their feet in the process. Bodies trampled him, and he squinted in a feeble attempt to get his bearings.

He couldn't see, couldn't hear, couldn't think.

Pain tore across his body, but he'd been through the ringer before. It was all superficial — no bones were broken, which meant he could ignore the sensations entirely. He pulled himself upright halfway down the stairs and searched the screaming crowd for any sign of Iosif.

Nothing.

The guy had disappeared.

Fuck.

It was all he could think. He repeated the curse over and over again under his breath as he covered the last few steps and leapt down onto the pavement underfoot. Another couple of bodies crashed into him, sending him spiralling in different directions. He caught his breath and finally shoved a sprinting man aside, sending the guy sprawling across the icy asphalt on the road — otherwise, the guy would have barrelled straight into Slater and taken him off his feet for the second time in the space of five seconds.

Composing himself, he took a moment to pause in the middle of the pavement, ignoring the pressing urge to duck below the line of sight in case the gunman deemed it necessary to take out anyone attached to Viktor.

He searched desperately for Iosif, still finding nothing.

Then the man himself hurried straight past Slater, materialising out of nowhere, his gaze fixed on something in the distance. Slater wheeled, snatching out a hand to grab at the bottom of Iosif's jacket, but he missed by inches. He considered pulling out the Grach in his waistband and firing a shot into one of the man's limbs, but that wouldn't guarantee survival in any capacity. Any direct impact had the chance to sever an artery, and Iosif would almost certainly die from massive blood loss unless an ambulance arrived in minutes.

Slater didn't think the man deserved to die just yet.

He didn't even know who he was.

So he watched miserably, helplessly, for the three seconds it took for Iosif to reach a jet-black van with windows tinted to the highest degree that had screeched to a stop in the midst of the procession of terrified train passengers.

Slater grimaced as a woman running full-pelt across the road didn't stop in time. She bounced off the hood of the van and sprawled across the asphalt, tearing off skin in the process. The occupants of the van barely noticed. A man in heavy tactical gear with a balaclava covering his features leapt out of the passenger seat and grabbed hold of Iosif as soon as he surged into range. The side door slid open on its tracks, and the guy in the combat gear hauled Iosif into the dark space. A second later the door slammed closed and the passenger dove straight back in the van. Its tyres spun, accompanied by the sound of screaming rubber, and the van shot off the mark. It veered around a cluster of civilians, clipping one man who couldn't get out of the way in time, spinning him off to the side where he collapsed in a heap.

Then it screeched around a corner and disappeared from sight.

Slater stood motionless in the midst of the crowd, the

only one not panicking. He searched the windows across the street for any sign of a gun barrel, but found nothing.

The gunman was gone.

Iosif was gone.

Viktor was dead.

Slater stood alone in a desolate stretch of Vladivostok and wondered how he'd managed to lose a grasp on the situation so completely, all in the space of a fleeting moment.

17

He didn't know what to do.

Slater walked dejectedly through the streets of downtown Vladivostok, one road blurring into the next, everything clouded in a hazy fog of grey sleet.

Including his own mind.

He couldn't believe how quickly things had changed. He had been willing to let Iosif escape if worse came to worse, given the fact that it would have been hard to control the actions of a man who wanted nothing to do with him. But he'd been relying on Viktor as a back-up plan — he could have wormed out more information as soon as they found a safe place to bunker down.

But the man had not been lying.

He'd come to Vladivostok to die.

And the people organising his departure hadn't wasted any time in doing so.

They must have known exactly what train he'd been on. They'd had a man in position to take him out as soon as he filtered into the streets — they hadn't known that Slater had intervened and caused a critical incident on board the train, but in the end that hadn't mattered. Whether he was fleeing for his life or not, Viktor had ultimately walked straight through those doors all the same, effectively signing his own death warrant.

Misery washed over Slater. He lowered his head and cursed — it was a two-pronged assault on his senses. On one hand he was furious at himself for allowing Viktor to succumb to his enemies so quickly and Iosif to escape into the hands of his friends, but on the other hand he couldn't believe how little information he'd been able to gather.

One man would carry his secrets to his grave, and the other was gone forever, vanished into the dark underbelly of Vladivostok, never to rear his head again at risk of Slater finding him. Iosif had seemed genuinely scared of Slater.

Slater doubted he would ever see the man again.

No-one would be that foolish.

Which left him in an odd kind of limbo, where he had almost nothing to investigate other than a loose connection to the Medved Shipbuilding Plant.

Wherever the hell that was.

Even when he managed to locate the plant, what on earth was he supposed to do? Run around kidnapping construction workers until he managed to get someone to spill their secrets?

If there was some kind of illegal operation unfolding within the plant's limits, then nothing Slater could do would uncover it. As soon as one member of the guilty party sniffed trouble the entire entity would pack up shop and move on. Perhaps that was already taking place, as Iosif revealed that a strange American man had seemingly come all the way to Russia to investigate their dealings.

You can't do anything, a voice told him.

He decided on sniffing around Medved Shipbuilding

Plant at the earliest available opportunity, just for the hell of it. There was a ninety-nine percent chance he would turn up with nothing, but he had come this far, and he wasn't going to book a trip back toward Moscow for at least a few days.

The same voice in his head told him it was over, but he reminded himself of his past.

It never ends up being over.

Learn from history, Will.

So he would investigate.

Because that seemed to be the only way his life unfolded.

But not now.

He had just watched a man's head explode from less than a foot away.

Now, he needed a drink.

He tightened the thick overcoat around his torso to mask the droplets of blood staining his undergarments. He'd taken care of the blood on his face and neck by melting snow in his hand and rinsing it off.

He stepped into the first bar he found. It was an old-school traditional Russian tavern, complete with exposed wooden ceiling beams and a hearty fire on the far wall. The tables were populated with locals, all of whom turned to the entrance with raised eyebrows as a black man stepped into their local drinking hole for what Slater imagined was the first time in years.

Most of the patrons looked to be well over two hundred pounds — Russians sure enjoyed their drink.

Slater found himself consumed by the thirst for alcohol — he had used all manner of substances to dull his senses for the better part of a decade now. It probably wasn't the healthiest use of his downtime, but he didn't care. He preferred it over therapy.

This way, he didn't have to talk to anyone.

He could stuff all his emotions up into a tight ball and shove them down deep inside himself and suppress them with a steady stream of drink.

It had worked so far.

He wasn't about to unpack his mind. He simply moved through life at a blistering pace and dwelled on nothing. Maybe he figured he'd die before slowing down, and then he could take his twisted mentality to his grave, never having to deal with it if he departed from the land of the living.

Quite a sinister worldview, all things considered.

Once again, he didn't care.

He liked the taste of a drink, and all else be damned he would allow himself that reprieve. The rest of his life consisted of throwing his broken body into the line of fire for anyone he could help.

He wondered what Jason King would think of all this...

He wondered how King dealt with his demons.

He zigzagged his way around the wooden tables spread across the floor of the tavern and drew up a stool at the bar, ordering three fingers of vodka in a tall glass. The bartender was a stout man with thick white hair and a creased, weather-beaten face. He seemed to be in his early sixties.

'English?' Slater said, more to fill the silence than out of genuine interest. He couldn't care less whether this man spoke English.

His thoughts were consumed by the memory of the top half of Viktor's head separating from the rest of his body.

'Da,' the man muttered, then smiled at the irony. 'Sorry. Yes. I have to. Tourists end up in here every now and then. Like yourself.'

'Seems everyone I've run into in Russia speaks English in some capacity.'

'Changing world. Have to keep up. I am online now. Search for "Vladivostok bar" and I'm the first result. My son helped me with that. Best to speak English if you want to do well.'

'Fair enough.'

'You looking to stay the night?'

Slater looked around. 'I don't understand.'

The bartender jerked a thumb toward the ceiling. 'Rooms upstairs.'

Slater shrugged. 'Maybe. Let me think.'

He tipped the contents of the glass into his mouth and swallowed in one massive gulp. It was strong and didn't taste cheap, and it burned its way down his throat before settling in his stomach, warm and satisfying. The effects would take a few minutes to hit.

Until then, Slater ordered another.

As the bartender poured, he cast a look over Slater's shoulder. 'You here to visit your friend?'

'What?'

The man cocked his head. 'You two don't know each other?'

'What are you talking about?'

'Just a coincidence, you know. Two Americans in this place. Very odd.'

For a moment Slater tensed up, wondering how his past had caught up to him. There could be any one of hundreds of people sitting behind him right now, enemies long forgotten who had stalked him through Russia and finally lay in wait in this tavern, ready for him to come strolling through the door to put a bullet in his head.

Then he realised how ridiculous of a concept that was,

considering he'd made the decision to walk in here less than a minute earlier.

And he didn't think he had psychics for enemies.

He craned his neck as the bartender poured another couple of fingers of the top shelf vodka into the same glass, and noticed the woman across the room staring at him from the shadows.

It was hard not to notice her.

Her green eyes were piercing, as if she could see exactly who Slater was without a word exchanged between them. Her hair was curly, the colour of autumn leaves, and her figure was lithe and athletic — although it was wrapped up in winter gear, Slater found it hard not to notice. He held her gaze for a brief moment before turning back to the bar.

'Don't know her,' he said.

The bartender grinned. 'She's staying upstairs. Maybe you should get to know her.'

'I don't think she wants to know me.'

'That's...'

Slater stared at the man as he battled to find the right words.

'...pessimistic.'

The bartender seemed pleased with himself for nailing a difficult English word.

Slater smirked. 'My life is pretty pessimistic.'

'You are young. Strong. Healthy. Your life seems okay.'

'Healthy physically, maybe.'

The bartender tapped the side of his head. 'We are all fucked in here. Can't be mad about that.'

'Think I should I go introduce myself?'

'What do you have to lose?'

The alcohol started to warm Slater's insides, and the dulling sensation settled over him. For the first time since the incident had occurred, he found himself drifting away from the thought of Viktor's headless corpse lying slumped in front of the train station.

'Nothing,' Slater admitted, and swung off the bar stool as he downed the second giant mouthful of vodka.

18

The woman watched him approach with the hint of a sly smile creeping across her features. She sipped at her beer as he pulled out a chair and sat down across from her. There was enough of a pleasant murmuring throughout the tavern to make conversation comfortable. Slater didn't want to introduce himself with the whole place listening in.

'The bartender thought we knew each other,' he said.

'I don't know you,' the woman said.

She smiled, flashing brilliant white teeth. It stirred something inside Slater, and he grappled with how long it had been since he'd been with a woman. When in active service with the United States government he'd satiated any vices with the ruthless pursuit of one-night-stands, something he'd become rather adept at after a lifetime of travelling across the globe.

It helped being in peak physical condition, and he thanked his parents for the genetics they'd passed down.

Now, though, he realised his life had been chaotic for so long that his mind hadn't even floated over to the concept of romance. Sitting across from this woman gave him a stillness he hadn't experienced in quite some time.

He was present in the moment.

He wasn't dwelling on his past.

This was exactly what he needed.

'Texas?' Slater said. 'You've got the accent.'

'I spent most of my childhood there. Now I live everywhere.'

'You a dock worker?'

She nodded. 'I take what I can get.'

'I hope you don't mind me coming over. I've got nowhere else to be. Figured I'd try to find some company.'

'That's okay,' the woman said. 'Helps that you look so good.'

'Straight to the point,' Slater noted.

'We're in Vladivostok. Might as well cut to the chase.'

'You single?'

'Straight to the point yourself.'

'Like you said...'

'As a matter of fact I am. But what does that have to do with this conversation?'

'Nothing. Yet.'

'You are forward, aren't you?'

'Best way to live.'

'Well, yes, I am single. Are you?'

'What do you think?'

'Wouldn't have a clue.'

'I came over here.'

'Doesn't mean a thing these days. Married men are worse, usually.'

Slater shrugged. 'Guess I haven't been around normal society in a while. I don't know how things are.'

'Are you a hermit or something?'

'My job kept me busy.'

'What did you do?'

'This and that.'

'You're not giving much away, are you?'

Slater put his elbows down on the rough surface and made direct eye contact with her. 'I don't want to talk about work.'

Perhaps he'd said it too forcefully — then again, he *had* just seen a man die in his arms less than an hour earlier. He meant what he said.

She nodded respectfully. 'Understood. Can get a bit like that, can't it?'

'You have no idea,' he said. 'Sorry. I just ... I need a break.'

'Well, talk to me then.'

'I am.'

'About life.'

Slater paused. 'What about life?'

'You know ... hobbies, personal stuff, anything. I figure we can skip past the small talk, considering we're in a place like this. We may as well get to know each other.'

At a loss for words, Slater drummed his fingers on the coarse wooden surface of the table and allowed the hint of a smile to touch the corner of his mouth. 'I guess I'm boring. Don't have much to say. Work was my entire life for as long as I can remember. I only got out a few months ago.'

She raised her eyebrows. 'Retired? You must have done well for yourself. You don't look a day over thirty.'

'I worked hard.'

'For someone who doesn't want to talk about work, it seems like it's all you're dwelling on.'

'Sorry. I've got to learn how to detach, you know?'

'I know,' she said. 'That's not a foreign concept. Seems

like when I get off the job all I want to do is sign up for more. It pays well being out here.'

'What do you do?'

'Construction admin. Nothing impressive.'

'You're all the way out here for work. That's pretty impressive.'

'And if you're retired, then you're all the way out here by choice. I don't know whether that's impressive or psychotic.'

'Maybe I like the cold.'

'Maybe. I don't think so, though.'

'Construction ... you wouldn't happen to work at the Medved Shipbuilding Plant, would you?'

She smirked. 'You know far too much about this place for a retired man.'

'I'm curious.'

'You're curious about shipbuilding, and you like the cold. You certainly are unique.'

'Humour me.'

'Yes,' she said. 'I work there. But today I'm like you. I don't want to talk about work.'

'Can I ask you a question? It's forward.'

'I like forward.'

'You haven't seen anything dodgy going on, have you?'

'Define dodgy.'

'Something seriously bad.'

'You know something about that sort of thing?'

He shrugged. 'You hear rumours.'

She shook her head, adamant, innocent. Slater knew how to read people, and she read like someone genuinely oblivious. 'I mean, I guess I'm not paid correctly. Most of it's cash. Tax savings, that kind of business. But I just manage the rosters for the labourers. I'm very good at it — hence why I'm out here. I can be a real bitch when I need to be.

And I think upper management realised independent contractors won't retaliate against a woman if she's bossing them around, so they keep me busy. I'm useful to the plant. But I don't know what business goes on behind closed doors. The place is enormous. I'm sure there's a bunch of unsavoury shit going down, but quite frankly it's none of my business. You understand? I just turn a blind eye and do what I get paid to do. Blissful ignorance, I guess.'

'That's a lot to tell a stranger.'

She shrugged. 'You don't want to talk about your work. You're rich. You're young. You're retired. I figure you're about the furthest thing from an undercover cop imaginable.'

'You figure correct.'

She smiled. 'Give me a hint.'

'About?'

'What you used to do.'

'I can't. Maybe later.'

'Later?'

'You working right now?'

'I've got today and tomorrow off. Ten days on, two days off. Coming up to the end of a four-month stint. Then it's back home to count my purse.'

'They pay well?'

'Very well. Because no-one else wants to do it.'

'Now that's something I can relate to.'

Her gaze bored into him. 'You *are* mysterious.'

'Doesn't take much effort,' he said. 'A black man in Vladivostok. I may as well be a Martian.'

She laughed. 'Well, you're good company for a Martian.'

'What have you got planned for your time off?'

She cradled the beer bottle and drained the dregs from the bottom, then placed it gently on the table. 'I plan to sit here and drink and go upstairs and sleep and repeat that until a handsome man walks through that door and sweeps me off my feet.'

Sarcastic, but with an underlying tone of truth.

'Don't know if I'm handsome, but I gave it a shot, didn't I?'

'You're handsome.'

'I'm flattered.'

'I doubt that's the first time you've heard that.'

'It's been a while.'

'I don't believe that for a second.'

'I've been ... busy.'

'Work?'

'Work.'

'Well, isn't it convenient that you're retired, then?'

'Why don't we go upstairs?'

She raised an eyebrow.

'I just want to see your room,' he said. 'That's all.'

'Oh, I'm sure.'

He shrugged and put both elbows down on the table. The confidence was returning. 'I mean, we could keep talking. But I think it's pretty obvious what we both want. And we have all the time in the world to talk later. So it's probably not politically correct to be so forward, but I'm a long way past caring about that.'

'Okay,' she said.

With a smile.

19

For the next few hours, all thoughts of blood and death and despair passed from Slater's mind.

He was utterly, completely free.

She led him up a flight of claustrophobic wooden stairs, and Slater had to duck so he didn't knock his head against the low ceiling overhead. He figured the barman didn't advertise the living quarters to all the patrons — only trustworthy ones. They stepped into a long low hallway with rustic wooden walls and antique furniture positioned on either side of a thick plush carpet. The central heating proved effective, eliminating the icy chill of the outdoors. A multitude of doors on either side of the corridor branched off into small private rooms, with a communal bathroom at the far end of the hall.

A quaint little setup, befitting the authentic atmosphere of the downstairs bar.

A place to call home in an otherwise desolate wasteland.

Slater pinned her to the wall as soon as they made it out of sight of the bar's patrons and kissed her hard, savouring the taste, sensing the quiver in her lips as she returned the gesture.

When they parted, he ran a finger down her cheek.

'I don't even know your name,' he said, flashing a smile.

She stifled a laugh. 'Shows how socially inept we are, doesn't it?'

'I don't socialise much. And I take it there's not much opportunity to talk to people all the way out here.'

'It's tough.'

'I'm sure people want to talk to you, though.'

'Most do.'

'Do you oblige?'

'Only when I feel like it. Which isn't often.'

'So I'm the exception.'

She kissed him again, pulling him close, breathing him in. 'There's just something about you.'

'I'm glad.'

'So am I.'

'Where's your room?'

'Come with me.'

'I'm Will.'

'Natasha.'

She took him by the hand and led him halfway down the hallway. Most of the doors lay open, revealing identical living quarters with neatly made beds and small fireplaces by the windows. There were ample vacancies — Slater wondered whether it was the off-season, or the simple fact that no-one ever came to Vladivostok.

He figured it was the latter.

They stepped into Natasha's room and she pounced on him, stripping clothes and locking lips as the door swung shut behind them. At first he found himself taken aback by the intensity, but that quickly faded away, replaced by a burning desire to fulfil his wildest fantasies. He hadn't planned on meeting a romantic interest this deep in the Russian Far East, and he figured she hadn't either.

And the warmth of the room created a reprieve, a safe haven from the harsh, cruel world that lay just outside the building. Slater relished it. He never wanted to leave.

Two bodies intertwined, they barely made it to the bed before she guided him inside her. They gyrated and writhed and moaned, and Slater gave thanks that the rest of the floor was mostly empty. He wondered if the patrons downstairs would hear, and then Natasha changed position and he stopped thinking entirely.

He fought for control, but she was something else.

They climaxed in unison, collapsing against the headboard in a sweaty heap. Slater breathed out the tension of the morning, letting it loose finally, and looped an arm over her supple shoulders. He kissed her on the forehead, breathing her scent, questioning how he'd managed to get so lucky after such a horrific arrival in Vladivostok.

'You're so good,' she whispered, kissing his chest.

'I'm surprised. It's been a long time.'

'How long?'

'Let's not get into that.'

'A guy that looks like you ... it had to be by choice.'

'I didn't have time to do anything other than survive before today.'

She stared up at him, her eyes full and her lips luscious. 'What do you mean?'

'I probably shouldn't have said that.'

She worked her lips up his body, planting kisses from his chest to his neck to his jaw. 'I'll just have to convince you to talk, then.'

'Are you good at that?'

'It's a certain kind of talent.'

'I haven't had an easy retirement.'

'Your career involved something dangerous, didn't it? Something ordinary people don't sign up for?'

'How'd you know?'

'It's pretty obvious, Will.'

He stayed silent.

She said, 'So you tried to retire, and you kept running into the same situations?'

He nodded. 'The same thing happened to an old co-worker of mine. I don't know what it is. It must be something about the job. We acted as a magnet for bad shit for so long, and then when we retired the magnet stayed there. Inside us. I attract trouble, it seems.'

'So maybe you shouldn't be hanging around with me,' she said. 'Maybe that's dangerous.'

'Maybe. It's your call.'

She raised a finger and tapped his forehead twice, as if knocking on a door to his brain. 'I think there's something hardwired up here. Some kind of neural pathway that formed over the years. It happens in anyone's career, but it seems like yours was more dangerous than most. So now, when you've got nothing to do, you go straight toward trouble.'

'Maybe.'

'I think I've got it.'

He ran his hands over her naked body under the sheets, relishing the moment, hanging onto the release of pure bliss that came with the surroundings. The room was small and cosy, and that meant everything. He felt secure in here. No-one would come kicking in the door looking for him. He could ease off his awareness levels just for a few hours, until the time came to activate his old tendencies.

'How long ago did you retire?'

He paused to consider. 'It's been nearly a year.'

'And how've you found it?'

'Terrible.'

'Trouble?'

'Lots of it.'

'But you went after it.'

'I'm not sure if I did. I think it found me.'

'Where'd you go?'

'Yemen first.'

'You expected a cosy retirement in Yemen? It's an active war zone last time I checked.'

'That was ... a turbulent period in my life.'

'You went to confront your demons?'

'Yes and no. I went to the most dangerous place I could find. I was still addicted to the lifestyle, I think.'

'And what happened there?'

He remembered the heat, the sand, the blood, the mercenaries, the war. He remembered killing more men than he could count. He remembered saving hundreds of thousands of lives from a weaponised virus in London.

'Nothing good,' he said.

'And then?'

'I stopped over in Macau for a while.'

'How'd that work out for you?'

He remembered lions, cells, casino lights, more murder, more death, more war.

'Even worse,' he mumbled.

'And then?'

'And then I came here.'

'And how are you expecting it to work out for you?'

He remembered Viktor's head exploding, Iosif disappearing into the crowd in the arms of a muscled bandit, blood staining his shirt, the cold chilling his skin, the dead men he'd sent to the afterlife on the train.

'I can't say I'm expecting anything good.'

'Then aren't you glad we met?' she whispered.

'I am.'

And that also scares the hell out of me.

But he didn't add the last part. He simply thought it. Then he rolled over and resumed his blissful ignorance of the dark stink below the surface of Vladivostok. There was corruption here, and something awfully sinister afoot, but in that moment he didn't care.

He only cared about Natasha underneath him, and the brief reprieve from madness in a tiny warm cabin above a bar.

20

At eight in the evening, daylight still filtered in through the foggy window. Slater had forgotten how late it grew dark in the Russian Far East, but at least it gave him time to run out for errands.

He rolled over in bed and kissed Natasha's sleeping form, planting his lips to her cheek. She stirred.

'Where are you going?' she mumbled.

'We need food,' he said. 'I'll try and find a convenience store.'

'There's one down the road. We can get a meal, though. There's a few restaurants around, even though it's the edge of the earth.'

'I think I'd rather stay in bed,' he said. 'Don't get many opportunities to do something like this.'

Through groggy eyes she smiled, reached up, and kissed him. 'Did I tire you out?'

'Seems like it's the other way around.'

'When I'm off the job I sleep as much as I can.'

'I'm sure.'

She playfully slapped him on the shoulder. 'You are good, though.'

'You keep saying that.'

'I mean it.'

He thought about leaving then, but something told him to stay another moment longer. He reached down and cupped her face in his hands.

'Listen,' he said. 'I just wanted to say ... this makes me happy.'

She raised an eyebrow. 'You're not going to get all lovey-dovey on me, are you?'

He smirked. 'No, no. I'm not about to propose. But I'm really glad I met you. You don't know how much I needed it.'

'I think I'm getting an idea.'

'Don't take it personally that I have to be vague. I'm vague to everyone in my life.'

'Secret business. I get it. I'm glad I met you too.'

'Nice break from the monotony?'

'You have no idea,' she said. 'It's a tough life out here. Sometimes I need to get away from it all.'

'Hopefully I helped.'

She sat up and whispered in his ear, 'I never take naps. You definitely helped.'

He smiled. 'Glad I could be of service.'

He dressed, taking care not to present the tiny specks of blood on the front of his shirt to Natasha. Sifting through the clothing he'd stripped off in a hurry earlier that afternoon, a sharp pang of realisation shot through him. There was no sign of the MP-433 Grach. Without an appendix holster on him, he'd opted to tuck the officer's gun into the back of his waist-band on the train. In the carnage, he'd forgotten all about it.

And now it was gone, lost at some point on his journey,

either tumbling out of his jeans or sliding down through his pant leg. It had happened at some point during his mad dash out of the station.

He grimaced, recognising he was unarmed, and tried to force the thought from his mind.

If all went peacefully, he wouldn't need a gun.

But when has that ever happened?

He sauntered out of the room and retraced his steps through the warm hallway, down into the bar. At this time of evening the space was livelier, sporting an amalgamation of Vladivostok's working class cradling beer steins and thin tumblers of vodka between their hands. Chatter filtered through the space, drowning out any silence. Every now and then a drunken uproar permeated through the room — a table of tradesmen piping up, embroiled in passionate conversation.

Slater met the gaze of the bartender across the room and they exchanged a sly nod.

The guy obviously realised Slater and Natasha hadn't been upstairs talking for the last few hours.

Before he ducked out to load up on supplies, he weaved his way into a gap at the bar and waved the barman over.

'Having fun?' the guy said, his accent thick, his eyebrows raised.

'Thanks for setting me up before.'

'I didn't do anything. Seemed like she couldn't wait to get her hands on you.'

'I'm a lucky guy.'

'You sure are. You should see the number of locals she's swatted away since she's been here.'

'She's popular with the townsfolk?'

'They are all in love. And so are you.'

'I wouldn't go that far.'

'You need a drink?'

'Thanks. Vodka. Make it heavy.'

The barman poured out two fingers of the top-shelf liquid and slid it over. 'Pay in the morning. I assume you're staying the night.'

'Thanks.'

'You sure can handle your drinks.'

'I've had practice.'

'Running away from something?'

Slater paused. 'You're perceptive.'

'We're all running away from something.'

'Are we?'

The barman reached across the oak countertop and tapped Slater on top of the head with a meaty finger. 'You're just running from something in here.'

'You know people too well.'

'I run a bar. I meet a lot of sorry folk.'

'I can imagine.'

'Enjoy your time with the woman. Make sure you don't let your demons get her, too.'

Slater didn't respond. Transfixed by how effectively the barman had pierced through his defences, he drained the vodka with a wince as the alcohol trickled down his throat, soothing his insides. He laid the empty tumbler down on the countertop, nodded once to the man, and hustled out of the building.

You should keep walking.

The insidious thought threatened to consume him as he braced himself against the chill, noting the darkness beginning to leech into the region. Everything outside was cold and grey and foreboding. But that matched perfectly with Slater's personality, and he found himself more comfortable out here in the chaos than inside in shelter.

He recalled what Natasha had said.

Neural pathways.

He'd conditioned himself over the years to embrace the pain. It had sent him to Yemen, and carnage had found him there as if he were a beacon of destruction. Then what was supposed to be a pleasant recovery in Macau had wound up in a dark place he never wanted to revisit. Both outings had almost destroyed him, but he'd emerged with enough traumatic memories to fill the heads of ten men.

So if he walked away from Natasha, opting to keep her safe and keep his problems to himself, then he would only be strengthening the neural pathways. He'd do the same thing he always did — run away from happiness, and leap into war with both feet.

No.

Forget about Viktor. Forget about Iosif. It's all in the past.

Start anew.

But how many times had he told himself that?

21

He found a food cart run by an elderly Russian woman on the nearest street corner, and one whiff of the smells emanating from the cart made him stop well before he located a convenience store. He paused to peruse, and she seemed to sense he didn't speak Russian. She gave a subtle nod and a warm smile and let him browse. He settled on steamed buns packed with beef and pork and cabbage.

'*Pyanse*,' she said, handing over a small plastic container of the buns.

Slater guessed that was their name.

He held up two fingers, and she filled another container.

Leaving her with far more rubles than the meals cost, he set off back in the direction of the tavern. The sun dipped fully behind the horizon and the light began to fade from the sky, plunging murky shadows over the freezing streets. The wind picked up in volume, howling icily across the sidewalks.

And then Slater saw it.

Across the road. Two men, both sporting receding hairlines, no older than thirty. Wrapped up in workers' clothing, gloves on their hands, moving frantically from pedestrian to pedestrian. There was panic in their demeanours — Slater had seen it a thousand times before.

It almost shocked him how quickly he could recognise the signs of distress. He'd spent his entire life around men and women in similar predicaments. These guys were desperate, and they seemingly had no plan to get what they wanted.

They approached everyone on the street, one after the other, waving a photo printed on white paper between their gloved hands, passing it back and forth, shoving it in people's faces. They spoke frantically in Russian, enquiring, interrogating, pleading for help. They probably figured they were doing it subtly, but Slater could see their intentions clear as day.

They'd lost something.

Or someone.

Slater froze on the opposite side of the road, steeling himself against the wind, shielding his face from the biting chill. The weight of the decision rippled through him. He knew genuine distress when he saw it. His whole life had revolved around alleviating that distress, usually by putting himself through the worst situations imaginable.

Maybe the noble thing to do would be to cross the street and offer his assistance. He had no doubt it would lead him down a dark path. There would be violence, and suffering, and bloodshed. It never seemed to go any other way. But he would suffer at the same time. He would be beat to shit — especially if he was chasing down a missing family member, especially if he ran into the types of undesirables he always seemed to cross paths with.

Neural pathways.

Every instinct in his body told him to help. He could see the anguish in the men's eyes, the suffering wracking their bodies, tugging at their souls. He knew no-one would be able to help. Not like he could. If Slater put his full attention to the task at hand, he knew he could disintegrate everything in his path. But that would mean abandoning Natasha, abandoning the brief window of comfort he'd carved out for himself.

And he wasn't prepared to do that.

So, against his better judgment, he turned and walked away from the pair. They didn't even get the chance to approach him. They didn't cross the street in time, so he put his head down and hurried forward with the containers of *pyanse* clutched firmly between his fingers.

Blissful ignorance.

It tugged at his conscience.

He couldn't deny it.

Because he knew he could help, and therein lay the dilemma. How could he walk away from suffering and wrongdoing to focus on himself?

It was selfish, undisciplined, unacceptable.

But he had spent his whole life in a career that forced him to be selfless.

Forced him to be disciplined.

Forced him to accept every burden.

So he didn't blame himself when he finally decided to pass the burden to someone else.

He stepped back into the tavern and crossed quickly to the staircase, taking them three at a time. Glimpsing the two men in their states of distress had made him anxious. His chest tightened and his stomach twisted. Because every part of him wanted to seek them out. Every part of him wanted to help.

Except a tiny morsel of self-awareness, somewhere deep inside his head, saying, *You've done enough.*

You've fought enough.

You've helped enough.

Natasha was still in bed, dozing against the headboard, propped up against an array of pillows. Slater stripped out of his heavy winter clothing and dropped onto the mattress alongside her. He breathed her scent, unable to resist smiling.

She smiled back.

'You're unusually perky,' she said.

'Have you known me long enough to know what I'm usually like?'

'When I first met you. In the bar. That's who you are. Quiet. Withdrawn. You never said anything more than you needed to.'

'And now?'

'Now you seem looser.'

'I feel looser.'

'Is it a good feeling?'

'It is.'

She kissed him again — he couldn't get enough of her. She was his one escape from the world he knew he couldn't avoid forever. It was ingrained in his nature, and she knew it. It was something far deeper than neural pathways. It was in his soul to fight, to attack, to never pause for breath.

But now, just now, he was learning to take a break.

And a break felt damn good.

He parted from her, touching a finger to her lips, resisting the urge to dive under the covers with her and never come out.

'There's time for that,' he muttered. 'We need to eat.'

They sat up in bed and gorged on the *pyanse,* savouring

every bite, filling their stomachs with the warmth and the satisfaction. Slater couldn't believe how amazing it tasted, and decided he'd return to the same food cart in the morning if it was still there. The elderly Russian woman needed to be rewarded for her cooking abilities.

Satiated, they rolled to each other and resumed. Slater could sense the passion in everything Natasha did — the way she ran her fingers down his back, the way she gripped him as she came close to climax, the way her mouth quivered as she pulled him close and they lost themselves in pleasure.

She needed him too.

It was a cold, brutal life out here. She had no friends. It seemed she kept her own company, just as Slater did. That was why she came all the way out to this tavern when she had time off the job. To distance herself from her co-workers. Maybe she knew some of them weren't who they seemed.

Another kind of blissful ignorance.

When they fell off each other, panting and short of breath, night had finally fallen outside. Wrapped up in the bedsheets, their naked frames illuminated by the fireplace Natasha had stoked to life against the far wall, Slater figured he could pry for information.

'Why are you here?' he said, cradling her in his arm.

'I hate the job. I don't want to be around the shipbuilding plant when I don't have to be.'

'You could be doing a thousand things stateside more pleasant than this.'

'I was taught at an early age to detach myself from what feels good, and do what's best for my future.'

'That's good advice.'

'My mother told me that.'

'Is she around?'

'Not anymore.'

'Mine isn't either.'

'I'm sorry.'

'Don't be. It was a long time ago.'

'Do you want to talk about it?'

Macau.

He'd put his demons to rest there. Deep in the bowels of Mountain Lion Casino & Resorts. He'd discovered something nightmarish, something raw and primal, something intrinsically connected to his past.

And he never wanted to think about that again.

'No,' he said. 'I really don't.'

She laid a hand on his chest. 'Holy shit.'

'What?'

'Your heart rate.'

'Sorry. I *really* don't want to talk about that stuff.'

She kissed him. 'We don't have to. Why don't you just sit back and let me take care of you?'

'I don't know if I've got the stamina.'

'I'm sure you do.'

'How long can we do this for? Realistically?'

She furrowed her brow. 'I have to be back at the plant the day after tomorrow.'

'That's all the time in the world.'

'You think that'll be it?'

He paused, pondering. 'It has to be, doesn't it?'

She nodded. 'I didn't want it to be a one-way street. But I hope you know I'm not looking for anything serious.'

'I wanted you to know the same.'

'You sure?'

'My lifestyle wouldn't survive a committed relationship. At least until I change it.'

'You got plans on changing it?'

'I'm trying.'

'Doesn't seem like you're trying too hard. You came all the way out here. You know what happens out here.'

'Do I?'

'I'm sure you have an idea.'

'Do you?'

'I know the shipbuilding plant's a cesspool of unsavoury types. I'm sure the rest of Vladivostok isn't much different.'

'When we're done,' Slater said, taking a risk, 'could you point me in the direction of those unsavoury types?'

'And lose my job? I don't think so.'

He shrugged and settled back as she worked her way down his mid-section, trailing soft kisses along his abdominals, heading in a certain direction.

'What would you do to those people?' she mumbled into his flesh. 'Is that why you came here?'

'I don't know why I came here.'

'That's a lie,' she said, and took him in her mouth.

Then Slater ceased thinking about the bad, and focused only on the good.

22

The next morning, he set out in search of a mixed martial arts gym.

As he dressed in his clothes from the night before he made a mental note to purchase athletic gear as soon as he could find it. At that point the last thing he wanted to do was venture out into the ice-cold dawn, wrenching himself out of the warm cocoon of the bedroom. Natasha grumbled in her sleep as he slipped out of the covers, and he turned and placed a hand against her cheek.

'Where are you going?' she mumbled.

'A couple of work things I need to take care of,' he said.

'Thought you were retired.'

'Sometimes I take on contracts.'

'From who?'

'Whoever needs them.'

'You're going now? To fulfil a contract? Is that why you came here?'

He gave a wry smile. 'No. I'm free now. But I need to do some maintenance work to make sure I'm ready.'

'Maintenance of what?'

'Myself.'

He slunk downstairs, moving like a ghost through the empty bar. Before he'd closed down for the night, the barman had placed all the stools up on the tables and killed the lights. Pale blue dawn light filtered in through the windows, draping elongated shadows over everything in sight, but Slater didn't feel the slightest bit perturbed. Exhaling foggy clouds with each breath, he realised the uncertain environment gave him strength.

He couldn't stay comfortable for too long.

It would drive him insane.

Neural pathways.

Thankfully, he'd made good choices early in his career, and forged them well.

Now, it was nothing more than second nature.

He walked the streets of Vladivostok with his hands in his pockets and his jacket drawn up to his face, shielding his features from view of any prying eyes. He stayed alert the entire time, checking each shadow and each alleyway for any threats. Finding none, he asked a handful of passersby if they could point him in the direction of a gym, and he went door to door interrogating the men and women behind the desks until someone identified a mixed martial arts training facility on the outskirts of the port city.

It might have been easier if he had a smartphone, but that was the furthest thing from what he needed at this point in his life. An instant connection to every corner of the globe would only exacerbate his issues.

He needed to unplug.

Disconnect.

Detach.

There was something oddly freeing about it. He would only find out about major news events if they were notable enough for everyone around him to discuss. Otherwise he remained in the dark.

Blissful ignorance.

He couldn't quite free himself from the shackles of that phrase. Probably because if he wanted any semblance of a normal life, he would need to ignore those who needed help in future.

Thankfully, he didn't see himself finding that peace anytime soon.

Jason King had.

But King and Slater were two very different men.

The incident the previous night had set him on edge. Half his conscious awareness was fixated on the two men he'd seen, wondering what their plight might be, speculating whether he could have helped or not. But that was in the past. He couldn't change what had happened.

So he did the next best thing.

He honed himself for the next one.

He located the grungy warehouse tucked into the industrial district only half an hour after leaving the tavern. Its roller door was up, and heavy *thwack*s emanated out into the cold morning air.

The sound of flesh detonating off leather, whether they be pads or bags.

The sound of combat.

Slater figured he'd get met with resistance, so he strode into the warehouse with his chin high and his shoulders back, exuding confidence. He surveyed the scene — wrestling mats spread over the concrete, heavy bags suspended from the ceiling, and an assortment of short, squat Russian men built like trucks punishing themselves in the early hours of the morning. Sweat flowed freely from pores, and testosterone hung in the air.

In unison, all the occupants of the gym turned to stare daggers at the newcomer.

A foreign newcomer, to be specific.

Slater walked right up to the guy he figured ran the place, a burly man in his late fifties with greying hair and a face that had seen decades of hardship. Vladivostok seemed like a cruel place to run a business, let alone a mixed martial arts gymnasium.

'I want to train,' Slater said, and raised both fists in demonstration in case the language barrier proved too cumbersome.

The guy treated him with the same disdain as the rest of the men in the warehouse. The stench of dried sweat permeated the atmosphere, seeping into Slater's nostrils, almost making him gag. But he held his ground and tried again.

'I want to train,' he said.

The giant Russian man shooed him away, pointing toward the entrance, dismissing him with a single gesture.

Slater pulled two thousand rubles out of the inside of his jacket pocket.

The hand went down, and the owner gave a solemn nod. He held out a hand for the money, transfixed on the crumpled bills.

'I need gear,' Slater said.

The guy raised an eyebrow.

Slater pointed to his clothes. 'Training gear. I only need to borrow it.'

The man nodded, and ushered him deeper into the warehouse, out of the cold.

23

This is what I was born to do.

Slater stepped away from the bag, the sweat already flowing, sucking in lungfuls of the freezing Far East air.

All it took was a single timed round on a heavy bag to silence the entire gym. The odd jeer or dirty look fell away as Slater changed into Muay Thai shorts and a tight compression shirt, then proceeded to unload all the pent-up energy in his system into a heavy bag that weighed well north of two hundred pounds. Packed with grain or sand, the giant man-sized slab of leather jolted back and forth as Slater unleashed right hooks, left hooks, knees, twisting side kicks, scything elbows. It shuddered on its support, threatening to tear free from the chain it hung from.

Suspended in the air, bouncing left and right as Slater transferred kinetic energy with each resonating impact, the bag finally groaned to a halt when he stepped back, completing the round. He assessed the general atmosphere in the air — everyone seemed stunned.

The newcomer who'd seemingly used his daddy's trust

fund money to pay for a workout session in a gruelling Vladivostok facility had proved his worth.

Then the owner, who introduced himself as Nikita, became more welcoming than Slater had ever anticipated.

The giant man rushed forward, slipping pads onto his hands, gesturing for Slater to fire off a series of punches into the leather mitts. Now that his capabilities were revealed, everyone wanted a round with the new guy. Slater pushed forward relentlessly, never resting for a moment, finding the level of exertion that made him uncomfortable and then learning to live there, to embrace it with all his heart.

That was how he achieved so much.

Because he found his breaking point, and then he started to tread water.

The longer you hate your surroundings, the faster you adjust to them.

So, lungs burning, heart racing, sweat pouring, mind sharp, he never let up. He welcomed any challengers, donning head gear and accepting sparring rounds with any of the mixed martial artists who deemed it necessary to test their mettle. The men were hard and tough and cruel, their discipline honed by years of living in such an uncompromising city as Vladivostok. They took him down to the mat, controlling his position, and he relished it.

He bit down on his mouthpiece and fought tooth and nail to secure dominant position on his own, reversing some of the wrestling manoeuvres, implementing his Brazilian jiu-jitsu black belt wherever it seemed relevant. Sparring partner after sparring partner crawled away from the mats having absorbed far more blows than they expected, nothing but cowering shells of their former selves.

When the session drew to a close and Slater collapsed in a sweaty heap by the far wall of the gymnasium, he'd made six of his sparring partners tap out, dominantly controlled another two, and knocked one of them down in an unfortunate well-placed shot. He never wanted to hurt anyone badly in training, and luckily the guy had escaped without a concussion.

As a result, Slater could barely feel his limbs.

His muscles depleted and his energy sapped, he sucked down a couple of bottles of amino acids and electrolytes the gym owner sold at the front desk, and took a few minutes to catch his breath. He picked himself up off the mats, clambering out of a pool of his own sweat. Then he stretched out, showered using the facilities, and changed back into his original clothes, donning the winter gear once more.

A couple of the pro martial artists sauntered up to him as he finalised the payment at the front desk and offered handshakes. The language barrier separated them from an in-depth conversation, but Slater sensed the respect in the atmosphere. He might have lost a few rounds, and he might have collapsed at the end of the session, but he'd more than proved his worth.

Anyone from any corner of the globe respected hard work.

Even in a city as harsh and unforgiving as Vladivostok.

He shook their hands, exchanging knowing nods, and ducked back out into the mid-morning chill with a spring in his step. He hadn't pushed his limits like that since setting foot in Russia. It would take some practice to return to the physical conditioning of old — at the peak of his career, aided by an arsenal of designer steroids, he'd put himself through three separate training sessions per day, each close to two hours in length. That kind of schedule had wreaked a toll on his body, and retirement had been an important step in saving his joints and preventing any long-term damage.

But the burning desire to outwork anyone on the planet was still there.

It would never go away.

As he hurried away from the grid of warehouses, eager to return to the safe haven above the bar, he realised he hadn't given Iosif's fate a moment's thought the entire morning. The absence of a phone or any kind of electronic device proved paramount now — he had no doubts that the madness at Vladivostok's train station had made national news considering the public nature of Viktor's assassination.

But he was oblivious to all of it. Being out of touch made it easier to slip into a new life, even after the traumatic experience the previous day.

That seemed like an eternity ago.

Especially after what he'd been through since. A whirlwind detour with Natasha, and then a gruelling workout that reduced him to a shadow of his former self. But he would rebuild, as he always did.

Stronger than before.

He took his time on the walk back to the tavern, barely fazed from the cold. His muscles were so depleted that every step felt like a drag. It was a long hard slog to put one foot in front of the other. Thankfully, though, it was all he could concentrate on — he paid the turbulent arrival into Vladivostok no attention. He simply focused on the present moment.

It was the best way to live.

By the time he made it back to the bar, the barman had opened the place up for the daytime customers. A few surly individuals sat scattered around the tables, each cradling their beverages like their life depended on it. Slater sensed a different atmosphere to the unruly cheer of the previous night.

The daytime crowd were a sorry bunch.

He scanned the room, looking for the barman, but his search came up empty. A couple of patrons made uncomfortable eye contact as he stared at each of them in turn, but there was no animosity in their expressions. All of them were dull, tuned out, deaf to the world. They'd found the solution to their problems in the bottom of an empty glass. They noted the arrival of the new guy, but didn't pursue it any further. Most of them lost interest right away.

Slater paused at the foot of the staircase, finding it odd the barman would leave the premises unattended as customers loitered about. It wouldn't take much effort for one of them to reach over the counter and slip an expensive bottle of top-shelf alcohol under their jackets.

He took the stairs two at a time, disturbed by the odd development.

He reached the top of the staircase and froze.

Oh.

24

The barman sat in a bloody heap, propped up against the wall halfway down the hallway. Purple blotches covered his face. His cheeks were in the process of swelling, and soon the man would be unrecognisable. Slater didn't need to study him for long to recognise a broken orbital bone. One of his eyes was completely swollen shut, and the other drooped lazily toward the floor. He was semi-conscious — his body had opted to shut down and compartmentalise the pain instead of staying alert and experiencing it in full.

Better to dull the worst of it for now.

Besides, even if he stayed awake and alert, his body understood how inhibited it was. The man was in no state to put up a fight of any kind. If the people who'd beat him half to death wanted to return and finish the job, there was nothing stopping them from doing so.

Slater turned his attention away from the barman and studied the door to Natasha's room.

It hung ajar.

His stomach twisting and tightening with each breath,

he tiptoed silently over the plush carpet, making no noise whatsoever. He could be a ghost when he needed to be. He stepped over the barman, who muttered something indiscernible, and approached the open doorway with more trepidation than he thought possible.

Because a soft voice in the back of his head told him exactly what he would find.

Neural pathways.

Nothing changes.

Same actions, same results.

He stepped into the room. The bedsheets lay on the floor, hurled off the mattress in a panic. The mattress itself had shifted a few inches off its base, signs of a vicious struggle. The fire had died out long ago, reduced to smouldering embers. And, most notably, Slater spotted a dried patch of crimson blood on the headboard, smeared in a jagged pattern from left to right. He thought he could see a fingerprint in the mess. Someone clawing for a handhold as they were dragged from their slumber by hostile intruders.

There was no sign of Natasha.

Slater went through the motions, slipping back out into the hallway as soon as he confirmed the room was empty and checking each room on the second floor, one by one, for signs of a hostile presence.

Nothing.

This place was a crime scene.

The blackness appeared. He sensed it in the pit of his stomach, forming amidst the tight knots compressing his gut. In between the nausea and the anxiety and the impending sense of doom was something else. Something darker. The rage, threatening to bubble its way to the surface.

The rage he'd left behind in Macau.

And every fibre of his being wanted to unleash it.

Not yet.

Not here.

He finished checking the final room and crept back out into the hallway. The barman hadn't budged an inch — his face continued to swell, turning grotesque before Slater's eyes. Silence draped the corridor. From downstairs, the soft murmuring of the bar's handful of patrons filtered up the staircase.

How the hell had this happened with the bar itself populated?

Slater walked over to the barman and crouched down by the man's pathetic form. He reached out and tilted his head upward by prodding his chin with a single finger.

The guy stirred and returned to consciousness, his head lolling in place. 'Just finish it.'

'What?'

'Wait ... you're the guy.'

'What happened here?'

'I tried to stop them.'

'They got her out of here by turning invisible, it seems.'

'W-what do you mean?'

A thin line of blood ran out of the corner of the barman's lips. He coughed and reached up a hand to wipe the smear away. Slater batted it back down, slapping his arm away with an open palm, like a whip cracking, flesh against flesh. The man winced and cowered, dropping his head low.

'What do you want?' he moaned, and Slater sensed the desperation in his tone. 'They already beat me half to death. Are you with them? Is that why you wanted to talk to her?'

Slater paused. He reached out and clasped his fingers around the barman's throat.

'I just find it very convenient that you wound up here,'

he said. 'Hurt, but alive. And it seems like nothing out of the ordinary downstairs. None of the patrons had an inkling that something was afoot. And here you are. It all seems a little contrived, don't you think? So I'm not going to trust you until you break down exactly what happened, step by step. And you'd better be damn convincing. Because I quite liked that girl.'

'Is your name Will?' the man muttered.

'Yes. It is.'

'Then she liked you, too. It was the only thing she said when they came for her.'

'Who came for her?'

'Just a few guys. I'd never seen them before.'

Slater tightened his grip, restricting the man's air passage. 'You're going to need to be more specific than that.'

'P-please,' the man said, choking, gasping.

Slater loosened his fingers from around the man's throat. 'I trusted you when I stepped foot in this place. So I'll give you the benefit of the doubt. Speak.'

'If I speak, you might not believe me.'

'I'm not giving you an alternative.'

'But there is an alternative. And then you'll believe me.'

'What?'

The barman lifted a bloody finger to point at the shadowy crevasses over the staircase. Slater spun and followed his gesture, spotting the security camera skewered into the faded plaster. A single red dot blinked in and out of existence underneath the lens.

'That was rolling the whole time?' Slater said.

'Nature of the business,' the man said. 'I cannot survive unless I protect myself. The types of people who want to stay here usually aren't the most noble. Your American friend was the exception. That's why I was pleasantly surprised at her arrival. And that's why I fought to protect her.'

'You'd better be telling the truth.'

'We'll check the footage. But—'

Slater raised an eyebrow. 'This isn't the time for but's.'

'Just don't take it to the police.'

'Why on earth would I do that?'

'I don't know. I don't know who you are.'

'Clearly not. The police are the last thing on my mind.'

'So you are a bad man, too?'

'Bad enough. Why don't you want the police involved?'

'I don't run my bar the most honest way.'

'You pay taxes?'

'Nowhere near as much as I should.'

Slater shrugged. 'Nature of the beast. I don't blame you, living all the way out here. Thankfully I'm not here to audit you.'

'So you don't care.'

'Why would I care? I care about a friend of mine. That's all.'

'Then let's go to the cameras.'

25

In a small back room tucked into the far end of the hallway, the barman sifted through an assortment of ancient computer hardware that had spent the better part of five years collecting dust, unused and untouched for as long as the man could remember. In his sorry state, snivelling and dishevelled, Slater almost felt sorry for the man.

But he didn't implicitly trust him.

Not yet.

So he remained vigilant, hovering in the doorway, shooting a glance at the staircase every few seconds to make sure a curious patron didn't decide to wander upstairs and investigate where the owner had disappeared to. The barman fumbled with a blocky desktop monitor and fired the computer underneath the desk to life. As he set about navigating through loading screens, he winced and bowed his head as a fresh wave of pain coursed through him.

A side effect of the beating he'd taken.

Slater grimaced. This wasn't like him. He didn't ordinarily act so cruelly toward common folk, and he had little doubt this man was true to his word. There was no great conspiracy here. There was just chaos and confusion, and deep black rage below the surface of Slater's mind. All his conscious thought was directed at that particular hurdle, making sure it didn't explode outward. The last thing he wanted was to draw more attention to himself, especially in a sensitive situation like this.

If he set off on a rampage through the streets of Vladivostok, it wouldn't take long for the incident on the train to catch up to him. There were dark forces at play here, and he didn't yet know whether Natasha's disappearance was connected to any of it.

He sure hoped not.

Otherwise he might have to revert to old measures.

And old measures never ended well for anyone.

'I never got your name,' Slater said, noting the *deja vu* to the conversation he'd shared with Natasha. He wondered if there was any significance there.

Was he deliberately avoiding forming a personal connection with anyone until he absolutely had to?

Nonsense.

Otherwise he never would have gone upstairs with Natasha.

'Alexei,' the man said. 'I was not part of this. I swear.'

'I believe you. I just need to see for myself.'

'I tried to stop them…'

Alexei's face had swelled so significantly that it masked his emotions, but Slater thought he spotted the man openly weeping through his wounds. He stepped forward and laid a hand on the big barman's shoulder. The guy's chest heaved up and down.

'It's okay,' Slater said. 'You did everything you could.'

'Not enough.'

'It happens to everyone.'

'Does it happen to you? You seem too calm. You must be in these situations a lot. Do you ever not do enough?'

Slater pondered that. 'Not usually. But I put everything into it.'

'I tried that.'

'You don't have the experience I do.'

'I tried...'

'Show me.'

Alexei pulled up the requisite video file and let the footage speak for itself. It was grainy, but it painted a competent picture. Slater didn't need the barman to clear anything up. He saw it all for himself.

Three men sauntered up the staircase with as much nonchalance as they could muster, moving in single file. They were hard, cruel men — Slater could tell from their gait. They had the physiques of tradespeople with the demeanours of something much darker.

He'd seen their types a thousand times before.

Ex-military in some capacity, disciplined and tough and utterly lacking a conscience. Even in the grainy footage Slater could see the intense focus in their eyes — these men had committed themselves to a discipline, which was something sorely lacking in many in today's society, a noble gesture in itself. But they had directed their focus at something horrific.

Blood money.

Dollars for suffering.

He didn't know if they were the ones running the show or the henchmen recruited to carry out their superior's wishes. But, all the same, they transformed like chameleons as soon as they made it upstairs, out of sight of the regular patrons. The easygoing moods vanished, replaced by sociopathic intensity, and they made a beeline for the closed door to Natasha's room with renewed vigour. One of them knocked politely, keeping dead quiet, and all three of them poised over the threshold like coiled springs. The door swung open and the trio surged into the room, blocking the camera's view. Natasha didn't even get the opportunity to scream. They bundled her into the room, their fast-twitch muscle fibres firing, and all went quiet.

Slater sensed hot fury scratching at the cellar door deep inside him.

If they were going to...

But they didn't. They only spent a few seconds in the room before dragging her out into the hallway with a sleek gunmetal grey sidearm pressed to the side of her head. Her face was distraught, her lips flapping, her eyes streaming tears, but no sound came out.

They'd instructed her to remain silent. They didn't want to alert the customers downstairs.

'I realised something was wrong right about now,' Alexei mumbled through split lips. 'And I came up to investigate.'

The barman appeared at the top of the staircase on the surveillance footage, scorn in his eyes. Unblemished, Alexei surged forward despite the presence of the loaded gun and threw himself at the closest hostile. In any other encounter a violent fistfight would have erupted, alerting everyone downstairs to the commotion. But the guy Alexei chose to try and brawl with simply stepped back and unleashed a staggering uppercut into the underside of the barman's chin.

Alexei crumpled into the wall and slid down it, barely conscious.

The stocky thug threw three full-strength punches into Alexei's unprotected face, breaking his orbital, squashing his nose, causing immediate swelling across his delicate facial features.

Natasha watched the beatdown unfold with a horrified expression on her face, turning pale.

The guy with the gun twisted it against her temple, daring her to move, to make a sound.

She didn't.

The man leant forward and spoke in a low tone, undetectable by the surveillance camera's stock microphone.

'I was conscious,' Alexei said, stumbling over his words, slurring them. 'I h-heard what he said.'

'What did he say?'

'To walk out between the three of them like nothing was wrong at all. He told her if anyone suspected anything downstairs, he'd shoot her in the head without a moment's hesitation.'

'She obliged?'

'Watch.'

26

On the screen Natasha nodded, crippled by mortal fear, and her shoulders slouched as she became complicit in their demands. She followed them sheepishly down the corridor, trying her best to still her shaking torso. Before they descended the staircase and disappeared out of sight, one of the giant thugs laid a palm on her shoulder and whispered into the back of her neck.

'Telling her to relax,' Alexei said. 'They were treating it as a joke. As if they'd done it a hundred times before. I do not know who they are.'

'Maybe they have,' Slater said. 'Maybe they're experts.'

'Can I say something?'

'Of course.'

'I know you are an angry man. I can sense it. Even though I'm having trouble seeing anything. Do you think this had something to do with you?'

'I can't know for sure. There's only one way I can find out.'

'Will you go after them?'

'Yes.'

'Should I pretend I've never seen you before?' the man said. 'If anyone comes asking?'

'What if they enquire about your face?'

'An unruly customer, of course. There's no evidence of anything to the contrary.'

'You need a hospital,' Slater said.

'That is up to me to decide.'

Slater shrugged. 'I guess so. I'm not going to hold your hand.'

'I think I can deal with this on my own.'

'Who'll run the place when you're recovering?'

'I'll get help.'

'Who?'

'People I trust.'

'You know them well?'

'Of course.'

'Do you blame me for what happened?'

'I don't know what to think,' Alexei said. 'I fear you. If we're being honest. I don't know whether to get angry at you, because you might kill me.'

'I'm not going to kill you. You did an honourable thing.'

'Not honourable enough.'

'You did what you could. Those were trained killers.'

'You know their type?'

'Rather intimately.'

'What will you do?'

Slater paused, letting the silence of the upper level drown out their conversation. He thought long and hard. Then he said, 'You can take care of yourself from now on?'

'I've been running this place for ten years. I can take care of myself. Just have to clean up some blood, yes?'

'Then you never saw me.'

'And if your picture shows up in the newspaper tomorrow?'

'Then I'll be responsible for a few murders. And you definitely won't want to know me then.'

'So this never happened?'

'It never happened.'

'I'll never know whether you succeeded in finding her or not.'

'No, you won't.'

'Can you call me? If you manage to do it?'

'I don't have a phone.'

'You really are a strange man, aren't you?'

'Comes with the profession.'

'What's your profession?'

'Some things are best left unsaid.'

With that, Slater pivoted on his heel and disappeared from the room. He figured Alexei wouldn't even realise he was gone until the barman swivelled around in his computer chair and squinted through his puffed-up eyes.

But the man was tough. Far East tough. Vladivostok tough.

He would survive. He would continue. He would prosper.

And Slater would do what he was put on this earth to do.

Fight.

27

As he thundered down the staircase, he figured it had always been inevitable.

He'd come to Vladivostok for a reason. Any attempt to ignore it was futile. It would always catch up to him, like fate, destined to unfold the way it was always supposed to. He hadn't told a soul why he'd really come here, and he wasn't about to.

Because that centred around a time he would much rather forget.

But he couldn't forget about it until he'd put his demons to rest.

So it all seemed to fall into place. He strode straight past the groggy, zombie-like patrons and powered out into the street, sporting no possessions whatsoever. A free man in every sense of the word. He had nothing tying him down, no burden to shoulder, nothing to force him to loiter anywhere for longer than he needed to.

He'd always structured his life that way, ever since retirement.

Because it allowed him to react on the fly. It allowed him

to abandon his surroundings at the drop of a hat. And no-one had ever needed him to go through with that sort of drastic plan more than Natasha. He knew, deep in the bottom of his heart, that he was responsible. Iosif was out there somewhere, alive, and the shadowy figures connected to him slunk around Vladivostok. They were connected to the mercenaries. Somehow. Some way.

And Slater finally realised that the stars had aligned.

He needed Natasha back. Not because of his own sense of guilt, but because she didn't deserve what had happened to her in the slightest.

And if it had something to do with him, he wouldn't rest until he found her.

He made it out into the freezing street without being bothered by any of the patrons. Once again, they probably found him a curious enough sight to stare, but Slater's presence couldn't drum up enough interest for them to bother interfering. He left the tavern behind, silently wishing Alexei the best of luck in his recovery. He ran into people like the barman far more often than he ever expected — ordinary people who went above and beyond, even in the face of death.

Most would have hesitated at the sight of the three thugs, one of them armed, pressing a loaded gun to a hostage's head.

Alexei had hurled himself into the fray.

Maybe in another life he would have made an effective operative. If Black Force had caught him early in his evolution. If they'd honed him into a human weapon from day one. But not many received that path. Not many were offered the opportunity.

Slater had been.

He wondered if it had all been a colossal mistake.

Then he saw them again, and all extraneous thoughts shrank away.

The two men from the previous night were still pacing up and down the dreary Vladivostok streets. Their demeanours sported signs of wear and tear — Slater figured the pair had been up all night on their personal crusade. Even from the opposite sidewalk, Slater spotted the heavy dark bags underneath their eyes. They were both in their thirties if Slater's eye for detail held up, but the stress and the lack of sleep had aged them ten or fifteen years. They clutched the same crumpled paper between their fingers, but the elements had ravaged the printed photo, so all Slater saw from across the street was a faded silhouette printed out and folded in their hands.

Well, what's there to lose now?

Besides, something subtle told him it was all connected.

He crossed the street, barely checking in each direction before he stepped down onto the asphalt. At this time of year, when the cold bit deeper and harder than usual, Vladivostok became a ghost town. Slater wondered if news of the debacle at the train station had transformed the city into a collection of shut-ins — ordinary civilians terrified to leave their homes at risk of having their heads blown apart from a long-range sniper rifle.

Then Slater strode into range of the two men, got a proper look at the piece of paper clutched between one guy's frozen fingers...

...and he realised the incident hadn't made the news at all.

He knew the face staring up at him — an identification photo, taken at an upbeat moment, displaying the wry smile of the man who had died in Slater's arms the previous day. He felt a pang of sadness for Viktor. The printed ID made him seem jovial, a far cry from the terrified shell Slater had met on the train. An easier time, no doubt.

'Excuse me,' the man on the left said in broken English. 'Sorry to interrupt. Have you seen this man?'

Slater continued staring at the image. Something in his face must have given it away — both men paled at the same time.

'You know him,' the second guy said.

Slater nodded. 'I know him. You two haven't been watching the news?'

'What do you mean?' the first man said. 'Of course we have.'

I thought as much.

So the incident at the train station had been suppressed. There were a number of explanations — none of them good, yet some more sinister than others. In all likelihood, there was an ongoing investigation at the train station, and details of the murder hadn't been linked to the media yet. Or, also just as likely, there simply wasn't enough media in Vladivostok to get the information out in a hurry. Then there was a darker concept, one that Slater initially dismissed but found himself returning to time and time again.

Someone was actively covering up the details.

Hiding Viktor's death from the general public.

Someone in power didn't want anyone to know what had happened at the train station, for reasons unknown.

Unfortunately, Slater had enough experience in the field to get an idea of where this situation might be heading.

He bowed his head. 'We should talk about this somewhere private. Because you two might have something I need.'

'Where is he?' the first guy said, shaking the paper in Slater's face. 'Tell me!'

'Quiet,' Slater hissed, suddenly paranoid.

He threw a glance up and down the street. Now there were a few pedestrians about, directly juxtaposed against the dead streets Slater had stepped into upon exiting the tavern. Every passerby sent a pang of anxiety through his chest — it seemed like everyone was out to kill him. It seemed like everyone knew who he truly was.

'Not here,' he muttered. 'Come with me.'

But he should have paid closer attention to the mental fragility of the two men in front of him. They evidently knew Viktor well, and his sudden disappearance had torn them apart. Now they had a glimpse of what might have happened to their friend, and this strange foreign man was hiding information from them, preventing them from reaching the truth.

Slater realised all of that as the first guy lunged for him, his eyes manic and sleep-deprived.

Slater caught him by the lapels and hurled him into the brick wall of the adjacent building. The impact drove the breath from the man's lungs, but for good measure Slater kept hold of his collar. He wrenched him away from the wall and slammed him into the surface for the second consecutive time, adding insult to injury.

Then he let go, and hissed, 'I will help you as much as I can. But not here. I'm on your side.'

The unharmed man stared at Slater, wide-eyed, in disbelief at the outburst of violence. These men were physical labourers, but that didn't mean they were accustomed to the type of force Slater could unleash in the blink of an eye. They had spent their whole lives toiling away on construction sites, and he had spent his life toiling away in combat gymnasiums.

Big difference.

Overpowered into submission, the first guy nodded sheepishly, sucking air into his lungs in giant gasps, and beckoned into the nearest alleyway. 'Is this good enough?'

'It'll do,' Slater said. 'I can't hang around for long.'

'Why not?'

'Because I don't want to put the pair of you in danger.'

With that, he led them into the grimy stink of the alleyway, a narrow strip of land between two towering brick buildings. Overhanging awnings and lattices and balconies cast great shadows across the muddy ground.

And someone followed.

28

Slater didn't recognise the hostile presence until it was far too late.

He ushered the two men into the lip of the alley, and then sensed rapid footsteps directly behind him.

Close.

Too close.

He spun on his heel and threw a massive right hook without assessing the threat, figuring he didn't have time.

He was right.

The giant mercenary surged into range in unison with Slater's wild swinging, looping punch. He connected on the jaw and felt the vibration of the direct impact resonate up through the bones in his forearm, into his upper arm.

His shoulder socket rattled. A good, clean punch.

Lights out.

Or, maybe not.

The big Russian thug stumbled like a newborn giraffe and went down in a half-squat, almost losing his balance entirely. But he kept his legs underneath him and burst back to his feet, disorientated and thrown off by the attack but still composed enough to return the favour.

The guy was at least six foot three, standing a few inches over Slater, and built like a concrete slab. Slater didn't want to consider the arsenal of designer drugs the man was on. The real question was whether he could fight or not.

He could.

Inhibited by taking all five of Slater's knuckles directly to the jaw, he still had his wits about him enough to burst into motion. With his own survival on the line, the guy came in swinging with a serrated switchblade. The knife had been clutched between his fingers the entire time — he'd stormed into the alleyway ready to stab a series of holes through Slater's mid-section.

Knife fights were ugly, dirty, messy beasts. And Slater wasn't armed.

So he lurched away from the blade, opting to tumble back into the alley as if he were the semi-conscious one. The first swing of the blade narrowly missed his chest, slicing through the empty space a few inches in front of him. Slater's pulse redlined, beating fast enough to trigger a heart attack if he wasn't careful. The presence of the switchblade changed the dynamic entirely — now he found himself terrified for his life, fearing the death blow to slice an artery at any moment.

And that turned him into the one thing he'd wanted to put in the past.

A monster.

The next attack came in lazier than the first — recognising that Slater was unarmed, the attacker relaxed ever so slightly. Nothing perceptible to the common civilian, but even a millisecond's hesitation in this game spelled the difference between life and death. A combination of his compromised mental alertness, still rattled from the punch, and his supposed confidence in wielding a massive advantage over his assailant, led to a half-hearted swing of the blade.

And all that added up to a shocking reverse in momentum.

Slater reached out both hands at lightning speed and seized hold of the guy's wrist, so fast he could barely comprehend his own actions. But as soon as he had hold of the appendage he felt the white hot burning sensation of opportunity. He knew he would never get the chance to reverse fortunes again, and his body seemed to comprehend that.

Because he burst off the mark with inhuman strength.

Even though the guy had an advantage of close to thirty pounds in bodyweight, Slater wrenched him forward by the arm with all the bone-jarring torque he could muster. The man stumbled off-balance, his arm nearly ripped out of his socket, and Slater brought the guy's delicate wrist down to his knee with the strength of ten men. Possessed by fight or flight strength, he snapped the guy's forearm clean in two, rendering the limb entirely useless.

The knife spilled from the man's grip as shock set in and he lost all feeling in his right hand.

Slater let go of the guy's mangled wrist, reached out, and caught the knife by the hilt.

In one unbroken movement, he wrenched the blade up and shoved it into the guy's throat, tearing through flesh and soft tissue, destroying his trachea, brutalising his neck, severing all the important arteries.

He worked the blade left and right in two jerking motions, then let go of the hilt and lowered the bleeding, dying body to the alleyway floor.

Adrenalin and shock hit him in the chest, and the ease with which he'd murdered the man sunk in. Panting for breath, he dragged the corpse behind a collection of broken, disused furniture. Allowing the thug to pour his lifeblood all over the snow, he wiped his hands on his jacket and stumbled back out into open view, eyes wide and heart rate thudding incessantly.

The two workmen had no idea how to react. They stood in the middle of the alleyway, mouths agape, shocked at how ruthlessly it had all unfolded. Slater understood the sheer shock of the whole experience.

Violence up close and personal was something horrific, and it had taken him years to acclimatise to the brutality of killing another human being. He'd just done it in one of the most grotesque ways imaginable, and these men had probably never seen a dead body before, let alone watched the lifeblood drain out of a giant thug in a cold alley in a Russian port city.

Slater placed a hand on each of their backs, turning them away from the violent scene. 'Let's go.'

Neither of them budged an inch.

He shoved them hard, sending them stumbling deeper into the alleyway. Slater followed, charged with purpose. He couldn't linger around this place any longer than necessary. Already he sensed eyes on him, whether due to paranoid insecurities or a real presence. He hadn't spotted the man approaching, and that said everything that needed to be said about who he was up against.

He folded the switchblade up, still slick with arterial blood, and tucked it into his inside jacket pocket.

The fact that he wasn't armed had never been more apparent.

The two workers got moving and Slater stayed hot on

their heels. They took a left at the end of the alleyway and entered a complicated grid of side streets, all cutting between residential apartment complexes and retail outlets. The narrow laneways collected trash and disused furniture. Finally Slater found an open doorway leading into an abandoned building and ushered the two workers through. They stepped into a low dark space, illuminated only by the bleak natural light filtering in through the grimy windows. Years ago it must have acted as a reception area for a storefront, but the building had been decommissioned and surrounded by other structures, cordoned off from the populated streets, left to fall into disrepair.

Slater gestured for the two men to crouch down against the far wall, and he spent far longer than necessary staring out through a crack in the doorway, watching the laneway outside for any sign of trouble. He kept one hand poised tentatively against his chest, feeling the reassuring weight of the switchblade in his pocket. He knew exactly how to use it, and if the future had to get messy, he knew what to do.

But nothing materialised. There were no reinforcements, nor were there screams from the neighbouring alleyway as someone discovered the body. Slater sensed there were parts of Vladivostok that lay dormant for months on end, hidden away from prying eyes. Common civilians didn't venture into these alleyways. They were dark and decrepit and filled with the potential for suffering.

They belonged to the underworld.

Thankfully, the underworld was quiet today.

Slater shut the door behind him, took a deep breath, and set to work trying to decipher the bloody labyrinth he'd been dropped into.

He just hoped the two workers could keep up.

29

'Bogdan,' the first guy said, introducing himself.

'Pasha,' the second said after only a brief pause.

Slater studied them.

Bogdan was the larger man, rotund around the mid-section, barely squeezing into his high-visibility workers' vest. Despite his height and weight, he had the aura of a harmless giant. He waved his fat, meaty hands around every time he spoke, gesticulating wildly to compensate for the fear coursing through him. He spoke limited English, but he made up for it by conveying emotion with every sentence. Slater had no trouble understanding him.

Pasha was a different story. Short, thin, slightly more reserved. But still scared shitless. He had a better grasp of the English language, so Slater did most of the communicating through him.

Every now and then, Bogdan interjected with a passionate statement.

Slater found the man endearing.

'So,' Slater said, 'we're in quite a sticky situation, aren't we?'

'Where do we begin?' Pasha said. 'We want to help you. You just saved our lives.'

'I'm not sure about that,' Slater said.

'What do you mean?'

'I don't think that guy was interested in you at all. Everyone in this city seems to be trying to kill me. Or people I get close with. I think you two are safe.'

'No!' Bogdan exclaimed, pointing a fat finger at Slater. 'You are wrong. He was following us. Before you came.'

Slater glanced at Pasha. 'Is that true?'

The man nodded, icy fear in his pale blue eyes. 'We thought he was annoyed at us disrupting the neighbourhood. You know, going around and asking everyone in sight about Viktor. We thought he might come up to us at some point and start a fight. Try and push us around, tell us to shut up, take our problems elsewhere. That type of thing. We didn't know he had a knife...'

'It's all connected,' Slater mumbled.

'What?' Bogdan said.

'Sorry. Thinking out loud. But there's some serious shit happening in Vladivostok. Important enough to kill people without a moment's hesitation. You two work at the shipyard?'

'Yes.'

'What do you do there?'

'We are building an icebreaker. Actually, we just finished.'

Slater paused. 'This is news.'

'Is that important?'

'It might be. Viktor was working on it, too?'

'Yes. He was. Do you know what happened to him?'

'I do. But you're not going to like it.'

Both men went pale, anticipating what might come next, but it hit them hard all the same when Slater told them.

'At the train station?' Pasha said, disbelief in his tone.

'Yes. It happened yesterday. I'm surprised the authorities have managed to cover it up so well.'

'Do you think that's what's happening?'

'There's been no mention of it. If there was an ongoing investigation, the police would at least release some kind of prepared statement. They'd be vague about it, but they'd let everyone know there'd been an incident. They wouldn't completely blanket it like this.'

'But all the witnesses? You said there was a train full of—'

Slater held up a hand. 'You'd be surprised how effectively an entire train load of people could be silenced if they have control of the media. So what if people run around talking about it? If no-one reports on it, it never happened.'

'That kind of thing doesn't happen in today's—'

'Yes it does.'

'I—'

'You see what you're told to see. You hear what you're told to hear.'

'But why Viktor?'

'I think you need to tell me more about this icebreaker you're working on.'

'Why?'

'Viktor ran from the Medved Shipbuilding Plant when he stumbled onto something. He made it all the way to Moscow, and then they called him and threatened his family and ordered him back. He came back here to die. And he knew that. I thought I could stop it, but I was wrong.'

'So that's why he disappeared,' Pasha muttered.

'How did it happen?'

'He no show to work one day,' Bogdan said, complete with hand gestures. 'We think he sick, but no-one hear from him. And the days go on. And we get scared. Because many bad rumours about him. His family very worried.'

'Are his family safe?'

'Yes. We are checking in on them.'

'You're sure?'

'We check this morning. They safe.'

'So they haven't stooped to that level yet. That's something, at least.'

'Who is *they?*' Pasha said.

'I don't know. The people behind this. I assumed it was your employers.'

'They don't know where he is either.'

'Tell me about the icebreaker.'

'You have not heard about it? It's all anyone is talking about.'

'*Big* ship!' Bogdan said.

'Big ship,' Slater muttered.

'I can understand why Viktor saw something he shouldn't have,' Pasha said.

'Why's that?'

'It will be the largest nuclear powered icebreaker in the world when it's completed. We've been working on it for years. Good money. A stable contract.'

'Good money for tradesmen,' Slater said. 'I don't know if a stable income is worth killing people over.'

'No,' Pasha said. 'Not because of that. Because of the opportunity.'

'What opportunity?'

'The ship is finished. We are unveiling it later this week. A large ceremony. But no-one knows what for.'

'I don't understand.'

'The Russian government has a plan for its maiden voyage. But they aren't telling anyone what it is. It's all being kept quiet. They're very secretive about it.'

'Lots of tension,' Bogdan said. 'In government. Because of what happened last year. You know about that?'

Slater knew all too well.

Because he'd been the one to cause it.

30

He elected to keep that information away from Bogdan and Pasha.

What they didn't know wouldn't hurt them.

But the whirlwind of destruction he'd carved across the globe before his official retirement had created long-lasting consequences on the global political spectrum. It was why he didn't carry a phone, or check the news. Any day he expected to receive word of the breakout of nuclear war, but over the last few months the tension seemed to have dissipated.

It was half the reason he'd come to Vladivostok.

To tie up loose ends.

Because his last visit to the Russian Far East had left far too many unresolved problems to be comfortable with.

And therein lay the truth.

He'd always expected confrontation. Like Natasha said, he was a magnet for it. He knew when he'd rescued Jason King from an abandoned gold mine on the Kamchatka Peninsula the war wouldn't end there. They'd aggravated too many people in the upper echelon of Russia, the corrupt and powerful oligarchs and titans of industry. These faceless men and women had paid an arsenal of mercenaries to host a bloody tournament-style fight to the death in the bowels of the gold mine, run by an ex-KGB killer named Vadim Mikhailov.

Mikhailov had met his demise at the hands of King, but he wasn't the ringleader.

He was the puppet, dangling from strings wielded by billionaires and politicians at the very top.

So Slater figured if he strode back into the hell he'd left behind, it wouldn't take long for his past to catch up to him.

Then he could confront it, put it to rest, and move on with his life.

But it seemed he'd become entangled in something else entirely. And right now, barely treading water in the murky cesspool of Vladivostok's underbelly, he realised he was in way over his head. He couldn't keep running, playing defence, trying to piece the puzzle together before it caught up to him.

No.

He had to accept he didn't know anything, and move forward, directly meeting the resistance.

It was how he would get Natasha back. It was how he would avenge Viktor. It was how he would track down Iosif.

He couldn't achieve any of it unless he took a deep breath and leapt into motion.

The very thing he'd spent his entire journey trying to avoid.

You can't avoid the inevitable.

'Pasha,' he said. 'How much do you really know about the icebreaker?'

'What do you mean?'

'You've been building it. I'm sure there's a crew of dozens working on it.'

'Well over a hundred.'

'So it's an enormous project?'

'Did you not hear a word I said before?'

Slater nodded. 'I didn't put it together. So there's thousands of moving parts. It's a miniature city, basically?'

'Yes. Good for the economy.'

'And the illegitimate economy.'

'What?'

'You noticed any security around the ship?'

'Of course. The government would be mad not to protect it.'

'You talk to the security?'

'No. We've been explicitly told not to.'

'They're regular guards?'

Bogdan shook his head. There was fear in the big man's eyes. 'They are not normal guards.'

'Mercenaries? Special Forces?'

Pasha nodded. 'We can't be talking to you about this. This is a matter of national security. Sensitive information.'

Slater reached out and gripped him by the collar. He pulled the man in close. 'They killed your friend because he saw something he shouldn't have. You really want to hold back information in the name of national security? Then you're letting them get away with it.'

'I didn't know it was this serious,' Pasha said, withdrawing into himself. 'I've said too much already. I didn't know this was a conspiracy.'

'It's more than a conspiracy. I think the government might be involved at every level. What do you know about this maiden voyage?'

'Nothing. I told you. The workers are told nothing. Maybe it's not important.'

'Sounds like it's important.'

'How do you know it has anything to do with work? You're just guessing.'

'Everything leads to the plant.'

'What?'

'I just lost a friend of mine,' Slater said. 'This morning. She works there.'

'You lost her?'

'She was abducted. By ex-military types. They looked an awful lot like mercenaries. Big, tough. That remind you of anyone?'

Pasha sighed and nodded. 'There's a lot of men guarding the ship.'

'More than necessary?'

'I thought so, when we started construction. I didn't think there was any need for a force like that. But what do I know? I'm just a worker. I don't know a thing about national security. So I dismissed it.'

'I think they're protecting it for a reason.'

'What reason?' Bogdan said.

'I don't know. But it's important enough to slaughter any of the workers who find out about it.'

'What are you going to do?' Pasha said, although it sounded like he knew the answer.

'I'm going to the shipbuilding plant.'

'I don't think that's a good idea.'

'I don't recall asking what you thought was a good idea or not.'

'Viktor wouldn't want this.'

'How would you know?'

'Because he was my best friend,' Pasha said, and the cold

reality of the situation started to sink in. 'And ... I don't think he was as innocent as you think he is.'

Slater raised an eyebrow. 'Why's that?'

'Because he didn't stumble on something. He always knew about it.'

'He did?'

'They pay money,' Bogdan said, eyes wide. 'To Viktor. To stay quiet. He no talk to anyone. Not even us.'

'But he wasn't involved, was he?'

Pasha shook his head. 'That was the last thing Viktor wanted. I have a theory about what happened. He's too much of a good man to voluntarily involve himself. I think he *did* stumble onto it, but months ago. Instead of killing him, they paid him to keep quiet. Because they couldn't make too many workers disappear.'

'Seems like they don't care about that anymore.'

'The unveiling of the icebreaker happens tomorrow. I don't think they care anymore.' He paused for effect. 'Or...'

'Or?'

'You said a lady friend of yours was abducted.'

'Yes.'

'She worked at Medved?'

'Yes.'

'That might be something separate. Half of Vladivostok works at the plant. Especially because of the icebreaker. It's not as notable as you think.'

'So it might—'

Pasha said, 'It might have something to do with you.'

'That wouldn't surprise me,' Slater said.

'Why's that?'

'I attract bad shit.'

'Maybe this is good thing,' Bogdan said. 'Because you

deal with bad shit. It seem very easy. You kill man just before. No problem. You do this at Medved. You find bad thing.'

'Yeah,' Slater muttered. 'I find bad thing.'

31

Deep in the upper levels of a decrepit office complex, abandoned long ago as its tenants succumbed to the global financial crisis, a man sat at a desk.

The desk and its surroundings were a far cry from his previous occupation. But that was another life. He'd been reduced to this. Reduced to feeding off scraps. But for a man like Magomed Petrov, scraps was all he needed to succeed.

He no longer used his last name. Not to his co-conspirators. Not to anyone. Everyone knew him as Magomed, because any connection to his past had to be severed. It was the nature of the world he lived in. And if he was caught before he pulled off the impossible, he wanted to die as anonymously as he could. He would be carted off to a black site, tortured to within an inch of his life and then left to rot. And he wouldn't blame them in the slightest for it. Not after it came to light what he was attempting.

He wasn't even sure he was comprehending the consequences correctly.

It would probably turn out far worse than he was anticipating.

And that satisfied him, deep down to his core.

Nothing motivated a man like soul-crushing rage.

He hated the world. He hated everything about it. He'd spent what felt like a lifetime being careful, presenting himself with grace, choosing his words carefully, forming the right connections, climbing the political ladder, getting cosy with the right people, never voicing his own opinion, instead curtailing everything that left his mouth to what would impress the man in front of him.

So that he could ascend.

And then they'd thrown him out in the street and left him for dead.

Blamed him for things he didn't do.

Accused him of plots he couldn't fathom.

But Magomed had experience. He had a lifetime's worth of learning how to form connections, learning how to impress, learning how to blend in wherever he went. He'd been utilising those skills for the last few months.

And he'd almost reached the final hurdle.

The most important step of all.

Shivering in the cold, he pulled the winter jacket tighter over his broad shoulders and steeled himself against the wind howling in through the broken windows behind him. He had a desk, a computer, a phone, and a mountain of official-looking documents that almost weighed the same as he did.

If he pulled this off, it would go down in history.

If there was anyone left to record history, that is.

He dialled a familiar contact and raised the landline receiver to his ear. There was no central heating in the dilapidated office complex, but his voice came out calm and composed. 'Any updates?'

'None. They still think I'm running the show.'

'Of course they do. Your name's on all the documents.'

'The mercenaries work for you, but I don't understand what you want to do with them.'

'Today, nothing. Tomorrow, everything.'

'It's all been leading to this?'

'You don't know what I know.'

'Which is?'

'I know what the government is doing on its maiden voyage.'

'How?'

'Are you forgetting who I was in a previous life?'

'I didn't think you had the same connections.'

'They're not connections anymore. But I know who runs the show behind the scenes. I know how to get to them.'

'Threaten their families?'

Magomed smiled, but there was no joy in the expression. 'You are old school. You don't know the half of it. There are methods much worse than threatening their loved ones.'

'Such as?'

'I'll keep you in the dark. That way you can sleep at night.'

'What's the end game here, Magomed?' the voice at the other end of the line said. 'I've never questioned you. I've always trusted you. I've put my name on everything you needed me to. But I fear my old age has made me pliable. I fear you've been shaping me to cover for you. And that makes me think — why? We have the same values. We have the same aims. Or, at least, I think we do.'

'You have been incredibly useful, and I can't thank you enough.'

'I want answers.'

'You will get them. I won't be around to see the end of this. You will have to watch the show for me.'

'I am old and rich and disillusioned. You know this. Why do you think I care about what you have to show me?'

'Because it's going to be a fucking spectacle,' Magomed hissed. 'And I need to make sacrifices to ensure it happens.'

'But yourself? That is too great a sacrifice.'

'There is no other way.'

'If you're not around to see it, what's the point?'

'You have no idea how often I've been asked that.'

'You are telling people that you're going to martyr yourself?'

'It creates allegiance like you wouldn't believe. I hold every mercenary in Medved in the palm of my hand.'

'Surely they don't all believe you.'

'It doesn't matter what they think. As long as they follow through with what I tell them to do.'

'They will die too.'

'Maybe. We will see how it plays out. But they are savages. They don't know what they'll be doing tomorrow. So if we wind up in the end game, they will try to fight their way out. Some will probably get away.'

'You could get away. If you tried.'

'And if I get caught? Then they know it's all a ruse. I can plan well in advance, but I'm not impervious to interrogation methods. Not in today's day and age. I need to make sure they never know it wasn't legitimate.'

'*What* wasn't legitimate?'

'War.'

Magomed let the syllable hang in the air in all its intoxicating glory. It tantalised him, supercharging him with the necessary motivation to sleep only a couple of hours a night, spending the rest of his waking moments plotting, scheming, making calls, sending encrypted messages, co-ordinating a chessboard on a global scale in preparation for a single moment in time in which the world would tear itself apart.

'Is that why you needed my resources?' the old man said. 'For this phone call?'

'It's the most important piece of the puzzle.'

'What if I don't like where you're taking the world?'

'You are old and rich and disillusioned,' Magomed said, repeating the man's self-description back to him. 'You saw what happened in Russia. What the Americans did. They sent their operatives into our motherland and had their way. They killed our countrymen. And then we became the bad guys, because a rogue force attacked one of their supercarriers. A force we had no affiliations with.'

'No affiliations,' the old man said, smug.

'I know you bankrolled some of the operation. That's why I came to you.'

'Why do you think I want to watch the world tear itself apart?'

'Because you've done everything you wanted with your life. And you know where Russia is heading. You've seen the incompetence of the government. This isn't about making a better future. It's about tearing down everything that stands right now. And watching with a smile on our faces.'

'You won't be here to watch.'

'I don't want to spend another minute longer than necessary on this godforsaken planet.'

'What did they do to you? When they cast you out? How did they make you like this?'

'You don't want to know.'

Silence.

Magomed said, 'Did you get everything ready?'

'I've spent weeks on this,' the old man said. 'You have no idea about the favours I needed to call in. It's all in place.'

'He's on the line?'

'He's expecting your call.'

'And he thinks I'm Russian military intelligence?'

'Of course.'

'Just needed to confirm.'

'This is it,' the old man said, his voice weak. 'This is what you've been working toward for months.'

'I won't let you down,' Magomed said.

He ended the call and dialled another number, barely able to contain his nerves. It connected in seconds, and a gruff voice said, 'Yes?'

'Is this Admiral Ramirez of the U.S. Navy?'

'It is.'

'My warmest greetings, Admiral. I was told to contact you with information pertaining to the maiden voyage of the *Moschnost* icebreaker in Vladivostok. We have particulars about the route through the Bering Strait.'

'We were waiting on specific details about that. May I connect you to a conference call? We're all looking forward to co-operating with you and your government on this endeavour.'

'Certainly,' Magomed said. 'I'm looking forward to it too.'

He gripped the edge of the desk with white knuckles, sweating freely, barely able to believe his ploy had worked. They suspected nothing. He had control.

Waiting with bated breath as Admiral Ramirez rang through to a smattering of high-ranking U.S. military officials, Magomed prepared for the end game.

32

'I ... have seen something,' Bogdan said, his head bowed, his hands clammy and shaking.

Slater leant forward, ignoring the chill in the atmosphere. 'Bogdan.'

The man looked up.

'I need you to tell me.'

'I don't think so,' Bogdan said. 'You are American. What if you want to put me in jail?'

'I'm American. But I don't care if you've turned a blind eye to it. In fact, I don't blame you at all. This stuff is terrifying. What did you see?'

Pasha muttered, 'I didn't know about this.'

Slater said, 'If you did, would you have done anything differently?'

'Probably not.'

'I respect people who tell the truth.'

'There is place in Medved,' Bogdan said. 'It is off limits. No-one can go there. Just collection of empty warehouse. But sometimes I put my head in. I look around. See what happens.'

'You haven't been caught?'

'No. And if I caught, I good at acting. I pretend I'm lost. You see?'

'I see. But that's a dangerous game, Bogdan.'

'*Da.*'

'What do they tell you happens in the off-limits section?'

'They say guard live there. Temporary shelter. And some do.'

'The mercenaries?'

'Yes.'

'Had you ever seen any of these men before construction started? Protecting other sites, for example?'

'We didn't work there before,' Pasha said. 'We came when the work opportunities came. And the guards were already there.'

'How long have you been working on the icebreaker?'

'Years.'

'And they've always been there?'

'Yes.'

'So it could be normal?'

'It could be. But it seems like there's more and more of them every day. And the rules changed a few months ago. Any kind of contact was prohibited.'

'Who told you that?'

'Upper management.'

'Who controls upper management?'

'I wouldn't have a clue.'

Slater turned back to Bogdan and said, 'What did you see?'

'Two of the guards. Mercenaries, you say. They drag young man into one of the warehouses. Young man not happy. Crying. Not walking. They drag him by arms. And man in suit follow. Like rich man. Businessman.'

Slater thought of Iosif. 'Describe the businessman.'

'Young, too. Dark hair. Black hair. He look foreign. Caucasian.'

Not Iosif.

Slater bent down, put his head in his hands, and let out a groan. 'This is a mess.'

'What do we do?' Pasha said.

Slater looked up and realised the man was deadly serious. All his independence had vanished in the face of Slater's arrival, as had Bogdan's. They were both staring expectantly at Slater, figuring he had all the answers, looking to him for support.

After all, they were out of their depth.

I am too, Slater thought.

But he could take it step by step. He could investigate. He could win.

'You two can't stay here,' he said. 'Considering what you know. Your friend and co-worker died because he got scared. You two can't go back to work. You said you were on stable incomes for years. Good contracts. You have savings?'

'Yes,' Pasha said. 'Nothing to spend money on out here. We both have more than enough to survive for a while.'

'Then use that to stay afloat. Get as far away from here as you can.'

'What if they track us?'

Slater paused to consider how to phrase his next words. 'I don't think anyone will bother to track down construction workers who violate their contracts after what's about to happen.'

'What will you do?' Bogdan said, eyes wider than ever. 'How do you know what will happen?'

Slater clasped his hands together, rubbed them to stave off the cold, and took a deep breath. 'Want to hear a story?'

Pasha shrugged. 'We're in too deep to say no.'

'If I tell you this, you can never tell a soul. But I'm truly sorry about what happened to your friend. I tried to protect Viktor and I failed. So I owe you an explanation for who I am.'

'Okay,' Pasha said.

'I used to work for a division of the U.S. government that doesn't officially exist. Black operations. I was recruited to this division because of a genetic predisposition. My reaction speed is faster than almost anyone on the planet. You both saw that first-hand, just before.'

'I didn't think that was real,' Pasha said, turning pale. 'I can't believe how fast you killed that man.'

'That's what I do. And I did it for years.'

'Did you kill Russians?'

'Many. You won't miss any of them. I only targeted scum. I killed just as many Americans.'

'And you got out?'

'I tried to. It didn't work out. I ran away when I was sent to track down another operative. A man better than me. His name was Jason King. I found out that the orders from the top weren't always accurate, and I became disillusioned. I tried to lay low in Antigua and enjoy the fruits of my labours, but I couldn't do it. And Jason King went back to work. We swapped roles.'

'Wait a second,' Pasha said. 'A year ago. In Russia. Those were government operatives—'

'King was sent to the Russian Far East. He botched it completely. I flew halfway around the world to pull him out of a gold mine, but we found something down there that no-one wanted us to see. Then everything went to hell. I'm sure you saw it on the news.'

'I thought we were in for another World War when I

heard Russian paramilitary had attacked a U.S. Navy vessel. I couldn't believe it.'

'They were trying to finish us off. Because of what we knew.'

'What did you find in the gold mine?'

'Nothing I want to talk about. But that's why you two need to run. Nothing good follows me. I've been at the centre of all this chaos over the last year. It's all because of me.'

'Or maybe you are blessing,' Bogdan said. 'Maybe without you, world be much worse. Maybe life terrible for you. But good for everyone else. Because of you.'

Slater exhaled. 'You know what, Bogdan? I think you're absolutely right.'

'So you're just going to let us go?' Pasha said.

Slater paused. 'What makes you think I'm holding you here against your will?'

'We just watched you cut a man's throat. We're a little intimidated.'

'Get out of here. Both of you. And never come back. But give me one last thing before you go.'

'What?'

'I just told you my story. Or, at least, a condensed version of it. You can trust me. You need to give me access to the shipbuilding plant. Whatever credentials you have, whatever gate codes you know. I need it all. Everything in your head. If I'm going to have even the slightest chance at this.'

Pasha shook his head, shockingly pale, eyes wide and bloodshot. 'No. What if you get caught? Taken alive? Then they know what codes you used. It's in the system. You know we gave them to you. They track us down, they find our families, they kill them all. Like they did to Viktor.'

'You're just going to have to trust that I'll succeed.'

'I can't do that.'

'I can,' Bogdan said. 'V12XY. Gate code. Gets you in the front. Two guards there. Distract them, maybe. But they mercenary. Like the others. All bad. Do what you need to do.'

Pasha flashed his co-worker a dark look, brimming with rage. 'You just got our families killed.'

'Or I save lives,' Bogdan said, shrugging. 'This man is good man.'

'Thank you,' Slater said, his pulse quickening, his temples throbbing.

V12XY.

The code to get inside Medved.

The code that would help him begin to decipher the puzzle he'd stumbled across.

The code, potentially, to Natasha.

'It's okay,' Bogdan said.

'I mean it,' Slater said. 'You just did a bold thing. You trusted me. And now I might be able to save my friend.'

'Might be too late,' Pasha muttered.

'Could be. But there's something in that plant that needs my attention. Something to do with the icebreaker. And you know it just as well as I do.'

'You're getting involved with people far more powerful than yourself,' Pasha said, his voice cold, unwavering. 'You shouldn't be doing this. You'll get yourself killed.'

Slater got to his feet and wrapped a hand around the back of Pasha's neck. 'If I had a dollar for every time someone told me that, I could build my own icebreaker. And here I am. Not dead yet.'

'Yet,' Pasha said.

'We'll see.'

33

Magomed stepped out of the dilapidated office complex into the freezing afternoon. Breath clouding in front of his face, he winced and braced himself against the cold, then glanced in either direction for signs of trouble.

But the city was dead.

The chill seeped into everything. There were barely any pedestrians about. At the far end of the street he spotted a pair of silhouettes, hovering underneath a doorway, shrouded in shadow. At this stage of his life he had enemies everywhere, in every form imaginable. He didn't chalk anything up to coincidence. Fixated on the duo, he paused in the lee of the office complex for a moment longer than necessary.

Long enough to arouse suspicion.

Cursing his own stupidity, he turned on his heel and hurried along the freezing sidewalk, brushing between small groups of pedestrians passing by in either direction. He quickened his pace, tucking the overcoat a little tighter around his frame, feeling for the KAMPO Bayonet he kept in an appendix holster specially designed to fit into his waistband.

He'd never used the weapon yet, but he'd trained enough to know he could plunge it into delicate flesh without a moment's hesitation.

Although it didn't fit the job description of his previous career, Magomed knew what it felt like to take another man's life. If it came to that, he wouldn't be shy about it.

He sensed an unknown party on his heels. It could be the two guys he'd seen loitering in the doorway, but he knew nothing about them, not even their features. His paranoia gave him an endless list of possibilities, but he refused to spend too much time fixated on what could be. Instead, he concentrated on what was.

And there were certainly men on his heels.

He couldn't turn around and check. If he did, he would give away the fact that he knew they were there. So he strode even faster, covering ground at an impressive rate, shouldering civilians aside who got in his way. He was heading for the port, but he figured if they were closing in, they would intercept him well before he made it to the Medved Shipbuilding Plant.

So he would need to act before then.

Heart hammering in his chest, he realised he would need to use the bayonet for the very first time. He'd last killed a man over eight years ago. He remembered the feeling, but now he second-guessed himself.

Would there be hesitation there?

At this level of espionage and deception, there was no room for error. He would have to trust his gut and have confidence in himself that he could make the requisite moves when the situation called for it.

Now he heard their footsteps, concentrating on them so

fully that they thundered in his ears. Two men. Right behind him.

He suspected they were with the Federal Security Service. Or possibly a more covert division.

The secret police.

He would find out shortly.

He diverted into a tiny residential side street, the neighbourhood currently the equivalent of a ghost town. In drab Vladivostok, everyone in the surrounding apartment complexes was either at work or shut in for the day, sleeping through the afternoon if they worked nights.

The dead hours between the lunchtime and post-work rushes.

No witnesses.

Magomed assessed the street in one sweeping look, and determined that he would never get another chance to make the leap. He knew it would test him physically, mentally, and emotionally. If his plan succeeded he would cause untold suffering on a global scale, but there was a world of difference between making demands from behind the anonymity of a phone or computer and stabbing two men to death in broad daylight.

But he if refused to go back to his old tendencies, he knew exactly what the two men would do with him. He would spend the rest of his days at a black site, punished eternally for what he almost got away with, unless they dragged him somewhere private and executed him on the spot.

Wryly, he noted that his previous occupation worked in his favour.

They wouldn't expect him to retaliate in any capacity.

He turned on the spot, facing the men on his heels for the first time. A single glance was all it took. They wore bulky overcoats and fur caps, and their faces sported twin expressions of determination. Their mouths were sealed into hard lines, and their eyes were emotionless.

They had gone through the same transition phase as Magomed in preparation for a murder.

They had their target, and they'd been in the process of finding a quiet place to eliminate him.

Magomed's sudden change in direction made them hesitate. He made sure to sport an expression of total innocence — befuddlement, openness, as if nothing was wrong at all. He saw the flicker of doubt in their eyes as they rounded the corner after him, following him into the desolate street. The murky weather aided the conditions, darkening the sidewalk, leeching uncertainty into the air.

The pair exchanged a look after they made eye contact with Magomed.

More uncertainty.

Is this our man?

Magomed opened his mouth to speak, a subtle gesture that stopped them from reaching for their weapons. No doubt they would have fearsome sidearms concealed under their coats, but Magomed neutralised any hostility by staring them right in the eyes, wiping any fear or tension off his face, and taking a half-step forward to get into range.

Now.

Make the switch.

He prepared to kill. In one motion he slid the chunky steel bayonet out of his appendix holster, producing it from under his own coat in a heartbeat. But they didn't notice. Not instantaneously. He maintained eye contact with the pair of them as he brought the enormous knife into view. The grey steel, combined with the grey atmosphere, combined with the grey surroundings, shielded the knife from view for the vital half-second he needed to capitalise.

And then it was over.

They saw it at the same time, but Magomed shoved the blade into the gut of the first man before either of them could react. The steel tore through flesh and soft tissue and bone simultaneously, a fatal wound by any stretch of the imagination. Magomed made sure to move toward the man as he stabbed him, pressing himself chest to chest as he worked the blade left and right. It complicated the close-quarters nature of the incident, preventing the second man from getting a decent shot off even if he drew his gun.

But he didn't, because it wasn't immediately apparent what had happened. The first guy hadn't made a sound as Magomed slipped the blade into his delicate mid-section, instead opening and closing his mouth like a dying fish. Blood drained from his face, and poured from the wound in turn.

Magomed wrenched the blade free and thrust the guy aside, toppling him to his knees with a gentle push.

Then he was free to act explosively, darting toward the second man as the guy reached for his gun.

Too late.

Magomed shifted grip on the bayonet and raised it to shoulder height, jabbing it into the man's chest to the hilt, then pulling it out and bringing it down in an arc, finally completing the assault by plunging it into the same area of the stomach. He left the bayonet where it was, sensing the fight dissipate out of the man, draining out along with his blood.

Magomed lowered the second guy to the frozen side-walk. The mortal fear spreading across the man's face was justified. He would be dead in less than a minute. The first guy had seemingly accepted his fate, dropping to both knees and then pitching forward into the gutter by the side of the road, all the energy sapped from his limbs.

Magomed set to work dealing with the bodies. He'd been worried about personally transitioning two men into the afterlife, but corpses were a non-factor. He could handle them all day if he had to.

And, as the two policemen gave their final, pathetic groans, their eyes glazed over and Magomed realised the altercation hadn't fazed him in the slightest.

I'm back, he thought.

34

Slater couldn't babysit Bogdan and Pasha forever, but he could at least ensure them safe passage out of Vladivostok. Keeping that in the back of his mind, he elected to escort them to the outskirts of the port city, getting them on a bus or train and sending them as far away from this godforsaken town as he could.

They didn't deserve the same fate as their co-worker just because they'd learned unscrupulous details about their employers. As the nerves set in they withdrew into themselves, saying less, hunching over, shivering in the miserable cold. Slater watched them start to understand the ramifications of what he'd told them. Their friend, Viktor, had died a horrific public death. All because he wanted to run away.

So they knew they couldn't return to the plant.

They had to flee.

And he had to help.

He ushered them out of the warehouse where they'd had their impromptu rendezvous and guided them down a different alleyway, opting to take another path back to the street instead of having to look at the man he'd stabbed to death.

Bogdan and Pasha had reacted exactly how he'd expected two pacifistic manual labourers would react to witnessing a grisly murder up close.

They were both in shock, and neither seemed to believe that Slater was on their side. Every time he stepped too close, or reached out and laid a hand on one of their shoulders, they instinctively recoiled.

'I'm not going to hurt you,' he said, keeping his voice low.

They both nodded their understanding, but he could tell they didn't mean it. The shock wouldn't dissipate in a hurry. They would both remember what they'd seen for the rest of their lives.

When they reached the main road, they paused in the lee of the nondescript alleyway. Slater went through a rudimentary threat assessment. He scanned the street for a few beats, watching the cars rumble past, studying each passing face for any sign of hostiles. In truth, he didn't quite know what he was looking for. He was still just as much in the dark about the puzzle as when he'd first stumbled into it.

Iosif, kidnapped by gunmen.

Viktor, assassinated by gunmen.

Natasha, abducted by gunmen.

Bogdan witnessing a young man being dragged into a warehouse at the Medved Shipbuilding Plant.

Secrets surrounding a nuclear-powered icebreaker set to make its maiden voyage tomorrow.

It all added up, somehow.

Slater knew he wouldn't piece it together until he upped his pace. And that involved returning to a mindset he would have rather left in the past.

But things never go according to plan.

'I'll help you get out of here,' Slater said. 'The longer you spend in Vladivostok, the greater the danger.'

'Thank you,' Bogdan said, relief flooding his face.

Pasha seemed less grateful. 'We don't need your help.'

'Yes you do.'

'We're not kids. We can handle ourselves.'

'Just like Viktor could handle himself?'

'He couldn't,' Pasha said. 'But neither could you. You tried to help him and he wound up in the same place. So if we're going to die, it'll happen regardless. Besides, you need to go to Medved. The answers are there that you so desperately crave.'

'I can take a detour first. For my conscience. If your bodies turn up on the outskirts of the city I'd never be able to live with myself.'

'Why? Who are we to you? You don't know us. Why do you care?'

'The nature of my career,' Slater muttered. 'All part of the job.'

'You don't do that anymore.'

'I do a variation of it.'

'You're not employed.'

'I'm self-employed.'

'For what?'

'My conscience.'

'We'll be okay,' Pasha said, and Slater felt inclined to believe him.

Then the blood drained from the man's face as a pedestrian hurried past them. Pasha locked his gaze onto the back of the man's skull, and his hands started shaking. Slater turned to Bogdan to see whether he had a similar reaction and noted his wide eyes and frozen features, like a deer caught in headlights. He found himself so perplexed by their reaction that it took him far longer than it should have to search for the stranger who'd passed them by.

He spun on his heel, peering down the sidewalk, and saw a bulky man in a giant overcoat hurrying away from them, his back turned. He had thinning ash blonde hair and a confident gait. There was purpose in his stride. He was going somewhere in a hurry.

'You know that guy?' Slater said.

Both of them nodded in unison.

'If you want answers,' Pasha said. 'Start with him.'

'Who is he?'

'I've seen him around Medved. He only talks to the guards. I think he controls them.'

'The mercenaries?'

Pasha nodded. 'He might be their boss.'

'Might be?'

'We don't know anything about him. He avoids the workers. And he seems permanently angry. Like someone took something away from him. That's what all our co-workers think.'

'How long has he been hanging around the shipyard?'

'Ever since the manpower increased. So ... a few months.'

'That lines up with the increased interest in the icebreaker?'

'Yes.'

'You think he's the ringleader?'

'No way to know for sure.'

'I can find out.'

'Then you would have to let us go,' Bogdan said, voicing what they were all thinking.

Pasha nodded immediately. 'Do it. We can handle ourselves — I told you. Besides...'

He trailed off as he sensed a pair of men moving along the sidewalk, hustling past them in the lip of the alleyway. This time, Slater got a better look. The pursuers wore traditional Russian fur caps and were clad in similarly large overcoats. Their faces were hard, cruel, unwavering. They had their gazes locked dead ahead, and they moved past without acknowledging the presence of the three men standing in the shadows of the alleyway.

As soon as the pair strode out of sight, Slater said, 'They looked like—'

'The secret police,' Bogdan whispered, his expression pained. 'This is very dangerous world.'

'Be careful,' Pasha hissed. 'But go. They were going after the guy from the shipyard.'

'You sure?'

'I know Russia.'

'I thought this was government conspiracy,' Bogdan muttered, furrowing his brow.

Slater shrugged. 'I don't know what the hell this is. Maybe this is something else entirely. Maybe the secret police want to find out what's going on just as much as I do.'

'You shouldn't involve yourself with them,' Pasha said. 'No matter how desperate you are for information. They will turn on you and lock you up for the rest of your life without hesitation.'

'I'll be careful. You two will be okay?'

They nodded in unison.

'Just grateful we don't have to go back to Medved,' Pasha said, breathing a sigh of relief.

Bogdan joined him in the overt gesture, even going so far as to wipe his brow.

'Thank you for everything you did for us,' Pasha said.

'Don't thank me yet. Thank me when I figure this out.'

'I doubt we'll ever see each other again.'

'That photo of Viktor,' Slater said. 'Do you still have it?'

'Of course,' Pasha said, peeling the crumpled piece of paper out of his jacket pocket.

He handed it over.

'Why do you need it?' the man said.

'Got a feeling I'll run into some of the people responsible for his death. I want them to recognise who I'm talking about.'

'I hope you run into them. He didn't deserve what happened to him.'

'He was a good man,' Bogdan said.

Slater nodded.

He wanted to say, *The world's a bitch. Bad things happen to good people.*

But he figured it would be best not to inject absolute pessimism into the pair.

'Get out of here,' he said, realising how much time had elapsed.

He had some catching up to do.

Shaking each of their hands, he tucked his chin deeper into the winter jacket draped over his frame and hurried out of the lip of the alleyway, moving fast to catch up to the man from Medved and the two secret policemen hot on his heels.

35

They made a strange convoy.

The blonde-haired man from the shipyard taking the lead, seemingly oblivious to his pursuers. The two secret policemen hunched over, hands in their pockets, moving fast to cover ground and catch up to the lead guy.

And Slater trailing behind them, eyes boring into their backs, making sure he didn't lose them. This street was one of the busiest he'd seen in Vladivostok, and passing cars sent plumes of rainwater kicking up, drenching the roadside concrete. The wind bit deep, bypassing Slater's jacket and needling his core.

He shivered, steeled himself against the numbing chill, and quickened his pace.

The three separate parties moved rapidly in the direction of the port, heading for the icy Sea of Japan. Slater knew exactly where the lead man was headed.

Medved Shipbuilding Plant.

Finally, after hearing rumours about the place for so

long, he would soon be stepping foot inside, armed with a gate code and a death wish.

He didn't even have a gun.

The mercenary's blood dripped off the serrated combat knife wedged into his belt, staining one side of his jeans. He pulled his overcoat around the crimson stain and moved to close the distance, darting between a cluster of pedestrians to catch up to the two secret policemen. He wanted to be right on their heels when they moved to intercept the first guy.

Because he needed the first man alive.

He needed answers to the dark web of lies that had seen Natasha wrenched from her bed and carted off to an unknown location.

Natasha's involvement made him angry. And anger clouded his judgment. And a clouded judgment skewered his rational mind, putting vital tendencies by the wayside in favour of intense focus on a single point in front of him.

And it all added up to make him blissfully unaware of his surroundings.

He didn't consider the multi-faceted nature of his enemies in Vladivostok. He forgot how little it had to do with the secret police. He forgot about the other shadowy forces at work in the gloom.

So when the giant Russian man on the other side of the road weaved between cars, making a beeline for Slater's position, he didn't even notice.

He kept his gaze fixed on the secret policemen. He saw the first guy turn into a side street, and the pair of policemen quickened their pace to follow.

Then a giant tackled him around the mid-section, wrenching him off the sidewalk, dragging him forcibly through the open doorway of an abandoned shopfront.

An expertly timed move, utilising the weight advantage to knock Slater off-balance.

He was helpless to resist as he stumbled up the tiny flight of concrete steps and sprawled over the threshold, tumbling head over heels into the dark space that stank of rot and disuse.

He wondered if every building in Vladivostok was as rundown and deserted as he'd been led to believe.

The assailant loomed in the doorway, backlit as a dark silhouette against the gloomy sky outside. Slater lay sprawled on his back, out of breath, shocked by how hard he'd been thrust off-course. It took him a moment to regain his composure, and the big man made use of that opportunity to surge into the store. He reached down and grabbed two handfuls of Slater's jacket and hauled him off the ground, taking the burden of Slater's entire bodyweight.

Greco-Roman wrestling at its most fundamental.

All the reflexes and strength and brutal ability to beat down other human beings was rendered useless. Slater found his limbs flapping in the air, and the ever-mounting frustration of being wrenched away from his main focus sent chills down his spine.

Then the big man hurled him into the wall, crushing the faded plaster, sending him tumbling into the interior of the structure. One arm pinned against his side, both legs splayed at awkward angles, Slater scrambled to lever himself out of the hole in the wall. He planted one foot down on the rotting floorboards, started to worm his way out of the darkness...

...and sensed the big man stepping in to unleash a powerful right hook, heading straight for his chin.

If it connected, lights out.

Especially coming from a man of that size.

Slater hurled himself back into the dented plaster, slamming the back of his skull against the jagged material. Thankfully, it caved under his weight, preventing him from concussing himself in an attempt to avoid the incoming punch.

The fist sailed past, taking another vicious chunk out of the plaster beside Slater's head.

He caught the arm, used it to yank himself out of the wall, and thundered an uppercut into the guy's throat.

Choking, spluttering, wheezing, he went down.

Slater grabbed him on the way down and smashed the back of his head against the wall, crushing more plaster. He kneed the guy in the face, breaking his nose, then dropped an elbow into the top of his skull with enough technique and raw strength behind it to stun the guy into a semi-conscious state.

Fight over.

Just like that.

Panting with exertion, Slater crouched down and grabbed a handful of the man's hair. The guy was bleeding profusely from the mouth and nose. His alertness diminished, his eyes partially glazed over, he was in no position to fight back. All from a concentrated barrage of strikes from Slater that had lasted no more than a couple of seconds.

When he won, he made it look easy.

He stared into the big man's dazed eyes and said, 'You're going to answer a few questions for me.'

36

'You speak English?' Slater said, his voice resonating through the empty space.

In a rare stroke of luck, the rotting door frame had swung shut behind them as they'd stumbled into the shopfront, sealing them off from any prying eyes on the street outside. The room was dark and decrepit and dank, devoid of any furniture, a perfect interrogation site.

Slater hadn't anticipated having to deal with this, but he'd never needed to worm answers out of a hostile under such considerable time constraints.

The big man hesitated for a moment, then shook his head.

Slater punched him in his broken nose.

The guy howled, hands flying to his face, and a giant sob wracked his body.

Slater didn't feel a shred of remorse.

'You speak English?' he said again.

'Yes,' the guy mumbled, his voice stuffy, both nostrils clogged with blood, his septum mangled.

'I don't have much time,' Slater said. 'Why didn't you shoot me?'

'I don't have a gun. I wasn't expecting to run into you on the streets like that.'

'Who are you?'

'I work for Medved Shipbuilding Plant. I'm in security.'

'What did you do before this?'

'Russian military.'

'Most of your co-workers do the same?'

'Yes.'

'Tell me everything you know about what's happening with the icebreaker.'

The guy raised his gaze to meet Slater's, intensity in his eyes. 'You have to believe me. I don't know.'

Slater reached out and flicked the guy's septum with the tip of his finger.

As subtle as the gesture was, it brought about a world of agony. The man howled and cowered against the crumpled wall.

'What were your orders?' Slater said. 'Regarding me.'

'We're told to intercept you as soon as we find you in Vladivostok. All the guards have the same orders.'

'From who?'

'The boss.'

'Who's the boss?'

'I'm not telling you anything.'

Slater raised a fist, threatening a third consecutive shot to his shattered nose. The guy audibly whimpered.

'Okay,' the man hissed. 'Okay. But if I tell you the truth you won't believe me.'

'What do you mean?'

'We don't know who the real boss is.'

'What?'

'Our orders get passed through a shell corporation of sorts. We have people to report to, but they're just independent contractors or something. The real orders come from somewhere else.'

'And you're okay with that?'

'Most of us are desperate for work. We just do what we're told.'

'You're a certain type of worker, though, aren't you?'

The big man said nothing, wincing as pain seared through his broken nose.

'What are you talking about?' the guy finally said.

'All of you are waiting for something, and you know it. I assume there's a big payment coming down the line. When you go through with what you're ordered to.'

The man hesitated, and Slater raised a fist, taking aim at his nose.

'Ah!' the guy howled. 'No. Don't. Okay, okay, fuck. I specialised in counter-insurgency when I was in the military. I've killed people before. I don't have a problem with taking another man's life if the money's right. There we go.'

'Why the hell did you rattle all that off like it belonged on a resume?'

'Because that's what I was asked when I applied for the job. Those three specific questions. And I was told not to tell a soul, and that there'd be a certain kind of payoff at the end of the contract that would use all the skills in my arsenal. But I wasn't told what it was. We find that out tonight.'

'Who's telling you tonight?'

'The guy behind it all. He's heading for the shipyard now.'

'You just passed him. I was following him when you tackled me.'

The guy's eyes went wide. 'I did?'

'So you'll be in trouble if they find out you're talking to me?'

'I'm a dead man if they ever find out what you know.'

'Then you'd better hope I succeed.'

'What are you going to do with me?'

Slater glanced at the doorway. 'I'm on a tight schedule. I need to catch up to someone. I'm not going to kill you. But I need to make sure you're not going to follow me. And if I were you, I'd get as far away from Medved as you can. Because that's where I'm headed, and nothing good follows me.'

'I won't follow you,' the guy muttered, his nose starting to swell.

'Maybe. You already proved you don't have a conscience though. It wouldn't be hard for you to lie to me.'

'Please, just let me—'

Slater stepped back, creating space between them, and then launched a thunderous punch into the bridge of the guy's badly mangled nose.

A fourth consecutive strike, but this one had considerable weight and technique behind it, and the resulting *crack* sent a chill down Slater's spine.

The big man screamed and collapsed on the floorboards, passing out from the pain.

'You would have killed me,' Slater muttered to no-one in particular, his voice falling on deaf ears. 'This is a courtesy.'

He threw the door frame aside and ran out of the shopfront, hoping he didn't have to make up too much ground.

37

As soon as he stepped back out into the open, a dark chill worked its way down his spine. He sensed death in the air — some kind of sixth sense activated deep within him, letting him know that something had changed since his confrontation with the mercenary. There was nothing palpable, but he'd spent so long surrounded by combat that the mere presence of violence and bloodshed tickled his awareness levels.

Checking to see whether anyone had noticed his violent detour into the shopfront, he came away satisfied.

Everyone in Vladivostok minded their own business.

The pedestrians milling around when the big Russian had tackled him through the doorway were long gone, replaced by a fresh cohort of glib, unfamiliar faces. None of them gave him a second look.

He picked up where he left off, double-checking his combat knife still rested in the same position in his waistband. He shuddered at the thought of the blade slipping out of his belt in the previous fight. All it would take was a single scrape against the side of his thigh to sever an artery, considering how effortlessly he'd cut the throat of the mercenary in the alleyway.

There was no sign of the blonde-haired mystery man or the two pursuing secret policemen, but Slater could estimate where they'd been heading. He made for the port, heading in the direction of the ocean. The wind picked up, blowing a gale, coming off the Sea of Japan and lashing through the city streets. Vladivostok had long ago hardened itself against the conditions, its residents growing accustomed to the assault from the elements, but it would take Slater some time to adjust.

The cold seeped into his bones, stiffening his joints.

He gulped back apprehension, moving as fast as he could in an attempt to keep warm.

If anyone else ambushed him now, he would be unusually slow to react. He would need the extra half-second to loosen his joints, and that could kill him.

With a rare bout of fear coursing through him, he turned onto a side street as the light in the grey sky began to diminish. Surprised, he flashed a glance at his watch. It was approaching evening time. He shook his head at how fast the day had flashed by, a whirlwind of discovery after discovery.

He must have spent hours with Bogdan and Pasha, but it had seemed like minutes at the time.

He hoped like hell they'd made it to safety.

He would never know.

Oh, shit.

The sight ahead froze him in his tracks, barely discernible amidst the quiet residential street but easily apparent to someone with Slater's experience.

The bodies of the secret policemen lay splayed across the dirt under the shadow of a bush. The brambles draped over their bloody features, their cold dead hands already freezing over in the arctic conditions.

Slater felt sick to his stomach.

He'd missed it. The blonde guy had slaughtered the pair of them for even daring to follow him, and now he was gone.

No, not gone.

There.

Slater saw it at the edge of his peripheral vision, a brief flash of an overcoat disappearing around the corner of the next street, hundreds of feet in the distance.

He didn't even have time to determine a cause of death. He didn't know whether the secret policemen had been stabbed, shot, beaten to a pulp...

He simply had to *move.*

Reeling from one objective to the next, he broke into a flat out sprint down the quiet residential avenue. Dusk fell, and the sounds of the city fell away, replaced by the industrial uproar of the port. Slater imagined Medved Shipbuilding Plant was just one node of a gargantuan industry operating at the edge of the Russian Far East. And such an isolated location would be rife with exploitation — it was the nature of the beast. He recalled his last visit to the Far East and the nightmare he'd freed Jason King from. He recalled the horrors King had discovered in the depths of a gold mine.

Vadim Mikhailov. An ex-KGB executioner. The man who had led an army of hired guns, kidnapping innocent aid workers and villagers from the Kamchatka Peninsula and forcing them to fight to the death in a shocking tournament-style display of entertainment, live streamed from the pits of the gold mine to the faceless Russian billionaires and oligarchs bankrolling the bloodsport.

The very thought of the setup brought up nausea in the pit of Slater's gut.

But he wasn't naive enough to assume that was the only outrageous breach of justice happening out here in the cold, dead plains.

Vladivostok might have been a populated city, but anything outside its limits gave way to a freezing wasteland, barely inhabited by human civilisation.

And that left room for all kinds of horrors to take place.

Slater forced the thought from his mind. He'd returned to the Far East to round up the remnants of the mine operation and crush them forever, but that noble pursuit paled in comparison to what he'd stumbled on here.

So he pushed himself faster as the darkness closed in, rounding the corner and glimpsing the blonde-haired man hurrying down the next street. The houses in the quaint neighbourhood fell away, replaced by large swathes of unused land, which eventually gave way to industrial warehouses and fenced-off facilities. Slater shivered and gasped in the chill and hurried past towering factories, some belching smoke from their rooftops. The street lights barely illuminated the road, piercing through the fog that settled over the city in the evening time.

He moved quicker. The blonde-haired man had almost disappeared from view, and that was Slater's only connection to the conspiracy surrounding Medved.

He sensed they were approaching the shipbuilding plant.

There was a stench in the air.

The stench of fear. The stench of metal and ocean and darkness.

Night continued to fall, and Slater implemented every trick in his arsenal to stay invisible behind the blonde man, stalking him through the southern stretch of Vladivostok. He kept to the shadows, making use of the concealment, staying ever vigilant of threats on either side. He wasn't taking any chances after his encounter with the mercenary from Medved. If the man had been armed in public, he would have shot Slater down in the street.

And Slater wouldn't have known the kill shot was coming until it was far too late.

They rounded a corner, entering a new stretch of the industrial sector closer to the open ocean, and the Medved Shipbuilding Plant revealed itself in all its impossible size.

38

Pasha hadn't been exaggerating.

The plant was effectively a miniature city within Vladivostok. A high-walled perimeter fence built of concrete and topped with barbed wire flanked the entire perimeter of the grounds, but the colossal ships being constructed on the other side of the wall towered over everything in sight. They were the size of ten skyscrapers mashed together — some merchant vessels, some icebreakers, some container ships. They hung ominously in the dusk, backlit ever so slightly by the dark blue sky.

Despite the late hour, Slater sensed the electricity in the air. He couldn't hear voices, but the unmistakeable hum of operating machinery trickled over the wall. He identified the familiar beeping of forklifts — the construction sites were alive, and the workers in the shipbuilding plant were hard at work. But at the same time Slater sensed desolation — no matter how many men toiled away over the wall, there were vast swathes of dead land, home to dozens and dozens of warehouses and storage facilities and head offices and loading zones. The sheer amount of resources necessary to construct these behemoths was an operation unto itself.

The blonde-haired man tucked the overcoat tighter around his mid-section, hunched over a little more, and approached an unimpressive metal door in the side of the perimeter fence. It rested in a small concrete indent a few feet off the sidewalk, effectively hiding in plain sight. The man strode up to a simple numerical keypad in the side of the alcove and thumbed five consecutive commands — Slater loitered halfway down the street, watching closely, fixating on the number of times he stabbed down with his finger.

Five.

V12XY.

Adds up, he thought.

The door unlocked with a soft click that seemed to echo down the empty street, passing over gravel and potholes and sleet, and the blonde man hurled the door open and disappeared inside Medved.

Slater touched the knife in his belt in a rare moment of vulnerability. He'd spent years learning the ins and outs of urban warfare in an attempt to eliminate hesitation entirely. If he had to move on a target, he didn't want to stop and pause for a moment.

It was dead time.

Wasted time.

But now, something was different.

His sixth sense had aggravated again, kicking into high gear as he stared at the tops of the half-finished ships and the cranes towering over the rest of the site. Something lurked in that darkness, something he knew would rattle him to his core. There was no way to avoid it.

All roads lead to this.

He took a deep breath. Took his hand off the knife. Adjusted his jacket. Hardened his mind using a brief meditation tactic to inhale resolve and exhale doubt.

He envisioned his brain as a bundle of endless neurons, and in his mind's eye he destroyed anything that might make him waver in the face of a deadly threat.

Then he stepped out of the shadows and strode for the metal door, crossing the road and skirting around a handful of jagged potholes. The weather worsened along with the feeling in his gut, and a light rain began to cascade from the heavens. He hunched over, imitating the blonde man's actions, both to shield his face from any surveillance cameras and to avoid getting rainwater in his eyes.

He made it to the door, savouring the shadows, and punched in the code Bogdan had given him, letter by letter.

Now he had the chance to see whether the construction worker genuinely wanted to help.

V.

1.

2.

X.

Y.

A sharp electronic beep, a trio of green lights above the small keypad, and the door clicked open.

Slater took the handle and pushed inward, slipping through into the outer recesses of the shipbuilding plant. He quickly realised Bogdan's code wasn't exclusive to this particular door, for there must be hundreds of points of entry scattered across the grounds. This door led to a swathe of gravel and mud spreading as far as the eye could see, culminating underneath the bowels of a gigantic, half-finished container ship in the distance. This close to the Sea of Japan, the wind came howling off the ocean at an unprecedented rate and blew a shocking gale across the open stretch of land.

Slater shivered and took in the sight of an arsenal of machinery spread at random across the gravel, forming a rudimentary maze through the shipbuilding plant. But this section was only one tiny fraction of the larger picture. Slater could spend weeks searching the place and still fail to account for everything here.

He had entered a new world. A community of its own.

Then he turned and saw the guard booth resting in the shadow of the perimeter wall. He locked eyes with a gruff Russian guy in his early thirties, sitting slumped on the wooden steps leading to the booth, the embers of a cigarette glowing between his lips, his shoulders hunched to brace against the cold.

Slater froze, then nodded once, upturning the corners of his mouth despite his violent instincts to neutralise the threat.

Maybe he could pass himself off as a worker.

Maybe.

Then the guy stood up, tossed the cigarette away, and strode forward. He fired off a string of accusations in Russian, giving Slater the evil eye.

Maybe not.

39

Slater spotted the blonde guy in his peripheral vision. The man was nearly invisible, swallowed up by the vastness of the shipbuilding plant. He was a few dozen feet ahead, weaving between dormant machinery and oversized forklifts, about to disappear behind a mountain of wooden planks arranged in haphazard fashion. Slater forgot about him for the time being. The guy seemed set on his current path, refusing to check over his shoulder at any point, moving fast for the colossal unfinished container ship in the distance, propped up on giant supports the size of buildings.

He wouldn't be going anywhere in a hurry. The greatest threat had dissipated — Slater hadn't lost him in the streets. There were more variables out there, more laneways to vanish into, more collateral damage to take advantage of. Medved was a separate world, and Slater no longer worried about losing track of the blonde man.

Instead he turned his attention to the guard posturing up alongside him, ready to haul him out of the plant unless he was credentialed.

Didn't you see me use the gate code to get in? Slater thought, flustered.

He didn't want to cause any more damage than necessary. He'd hoped like hell the guard would simply assume Slater belonged in the plant.

Apparently not.

The man squared up to him, unquestionably aggressive, and hurled another insult at him in Russian. Slater spotted the appendix holster slotted into the guy's belt and noted the handle of the Makarov pistol protruding out. There was no mistaking the threat. But he also sensed opportunity — a chance to arm himself, finally.

He almost licked his lips at the sight of the weapon.

But he kept his composure, and as the Russian guard reached out and seized him by the collar, flummoxed by the lack of response, Slater let out a whimper. He dropped any shred of an aggressive posture, and took the defensive. Hands shaking, he reached out and urged the man to wait before hitting or kicking him. He gestured to his jacket, and raised an eyebrow.

I have credentials. Let me show you.

The guard paused, still sporting a white knuckled grip on Slater's collar, and nodded once.

Slater reached into the inside of his jacket and seized hold of the empty air, gripping nothing in particular. But now he was in an advantageous position, his arm bent at the elbow, raised to shoulder height.

He didn't need to unleash a big looping haymaker from a mile away and give the guard a chance to retaliate.

Expression smug, as if he were about to prove he belonged at the plant, Slater straightened up. But inside of withdrawing ID from his jacket pocket he scythed the elbow horizontally through the air, smashing delicate bone in the guard's jaw. The almighty *crack* poised in the air for a moment, then the wind carried it away.

The guard went down in a silent heap, not unconscious, just shocked.

Slater had broken his jaw with the elbow, and that carried with it all kinds of long-term repercussions. But they were avoidable if the guy took his recovery seriously. And Slater didn't have time to ascertain how innocent the guard was. For all he knew, the man had no knowledge of the dark side of Medved. So he guided the guy into a seated position on the guard booth's staircase, watching the blood drain from his face and the shock set in.

Slater reached down and gently extracted the Makarov from the holster. He gripped the gun one-handed, leapfrogged the short flight of stairs, and entered the guard booth. The space was tiny, claustrophobic, humid in an uncomfortable way, warmed by nothing but the guard's own body heat. The sole window was fogged and the silence permeated everything.

Slater found what he was looking for — a set of handcuffs resting in the far corner of the desk, tucked underneath a mountain of paperwork. They'd likely never been used. He left the booth, locked one manacle around the frozen guard's left wrist, and clamped the other around the banister at the bottom of the short flight of stairs.

The guard wouldn't be calling for help in a hurry.

Satisfied that he'd made his entrance undisturbed, Slater gripped the Makarov tighter and disappeared into the night, leaving a pale, sweating shell of a man in his wake.

40

Thirty minutes earlier...

Still high off the endorphins released during cold-blooded murder, Magomed stormed up to the Medved Shipbuilding Plant and entered a code into the metal door. He'd known the code all along but never had to use it. This was his first foray into the physical realm — all his previous orders had been conducted at a distance, using scapegoats and middlemen to take official employ of the army of mercenaries he had stationed around the plant.

The excitement of putting everything into action thrilled him. And it gave him immense satisfaction to know that stabbing the two secret policemen to death had barely fazed him. His mind was more battle-hardened than he thought.

He was ready.

As he opened the door, he ran a hand through his hair.

Coarse, jet black hair.

He hurried into the site, shooting daggers at the solitary guard stationed at this defunct corner of Medved. The guy looked miserable, slumped over the wooden stairs, puffing restlessly at a cigarette. As soon as he saw Magomed he gave an exaggerated double take, identifying the face but sporting disbelief that the man had actually arrived.

Because key individuals on Magomed's payroll had been briefed on his identity earlier that day.

Not all.

But some.

They were expecting him.

But the guard hadn't anticipated he would enter from this entrance.

'Magomed,' the guard said. 'This is all happening fast. Are we ready?'

'Almost.'

'Where is Ruslan? The rest of the men are waiting on him. They're getting restless. They're not sure if this is going ahead.'

'Ruslan is out there somewhere,' Magomed said, gesturing past the wall. 'In the city. I sent him out to make sure no-one thought there was foul play afoot. He contacted me earlier. We're in the clear. No-one suspects a thing.'

'The men know him. They don't know you. I think they will listen to their orders better if it comes from him.'

Of course, Magomed thought, stifling his frustrations.

Who did he think he was, revealing himself for the first time and expecting them all to bow to his commands? But that was exactly what he was paying them to do. He had to accept that everyone worshipped Ruslan — that's why Magomed had used the man to co-ordinate the mercenaries over the past few months.

Ruslan was their de facto leader, a fearsome ex-military thug himself.

And he looked the part, too. Six foot four. Packed with muscle. Blonde haired. Blue eyed. The perfect specimen to order a ragtag army of soldiers of fortune aboard an icebreaker.

So what use was it if the man was still out there in Vladivostok?

Magomed needed him back at Medved.

And he'd made that explicitly clear.

For a moment, doubt ran through him. Perhaps the secret police had planned a simultaneous attack. Maybe they'd sent their forces to sabotage all the leaders of the plot in unison. Maybe Ruslan had succumbed.

But that didn't align with the Ruslan he knew.

Still, Magomed stewed silently. 'Ruslan comes through this entrance, yes?'

The guard nodded. '*Da.* I'm expecting him at any moment.'

'Right. Carry on.'

'Are we still supposed to meet at midnight?'

'Yes. That's still on. Proceed according to plan. Nothing's changed.'

'You're worried about Ruslan.'

'He'll be fine.'

'He's...'

The guard trailed off, clamping his mouth shut as he realised he shouldn't be speaking.

Magomed cocked his head. 'What is it?'

'I shouldn't have said anything.'

'Now you have to tell me. You know this.'

The guard nodded, pale, sheepish. 'Shit. I really wasn't supposed to let this out.'

'Has he got himself involved with something?'

'You see ... there's a hell of a lot of waiting around, Magomed. These are violent men protecting the icebreaker. I'm a lowly perimeter guard and I can see that much. So

Ruslan and a few of the others decided to put their skills to use. It might have come back to bite them. That's why I'm worried about him. I don't know what kind of enemies he formed.'

'What's he been doing?'

The guard began to speak, apprehension drenching his features as he pivoted from one line of thought to the next, revealing details of something dark and sinister, something meant for the shadows, something never supposed to see the light of day.

'Christ,' was all Magomed could think to say. 'You think he's made enemies?'

'I can't see how he hasn't.'

'When was he supposed to be back?'

'He told me he was on the way. An hour ago.'

'I don't like the sound of that.'

'Neither do I.'

'There could be valid reasons for it, though. I ran into trouble. Out there. On the streets.'

The guard went pale. 'What kind of trouble?'

'There's certain authorities who actively don't want this to happen. I trust you'll do your job well for the remainder of the evening. Don't let anyone into this place who doesn't belong.'

'Of course. When have I ever?'

'Now is the most important time to be vigilant.'

'Of course,' the guard repeated.

Magomed nodded and continued into Medved's grounds, putting distance between himself and the guard booth. He let the dusk completely swallow him before pausing for a beat in the shadow of an enormous forklift. He threw a glance back at the booth — already, the guard had returned to sucking his cigarette down like his life depended on it. He wasn't watching the door. Instead he stared vacantly at the space between his feet. The man would prove utterly useless if anyone decided to force their way in through the door. He had a Makarov pistol, but he would be hesitant to use it if he met any resistance. His life was a sedentary one, spent endlessly searching for threats that never materialised.

When a problem did in fact surface, he wouldn't know what to do with himself.

And the secret police had set Magomed on edge.

So he decided to stay. He wanted to see if Ruslan returned, and whether he was followed.

He slid the bloody KAMPO Bayonet from its holster and stalked into the darkness, blending in to the point where he became completely invisible.

And then he watched, and waited.

41

Slater kept his gaze locked into the back of the blonde man's head, tightening his grip on the combat knife between his fingers, moving as fast as he could across the gravel without disturbing the ground underfoot. He remained silent, zeroing in on the target, having put every last obstacle behind him. Now there was nothing but the man ahead and the container ship in the far distance. The machinery had fallen away, replaced by dead ground.

No man's land.

Slater kept his distance, but night had fallen so completely that even if the blonde man twisted on the spot and peered behind him, he would see nothing but darkness. Slater's eyes adjusted to the night, his pupils expanding, and he decided to quicken his pace, closing the gap by a dozen feet. All was quiet in this desolate stretch of Medved — there were no workers around here, just emptiness. Space for more construction projects, perhaps. There were always more ships to build.

It didn't take him long to ascertain the blonde man was heading for the underbelly of the container ship by the shoreline, its enormous supports spearing into the heavens. The buildings underneath were a collection of warehouses, offices, and half-finished storage spaces. Everything seemed haphazard, thrown together at the last moment. There was all sorts of room for discretion in the shadows.

Alone in the middle of nowhere, Slater turned a full three hundred and sixty degrees, taking in the sheer magnitude of the Medved Shipbuilding Plant. His chest tightened, and a trickle of anxiety lodged in the back of his throat. He hesitated, unsure what caused the adverse reaction, and his heart rate seemed to double in the space of ten seconds. He realised instantly what it was — the shipbuilding plant was so vast, so impossibly enormous, that he hadn't a clue where to start.

He could track this blonde guy to his final destination — but then what?

Where did he go from there?

How did he get Natasha out of harm's way?

Was she even still alive?

How did it all connect?

He stilled his racing mind, took deep breaths to calm his central nervous system and still his shaking hands, and continued on. It was a rare moment of vulnerability in a life that had been marred by compartmentalising his emotions, pretending they didn't exist.

Pretending the natural reaction to any high-stress situation wasn't there.

Moving forward regardless of what his base instincts told him to do.

It took ten minutes to cross the stretch of land and stalk into the shadows around the half-finished container ship. The colossal structure stretched hundreds of feet above his head, carrying with it a sense of impending doom. If the supports shifted and the entire ship came toppling to earth, Slater wouldn't stand a chance in hell of clearing the impact site in time.

He clenched the Makarov in one hand, the combat knife in the other, and stayed hot on the heels of the blonde man in the overcoat.

The guy made a beeline for a grimy one-storey building on the outskirts of the construction site, made of giant slabs of concrete and seemingly thrown together without a care in the world. It acted as a buffer against the wind howling off the ocean, and the blonde guy hurriedly entered through a side door and disappeared into the dark interior. There were no lights on inside. A couple of exterior LED bulbs cast a weak, pale glow over the surrounding gravel.

Slater skirted around the edges of the exterior lighting and braced himself against the cold. He crouched low, poised in the middle of the wasteland, and counted out a long series of breaths. Then he raced across the dimly lit stretch of land and pressed his back against the faded concrete wall beside the door. The door was set a half foot into the wall, creating a small portion of darkness the exterior lighting couldn't reach.

He ducked into the alcove, now hovering a few inches from the door.

It rested slightly ajar.

He lowered himself to waist height, leant forward, and listened intently for any sign of a hostile presence. For all he knew, the blonde guy could be rendezvousing with the entire army of mercenaries, ready to make their final approach to the icebreaker for…

For God knows what, Slater thought.

But he didn't get that sense here. At first he'd assumed the blonde man was en route to his final destination, moving fast so he could implement his master plan, but this portion of the shipbuilding plant seemed dark, toxic, off the beaten track, hidden from the rest of the workers. He wondered how long the container ship had lain dormant — perhaps no-one had worked on it for years.

This was a dead zone.

Slater doubted the blonde man would lead a small army of security this far away from the main objective.

So what is this?

Perched in the shadows, he heard distant voices pass through the gap in the door. They washed over Slater for a brief moment, then passed through the alcove and disappeared in the wind.

But he heard every word before they vanished.

'Enjoyed yourself?'

'Of course.'

Slater froze, gripping his weapons tighter. He recognised that voice. He knew the inflection...

Above everything, he heard the sound of a running tap, and splashing water.

The unknown voice said, 'Time for payment. You're our last customer.'

The familiar voice said, 'Last?'

'I'm shutting down this operation tomorrow.'

'Why's that?'

'Myself and the rest of the men are needed for bigger and better things.'

'It doesn't have anything to do with the maiden voyage of the *Moschnost* icebreaker, does it? Because that timing would be awfully coincidental.'

'It might.'

'You're not supposed to be talking to me about it, I assume.'

'I don't care what you know. Who are you going to go to? The police? I'll simply show them footage of what you just did.'

A pause. Icy in intention. 'You recorded it?'

'I need reassurance, don't I?'

'Piece of shit. I'm not paying you a cent.'

A harsh laugh. 'Really? I don't think you're considering the ramifications of what I have on you.'

'You're a real piece of shit. You motherfucker. You're violating everything we agreed on.'

'You don't have room to take the moral high ground here.'

'Piece of—'

'You will pay me every cent you owe me. It wasn't easy to get what you wanted. We had to storm a fucking bar. You know how risky that was? Not much merchandise in Vladivostok like what you requested…'

Slater didn't hear another word, because rage as black as night seized hold of his insides. The beast returned, arriving before he could even think about preventing it, and then he lost all control of his motor functions. His limbs took on a life of their own. He let the darkness back in as soon as he pieced together what they were talking about.

He swung the door open, raised the Makarov, and had it pointed square between the eyes of the blonde guy in an instant.

Then his gaze moved to the second man.

Iosif.

The sleeves of his dress shirt rolled up past his forearms.

Hunched over a rusting metal sink.

Washing dark red blood off his hands.

42

Still dressed in the same business suit he was wearing on the luxury train, Iosif straightened up with his cheeks paling and his eyes widening. Slater kept the gun pointed squarely at the blonde man, because he figured Iosif wasn't armed.

Which proved correct.

For the first time, Slater could get more of a look at the blonde guy than the back of his head. He was enormous, at least four inches taller than Slater with piercing blue eyes and a rigid jawline. In another life, he might have graced the cover of an international magazine — he was good looking enough to qualify for that. But at the same time there was a certain coldness to him, a chill that hung in the air, pouring out of his eyes and catching Slater in its icy grasp. He didn't display any emotion as Slater announced his arrival, but behind the pale blue irises there was silent fury dwelling in the chasm.

'Who are you?' Slater said.

'My name is Ruslan,' the blonde guy said with barely a hint of an accent.

'You work for the shipbuilding plant?'

'Not exactly. I am contracted to work here. Who are you? Seems like you are not law enforcement. Which makes me curious.'

'If I was law enforcement, you'd be feeling sorry for yourself. Seems like I've caught you at an awkward moment.'

'No,' Ruslan said, his lips barely moving as he spoke, supremely confident. 'If you were law enforcement you would hesitate and try to arrest me and take me alive, at which point I would strip you of that gun and shove it down your throat until you choked on it. But you are something else, and I've never seen you before, so I assume you don't work for Medved. In fact I think you've never been here. And, let's see ... yes. Yes, of course. The woman. She spoke of someone like you.'

Slater tried to control himself, but he couldn't. He strode across the space, closing into range, despite Ruslan's dangerous confidence. To his credit, the man tried to put up a fight. As soon as he sensed opportunity he lunged, making a snatch for the outstretched Makarov, but in a one-on-one confrontation with no surprises he didn't stand a chance.

He almost got his hands on Slater's wrist, too.

Almost.

Slater whipped his hand back, satisfied that the bait had worked. He thundered a boot into Ruslan's groin, crushing his genitals under a steel-capped toe, and as the big man went down he stepped in with an elbow that sliced across the top of his temple, tearing the skin and causing a cascade of blood to run down the front of his face. Ruslan collapsed at Slater's feet, bleeding uncontrollably, effectively rendered blind by the injury.

Slater planted a foot on his chest and levelled the Makarov at his head.

'Still confident?'

Despite his ego, Ruslan shook his head. 'What do you want?'

'You just bragged about the woman. What the fuck do you think I want?'

'You're too late.'

'What exactly do you do here?'

His face a crimson mask, Ruslan turned to look at Iosif. 'I serve the customers.'

Iosif cowered, guilt riddling his features, grotesquely morphing his face. He hadn't managed to wash all the blood off his hands. Some of it had caked dry on his palms.

'If you move,' Slater said, 'I'll shoot you in the head.'

Iosif nodded, traumatised by the thought of instant death. He wasn't going anywhere in a hurry. He was weak.

Slater hauled Ruslan to his feet and kept the Makarov barrel trained on the back of his skull. Blood had stained the blonde hair crimson.

'Show me,' he said.

'You do not want to see.'

'Show me.'

'You are better off killing us both now.'

'Show me.'

Ruslan sighed, steadied himself against the wall, and gestured to a doorway set into the far wall, cast in shadow. 'Through there.'

Slater jerked the barrel of the Makarov, commanding the big man to lead the way. Ruslan took the lead, sauntering slowly across the cold concrete. Dread hung in the atmosphere — it seeped from Iosif in the form of shame, it seeped from Ruslan in the form of frustration, and it seeped from Slater in the form of acceptance.

He already knew what he would find.

He just hoped it wasn't as bad as he thought it would be.

Ruslan and Iosif entered a concrete chamber the size of a double garage, skewered into one corner of the building. There were no windows or secondary doorways. It was a private space, stripped bare of all furniture, devoid of any kind of decoration.

Except for Natasha's corpse, dangling from a rope in the centre of the room, her body mutilated.

This time, Slater was ready to tame the beast. It roared inside him, telling him to make it as slow and painful as he could, but before he could give way to his darkest thoughts he recognised the need for answers.

And Iosif would be useless.

So Slater walked up to him, spun him around so he knew what was coming, and pressed the barrel into the man's sweaty forehead.

Iosif's eyes went wide, and his mouth dropped open. 'No, wait, if you really want to know what—'

Slater fired, deafening in the confined space. Brains blew out the back of Iosif's head. His body hit the concrete with a wet smack.

'I don't,' he said.

43

He twisted on the spot and had the barrel aimed at Ruslan's head before the big man could even think about capitalising on an opportunity.

He jerked it back toward the main space. 'Out there. I've seen enough.'

Ruslan nodded and strode out of the room, barely giving Iosif's corpse a second glance. The old businessman meant nothing to him. Just another customer. The only annoyance about the man's death would be the lack of payment. Slater had run into a thousand men like Ruslan before.

As soon as they stepped out of the chamber, Slater unlocked his hips and pivoted on the spot, lightning fast. Ruslan didn't even have time to raise his hands in defence. Slater's shinbone drilled into his gut, crushing muscle tissue and possibly breaking a rib, and the big man spat blood and slumped into a defeated seated position against the wall.

Slater pulled to a halt in front of the broken man. 'What's your background?'

'If you think I am going to apologise you should kill me now.'

'No, I know your type. But this is a certain kind of cruel. And it makes me suspect something.'

'Suspect what?' Ruslan said, gasping for breath.

Slater remembered Pasha's words.

He seems permanently angry. Like someone took something away from him.

Slater crouched down and touched the Makarov's barrel, still warm, to Ruslan's bloody forehead. 'What's your last name?'

'What does it matter?'

'I ran into something just as cruel as this the last time I visited the Far East. I found it at the bottom of a gold mine, not too far from here. And I think it runs in the family.'

Ruslan's eyes flashed brilliantly, sparkling with a second wind, brimming with rage. 'You—'

Slater tilted the Makarov's barrel upward and smashed the butt into Ruslan's forehead cut, aggravating the bleeding. The man crumpled and cowered and winced, his accusation cut off before he could make it.

'Yes,' Slater said. 'If my suspicions are right, then I did exactly what you think I did.'

Silent and seething, Ruslan stewed in agony.

'What's your last name?' Slater repeated.

'Mikhailov.'

'Thought as much.'

'Did you kill my brother?'

'No,' Slater said. 'I didn't have the honour. A close friend of mine killed Vadim Mikhailov. But I watched him do it. And I enjoyed every second of it.'

'Fuck you.'

'Being a monster is genetic, I take it.'

'I do what I need to do to make money.'

'There are a million things you can do for money that don't involve ... this.'

'We are good at this,' Ruslan said, as if that said everything that needed to be said.

'*We?*'

'My brother and I.'

'The gold mine,' Slater said. 'You were part of the crew that abducted people from rural villages. You brought them to the mine. You let your brother make them fight to the death.'

'Like I said, we are good at getting profit from blood.'

'Who was Iosif?'

'Just a businessman,' Ruslan said. 'No-one special. Another guy with money to throw around and some suppressed sadistic tendencies. Those types pay well.'

'You run this operation? You take people and let rich bastards have their way with them?'

'I've been waiting around this godforsaken place for months. Sitting with nothing to do, waiting for the day I can avenge my brother, and it kept getting delayed. So I turned to what I knew well to make some extra cash as I waited. There's enough alcoves in this plant to do anything with discretion.'

'Delayed? What's delayed?'

Ruslan gave a sickening smile. 'Oh ... you don't know.'

'Know what?'

'You think I run this place.'

'I assumed.'

'I'm just one of the grunts with some spare time and some knowledge about how to get what I want from the world.'

'You said you were going to avenge your brother with this grand scheme.'

'But I don't call the shots. Thankfully my aim aligns with the boss.'

'And he is?'

'No-one really knows.'

'Awfully cryptic.'

'He was a powerful man in a previous life. That's all I've heard.'

'What the hell is that supposed to mean?'

'I don't think he wants to show his face. Until the end.'

'What end?'

'Not my business to talk about that. Don't you have a girlfriend to avenge?'

Slater scraped the Makarov's barrel down the top of Ruslan's forehead, drawing more blood. 'I have a feeling what you've been doing in this building will pale in comparison to whatever's happening tomorrow. And, thankfully, I'm able to control my anger. So we have a little more time together. I'll make it count.'

'A little less than you think,' Ruslan said, smiling at something over Slater's shoulder.

He didn't have time to wheel around. As soon as he sensed something behind him he splayed forward, kicked so hard in the small of his back that for a moment he thought he was paralysed. Reaction speed and uncanny reflexes meant nothing when the concrete was rushing up to meet him, so as he brought both hands up to break his fall and save being crushed unconscious by the concrete, Ruslan fell on him in an explosion of high twitch muscle fibres.

At that point, Slater was helpless.

Ruslan tore the Makarov from Slater's grasp and stomped down on the combat knife, wedging it between his giant boot and the dusty concrete. In desperation mode, Slater grasped at the hilt of the knife with a couple of fingers, hoping like all hell he could dislodge it from underneath the boot before he lost all control of the situation.

Ruslan noticed, and stomped down with his other boot.

Crunch-crunch-crunch.

Three broken fingers.

Nauseated, shocked, thoroughly rattled by the reverse in momentum, Slater instinctively snatched at his hand. Someone came up behind him and grabbed a handful of his hair, smashing his temple against the concrete. Slater moaned and rolled onto his back, reaching for the newcomer, trying to immobilise them.

Someone shoved a gun barrel between his teeth.

He sighed, tasted the harsh acrid tang of metal, and lay still.

He couldn't speak, but he could think.

Fuck, he thought.

44

Before Slater could even get a proper look at the newcomer, Ruslan dashed over and stomped down on his forehead.

Crrraaaackkkkk.

For a moment, Slater thought his skull had exploded. Sandwiched between Ruslan's boot and the concrete floor, an ear-splitting impact resonated through him, rattling his brain, thundering against his temples.

As he fought to hold onto consciousness, he figured it was one of the more devastating blows he'd ever taken in the field.

Perfectly placed.

With an uncanny amount of power behind it.

As Ruslan removed his boot, Slater audibly moaned. An involuntary reaction to the strike. If the man had stamped on his head any harder, it might have caused irreversible brain damage. In any case, it rendered him useless. A small parcel of energy reserves he kept in the back of his mind for times of extreme emergency fizzled out. His brain reeled.

His vision swam. His ears throbbed. His temples screamed for relief.

Seeking reprieve from the agony, he wondered for a terrifying moment if he would ever be the same.

Then the initial wave subsided, replaced with something close to acceptance. To avoid hyperventilating he concentrated on his breathing at the expense of everything else, allowing Ruslan and the newcomer to drag him into the corner and drop him in a heap on the floor.

They backed off.

Slater shut his eyes, figuring if they wanted to kill him they would have done it already. He had to use every fibre of his concentration to prevent himself descending into a full-blown panic attack. Because the stomp to the head had rattled him in a way he wasn't accustomed to. In this state, he was actively flirting with permanent scarring. He couldn't think straight, couldn't see, couldn't here. The uncertainty threatened to compound, the fear adding to itself in a natural downward spiral, and he forced himself to avoid that chain of events with all the willpower left in his broken body.

Ironic.

He had tested the limits of the human body so many times he'd lost count. He'd been shot, stabbed, beaten to within an inch of his life, and still managed to push through to completion of the mission. But the brain was a fickle bitch. Sensitive as all hell. Knocked in a certain direction, pushed a sliver too far, and it could cause permanent, debilitating damage. Slater allowed the pain to seep away and hoped with everything he had left that he wouldn't be crippled by the injury.

But, piece by piece, his cognition returned.

Not enough.

Nowhere near enough.

But a piece of it came back, squashing down the anxiety building in his chest. He could string a cohesive thought together. He could open his eyes and look at his surroundings.

Not that they were any brighter.

Ruslan Mikhailov loomed over him, sadistic venom in his eyes, just waiting for the word to finish Slater off. But he was hesitating. Controlled by an invisible leash that belonged to the man behind him.

The newcomer.

This guy was short in comparison to Ruslan, no taller than five foot nine, but despite his age he kept himself in good health. Slater figured he was early sixties with a coarse mop of black hair swept back off his wrinkly forehead. He carried himself with an uncompromising air of superiority — despite the shocking violence carried out by Ruslan right next to him, he stood with perfect posture, his gloved hands clasped behind his back, his brow furrowed as he scrutinised Slater.

Slater figured the man could see right into his soul.

'I don't believe it,' he said. 'I figured one of you would be back.'

'Have we met?' Slater muttered.

At least, that's what he wanted to mutter. What came out was a garbled string of indecipherable vowels.

Oh, Jesus, he thought. *I'm messed up bad.*

The old man squinted. 'What?'

Slater took a deep breath and tried his best to calm himself down.

You're not dead yet. You can push through this. Just make it to the next second.

One foot in front of the other.

'Have we met?' he said, this time his speech clearing, his heart rate settling.

The panic at anything surrounding brain injuries had taken a backseat, and he realised most of it had been terror rather than actual physical consequences.

They would come later.

In his old age.

If he ever got there.

'No,' the old man said. 'I know who you are though.'

'You do?'

'Do you recognise me?'

'No.'

'You are concussed, I presume.'

'Are you important?'

'I don't want to talk about that. But I was a public figure. High in Russian government. If you piece it together yourself, then props to you.'

'Got a name?'

'Magomed.'

'That's it?'

'That's all I'm prepared to go by.'

'Suit yourself. Why am I still alive? You realise what you're doing, right?'

'The old trope?' the man said with a wry smile. 'Leaving you alive so you can catch a second wind and fight back? Of course. But, as much as it's a trope ... you have to admit it's goddamn *exciting.* When else do I get a chance to talk to someone on my level?'

Beside Magomed, Ruslan stood deathly still, too high on adrenalin to decipher the subtle insult. But he clenched the Makarov tighter, aiming it square between Slater's eyes, hoping for any excuse to pull the trigger. Slater wouldn't give him one.

Magomed shrugged. 'I figure I'll take my chances. You're dangerous, for sure. I know exactly what you did on the Kamchatka Peninsula.'

Slater paused. 'You do?'

'How else do you think I know you?'

'So you don't have a name? You don't know anything about me? You just watched me storm a gold mine on surveillance footage?'

'I was still in my old position back then. We did everything we could to track you down. You and your friend. Where is he?'

'Long gone. Trust me, I wish he was here.'

'Maybe you don't. Maybe this is really the end. You seem like a man with a lot of experience. Maybe it all comes crashing down here.'

'Probably,' Slater admitted, barely able to think straight.

Behind his eyeballs, a migraine roared to life.

He lowered his head into his palms, inciting an exaggerated reaction from Ruslan. The big Mikhailov brother leapt back, anticipating an attack at any moment, the Makarov shaking in his hand.

Slater looked up and smiled through bloodshot eyes. 'A little jumpy, Ruslan?'

'Shut the fuck up.'

'You're just as nice as your brother.'

'Don't talk about him.'

'Listen,' Slater said, turning to Magomed. 'I could spend all day bickering with this guy, but you're the real problem, aren't you?'

'I'm the one who has to decide what to do with you.'

'You should kill me. That makes sense.'

'I will. But I'm choosing how to do it.'

'Why?'

Magomed sat down with his back against the opposite wall, his posture still immaculate. He breathed in, and breathed out. Then he said, 'Because it will be one of the last things I do.'

'What?'

'In twelve hours, I will die.'

45

Silence fell over the desolate building. Wind howled at the exterior walls, muffled by the concrete, but the ghastly wailing filtered through the open doorway all the same. The overhead lights flickered, the bulbs flashing on and off intermittently, plunging the three occupants of the sparsely furnished room into darkness with a strobe-like effect.

Slater thought long and hard about what Magomed had just told him.

'What you're about to do...' he said. 'You're sure it will get you killed?'

Magomed looked up and ran two hands through his coarse black hair. 'Yes. Now, adhering to the tropes, this is the part where I would tell you every detail of my plan and allow you to break free and catch up to me, thwarting it at the last second?'

'Something like that,' Slater said.

'I'm afraid today isn't that kind of day. And I'm afraid I have to go.'

'What does that mean for me?' Slater said.

Something felt different about the atmosphere. He'd put his life on the line more times than he could count. He was almost numb to the effects. He'd survived close calls with death at such a consistent rate that at some point it had all blurred together into a never-ending stream of carnage, like he was destined to reach the brink of getting murdered over and over and over again.

Deep down, subconsciously, he barely thought about the consequences of his actions anymore.

Because he always knew he'd find a way out.

But this time...

This time, there was a finality to his words that he'd never experienced before. He couldn't see a single path to victory, no matter where he looked. He glimpsed the giant bayonet in Magomed's hand, slick with blood, and figured the man had attended to business before he entered the shipbuilding plant. He must have been following Slater, as Slater followed Ruslan.

Ruslan.

Then there was the matter of the giant, wielding both Slater's weapons in his hands. He was a trained mercenary, a force to be reckoned with in combat, and even though Slater could best him in hand to hand combat he hadn't a chance at victory when faced with a Makarov pistol and a serrated combat knife.

And that wasn't factoring in his horrific concussion and the three badly broken fingers on his right hand.

He didn't even think he could fire a weapon if he got his hands on one.

So, as he said the words, he truly believed them.

His life was in the palm of Magomed's hand.

No backups.

No Plan B.

Just hope.

Something about it humoured him. Whether due to the way Ruslan had scrambled his brain, or the sheer disbelief that he'd made it so far in life only to fall at one of the final hurdles, he began to chuckle.

Magomed narrowed his eyes. 'What?'

'I just didn't think this would be the place it all came to an end.'

The old man shrugged. 'Sorry to disappoint. Were you expecting a nobler death?'

'Maybe. Something like that.'

'Well, I think I owe it to you to give you a memorable one.' Magomed turned to Ruslan. 'You think you can handle him?'

Ruslan nodded without a moment's hesitation. Too fast. He was overcompensating for the way Slater had manhandled him earlier, separating himself from the past, trying desperately to reassure himself that he had control of the situation.

Slater might have sensed opportunity, had he not barely been able to raise his arms. He couldn't even consider mounting any kind of retaliation.

Not for a long time.

Not until some of the short-term concussion symptoms leeched away, replaced by a muddy middle ground before he transitioned into the months of recovery.

Because a good concussion scrambled your wires for half a year, sometimes more.

There was no guarantee Slater would be the same person, even if he made it out of this concrete bunker alive, even if he somehow managed to thwart Magomed and a literal army of mercenaries. It was all hopeless — impossible challenge stacked on top of impossible challenge.

'Good,' Magomed said. 'Because the men are expecting me.'

He crossed the room and crouched down next to Slater, the hand clutching the bayonet tingling with anticipation.

As if to say, *Try it. Something. Anything. See where it gets you.*

Slater had nothing to offer. Instead, he managed a wry smile. 'This is the part where you leave me to kill your henchman?'

'I guess,' Magomed said, staring into Slater's eyes. 'But we both know there's nothing left in there. There's no fight in you. This is the end of the road.'

'I beat your man before,' Slater mumbled.

'This time I'd say the odds are ever so slightly stacked in his favour.'

'Maybe.'

'So much hope in those words,' Magomed said. 'I spent my life reading people. Learning how they tick. And I know how you're ticking, right here, right now. You're in a world of trouble.'

'I am,' Slater said, nodding in agreement.

'I hope you find a way,' Magomed said softly, out of earshot from Ruslan. 'It'd make things exciting, wouldn't it? Instead of effortless. Now, *that* would be quite the way to go out.'

'Don't count on it.'

'I'm not. Wishful thinking. Truth is, I can't afford the risk. But it'd make a good tale all the same.'

'Yeah...'

Slater's head hurt. His brain hurt. His mind hurt. His *soul* hurt. He didn't know what to do, how to think, where to direct his final scraps of attention. Ultimately he elected to slump against the wall and focus on his breathing, the only thing he could control. He thought he'd known the limits of pain, but this headache was something unprecedented. He hadn't imagined the human body capable of producing this kind of agony. He was surprised he was even conscious.

Still, Magomed lingered.

The old man said, 'You're really not going to try anything, are you?'

Slater whispered, 'Are you expecting me to?'

He barely had the energy to talk.

Magomed shrugged. 'I don't know. None of this is what I expected.'

'You wanted a challenge?'

'I wanted glory.'

'You're becoming a martyr for your plan. Isn't that enough glory?'

'Probably,' Magomed said, and restlessness sparked behind his irises.

'Is this the part where I convince you to change your mind?' Slater said, putting everything he had into forcing a sardonic smirk. 'You know ... try to make you doubt your motivations.'

Magomed smirked too. He got to his feet, rested a palm on the top of Slater's head, and gripped his skull tight, fingers pressing hard into his temples.

A final gesture of farewell.

'This isn't that kind of tale,' he said, and walked straight out of the bunker.

46

'Who is he?' Slater said.

He hadn't budged an inch since Magomed left.

In fact, his situation had only grown more dire.

Ruslan hadn't taken any chances when left to his own devices. Slater figured the memories of the beatdown were still fresh in his mind. The big man had disappeared into an adjoining room and returned seconds later with a pair of steel handcuffs. He'd approached Slater, seized one of his wrists, and fastened it to the portable heater built into the concrete wall beside him.

Chaining him in place.

Now he was utterly helpless.

That had been his one chance to retaliate. Ruslan hadn't disappeared for long, but opportunity had screamed in Slater's face. He was alone. Magomed was gone, heading off to rendezvous with his forces somewhere else in Medved. The shipbuilding plant was enormous enough to swallow him up. Slater doubted he would ever see the man again —

even if he broke free, even if he shrugged off the effects of the concussion.

Which wasn't possible.

He'd tried everything possible to override his body's natural tendencies and shut the concussion symptoms away in an internal vault until he was safe. But nothing responded. He squirmed and grimaced and willed himself to his feet, to no avail. It would take hours for the initial symptoms to dissipate. Then every movement would be painful, possibly for months on end. In that state he could force his emotions aside and escape, but that would require an overnight wait.

Time he didn't have.

So he'd watched helplessly as Ruslan secured him, eliminating any hope of survival.

Now the giant man sat facing him, cross-legged on the concrete floor.

A strange sight indeed.

And Slater figured if he was still alive, he might as well find out as much about Magomed as he could.

Ruslan ignored his enquiry. 'That's not how this works.'

'You don't want to talk?'

'No.'

'Then why am I still alive? You realise how stupid you look, right?'

'You're not going anywhere.'

'I've been in worse situations.'

'I doubt that.'

It was true. Slater had a past stacked with impossible odds and miraculous second winds, but he'd never crawled out of a hole this deep. He was defenceless, and as incapacitated as it was possible to be.

He regarded the steel cuff biting into his wrist, swimming in front of his eyes as his brain mercifully pleaded for respite. But he couldn't hand it unconsciousness. Not yet. Because there was still a sliver of hope, no matter how frail.

With each passing second, that hope ebbed steadily out into the vicious wind.

Carried away forever.

Ruslan sneered. 'That woman ... she must have meant a lot to you.'

'I didn't know her that well.'

'But you wanted to get to know her.'

'That would have been nice.'

'I wanted to get to know my brother, too.'

'What didn't you know about him?'

'We didn't spend much time together. The business kept us apart. I was one of the scouts. I drove between villages in the Far East, searching for potential candidates. Vadim ran the mine itself. There was a lot of work behind the scenes. And before that ... we did not speak.'

'How touching,' Slater said. 'Reunited through bloodshed.'

'Reunited through business.'

'It's the same thing to you?'

'Don't take the high road,' Ruslan said, his handsome face twisting into a snarl, the blood caked dry above his lips. 'You are no better than me.'

'We'll have to agree to disagree. Now, back to the main point. Why am I alive?'

'You took my brother away from me.'

Slater laughed.

Harsh.

Cruel.

'Are you going to cry about it? Your brother made innocent people fight to the death at the bottom of a mine to please oligarchs. Do you really expect me to feel bad that you didn't get a chance to hold hands?'

Ruslan stirred, almost launching to his feet, but restraint seized him at the last second. He clenched his teeth, grinding his molars back and forth, and stayed seated.

'I know what you're doing. You want me to kill you. You know what I'm keeping you alive for.'

'I assume you'll try to make it painful.'

'As painful as you deserve.'

'Your brother,' Slater said.

Ruslan raised an eyebrow. 'What about him?'

'He didn't die well. Actually, if I'm remembering this correctly ... I think he squealed. Begged. I wonder if it runs in the family.'

'Try your hardest,' Ruslan said. 'Nothing you say will faze me. Don't bother.'

'Grit your teeth any harder and you might break one,' Slater said.

'Shut the fuck up, or I might make it even more painful.'

'How long does it take to brainstorm what to do? Unless you don't even have two brain cells to rub together. I mean, Jesus Christ, you're just making this painful for yourself, Ruslan. Don't think too hard or you might pass out.'

'You're going to regret this.'

Despite the helplessness of the situation and the complete lack of energy inside himself, Slater summed up the capacity to mockingly shiver. 'I'm terrified.'

'Why are you so confident?'

'Confident?'

'You ... don't seem to care that you're about to die. I find it fascinating.'

'I figure my luck's finally run out. About time.'

'You find yourself in these situations a lot?'

'I do.'

'I'm sure my brother thought he could kill you.'

'Actually ... he didn't know who I was. But he was clashing with a friend of mine.'

'Your friend?'

'Same line of work.'

'Where is your friend now?'

'Not here. And that's all that matters.'

'You don't have other friends?'

'None who can help me now.'

'I don't think anyone can help you now.'

'You're full of one liners, aren't you?' Slater said. 'What's the delay? I'm sure you know how to hurt me. You've made a side gig out of it. Get to work.'

'The icebreaker doesn't leave this plant until early tomorrow. Which means I have all night.'

'I'm sure Magomed wants you back in a few hours.'

'He doesn't. He's familiar with what happened to my brother. He knows what this means to me.'

'What's he going to do?'

Ruslan said nothing.

'I'm about to die,' Slater said, and he believed it. 'You can tell me.'

'Then what does it matter?'

'I want to know what I wasn't able to prevent. I want to take it to the grave.'

'I don't know what he's going to do,' Ruslan admitted.

Vulnerable.

Genuine.

'He's keeping you in the dark?'

'Yes.'

'You don't like it.'

'Not in the slightest.'

'Do you think—'

Ruslan laughed. 'We could team up? I don't think so. For as long as I can remember my world has been nothing but suffering. I don't know how much time you've spent in the Russian Far East, but it's hell. Cold, barren hell. That's the only way I can describe it. And everything around me has been suffering. Everyone suffers out here. And my line of work makes that worse. Just the way life goes. So I don't care what Magomed wants. It's going to be bad. The new Russia might not make it. He's got more suffering inside him than I've ever seen, and he wants to take it out on ... something. But as long as I get paid, I don't care. The world won't end. Even if it leads to war. There'll be some corner of the globe I can go and stick my head in the sand. And then I can forget about the fact that the only person in my life I actually cared about died brutally in the bottom of a mine. But at least I can make you hurt before it all goes to hell. Some kind of revenge. Vadim would like that.'

'I would never team up with you,' Slater said. 'The second you let me out of these cuffs I'll cut your throat for what you did to that girl.'

'If only you knew the rest of it.'

'I can imagine.'

'What's your name?' Ruslan said.

'Will Slater.'

'You're not going to like this, Will Slater.'

'Get it over with. Avenge your brother. Nothing I say will make you change your mind.'

'No speech?'

'No speech.'

'Then I need a cigarette.'

'That's a real dumb thing to do.'

'It would be,' Ruslan said. 'If you had any chance of

getting out of this. But I felt your skull under my boot. I know the hurt you're feeling. I know it won't get better. And I know you're not going anywhere.'

Slater said nothing. There was nothing to say. Every word Ruslan uttered was nauseatingly correct.

'I...' he started.

Ruslan shot to his feet, crossed to the portable heater, and shook the steel bars with all his might. Veins pumping. Muscles straining. Teeth bared.

The steel bars didn't budge.

'You're not going anywhere,' Ruslan hissed.

Then he turned and left the building, fishing a packet of cigarettes out of his gigantic overcoat. The concrete room lapsed into silence, an empty shell containing the remnants of a dark horror story. Cold and pain drenched the air.

Now, Slater's brain screamed.

As it had many times before.

And he'd always risen to the occasion. He'd catch a second wind, beat down his adversaries as if they were amateurs, mow through the competition without breaking a sweat. He always found a way.

Not this time.

His body refused to respond to his mind's commands. He wished for a resurgence that never came. He sat in the dark corner, dejected and broken, sucking air in giant lungfuls.

Hoping.

Hoping for a chance.

It never came.

47

Ruslan Mikhailov stepped out of the building and crouched in the lee of the brick wall, protected from the howling wind, dwarfed by the gigantic skeleton of the half-finished container ship spearing into the heavens behind him.

His heart pounded in his chest. He lit a cigarette and sucked in the smoke, steadying his shaking hands. He was not frightened by the broken man in the concrete room. Slater didn't scare him.

Magomed did.

He knew precious little about what would unfold tomorrow. None of the mercenaries did. They were all similar in their worldview, and Ruslan had to imagine that was a deliberate move on Magomed's part. He knew his screening process hadn't been as extensive as the rest of the security. His brother had paved the way for the Mikhailov name, and it hadn't been difficult to transition from scouring villages on the Kamchatka Peninsula to protecting a shipbuilding plant in Vladivostok.

It was a similar game.

Assisting the ruthless.

Because Ruslan and Vadim had learned decades ago that the ruthless paid the best.

And when lacking any kind of conscience ran in the family, they both realised simultaneously they might as well advance their positions in life at the expense of others. Hence the last decade of Ruslan's life. He would have preferred a gradual descent into the person he'd become.

But he knew it wasn't the truth.

He'd just snapped.

One day in his early twenties, he used his fearsome physical stature and all the silent rage built up over his powerless youth to drag a helpless banker into an alleyway, beat him to death, and rob him of all his possessions, including a debit card he maxed out at a string of ATMs across Moscow.

It was all so ... easy.

And he regarded the corpse of the random civilian he'd plucked off the street without a shred of mercy.

With a coldness even he hadn't anticipated.

It had been a test. To see if he could sink to the same depths as his brother. And he could. From there it had been rather simple. He had a seven figure net worth now, squirrelled away in offshore accounts. Vadim had been worth eight digits when he'd died. The money had vanished. Untraceable. Ruslan would never find it. But he had enough. He'd inflicted unimaginable suffering, and gratefully he found he didn't care. So there was this last job, satiating the wishes of a man who'd been torn apart by the system he'd devoted his life to...

...and then nothing.

He'd done enough. He'd killed enough. He'd seen enough. Even if he didn't commit the atrocities, he certainly allowed them to happen. He profited from them. He tied up the victim, and handed the customer the knife. That was almost worse than doing the deed himself. He was enabling monsters.

But he didn't care. That was the golden ticket to a good life. To a happy life. To a free life.

When you stopped caring about other people, you could focus entirely on yourself.

Vadim had taught him that.

Vadim was everything Ruslan aspired to be.

He took another long pull on the cigarette, surveying the darkness. All quiet. The gravel fields spread out in every direction, dead and black and desolate. Wind howled through the empty shipbuilding plant. There would be commotion and activity at the other end of Medved, but that was far from here. No witnesses. No questions.

Just Ruslan, and the man who had aided in the death of his brother.

It had all led to this.

He would use a knife. He would make it slow. He would make it painful. Slater was a shell of his former self because of the concussion, but he would feel the agony all the same.

Ruslan turned on his heel, and drew the serrated combat knife from his appendix holster.

Whoosh.

He thought it was the wind, but in the final moment of his life he realised it was something else entirely. Something right behind him. Horrifyingly close. Something whistling through the air.

The garrotte looped around his throat and tore his skin apart.

Ruslan started to bring his hands up to his neck, but the

wielder wrenched with such ferocity that he didn't even get the chance to resist.

Because the man holding the steel wire was powerful.

Shockingly powerful.

With a sickening sound, Ruslan's head split from his neck.

His decapitated corpse slumped into the mud.

His retirement plans vanished.

Just like that.

48

It took Magomed twenty minutes to reach the other side of Medved Shipbuilding Plant.

By now, he didn't feel the cold. All sensation had been overridden by excitement — he knew his death was inevitable tomorrow morning, but that made him savour every part of life.

Including the suffering.

And there had been an awful lot of that lately.

Briefly, he wondered where it had all gone wrong. Well, he *knew* exactly where his life had dissolved into shattered fragments. But there had been a time beyond that when the malevolence inside him had festered, embedding the hate deep into his core, making him inseparable from it. And at that point he'd set the wheels into motion, step by gentle step. Now, he was almost at the end.

He couldn't quite believe he'd made it this far.

He left the shipbuilding plant through one of the dozens of side gates and ducked into the back seat of a waiting car. It was a nondescript black sedan pulled from a fleet of identical vehicles. Unimpressive and unassuming. The last thing he wanted to do was stand out and draw attention. He'd spent a lifetime doing that in politics, and it had resulted in nothing but pain.

Now he could turn the pain into something.

The driver wordlessly set off, taking him through the dreary streets of Vladivostok in the dead of night. The rendezvous with his men wasn't set for a couple of hours — he'd lied to Ruslan about the time constraints. In truth, he didn't want to spend any longer than necessary staring at the man he was supposed to be.

Bold. Confident. Young. Full of life. Relentless.

Sometimes Magomed envied the younger Mikhailov.

It was unfortunate what had happened to his brother, but now Ruslan could have his revenge. Magomed knew as well as Slater that the man couldn't achieve anything on his own. Not after Ruslan had stomped down on his head, scrambling his brain and ruining any hope of mounting resistance.

Shame, too.

Magomed had almost wanted the man to put up a fight.

He figured Will Slater was a one-man wrecking crew, judging by the confidence the man exuded.

Magomed had considered putting a bullet between his eyes and removing any chance of a miracle.

But not even miracles could heal a concussion.

So he'd allowed Ruslan his petty revenge.

Because how could he deny it when his own quest mirrored Ruslan's anger?

Instead of a single man, he was getting revenge against an entire country.

No.

More than that.

More than anything you can imagine.

In truth he didn't know the second and third order consequences of his actions. They would be vast. Enormous. Unparalleled in human history.

Good.

That's all this world deserves.

The silent driver pulled the sedan into the circular driveway in front of one of Vladivostok's most luxurious hotels. Magomed's life had become such a whirlwind of planning and scheming that he hadn't received the chance to learn the hotel's name. In truth, this particular journey had been thrown together at the last minute. He was going to send one of his mercenaries to do the job for him.

Discreetly. Under the radar. A professional killer doing professional work.

But his run-in with the two secret policemen had supercharged his confidence.

He'd learned much about himself earlier that day.

He'd learned what he was capable of.

He couldn't quite believe it when Ruslan had spoken of his own altercation with a pair of secret policemen. Magomed's suspicions of a co-ordinated hit on the major players had proved correct. Thankfully the pair of them had achieved similar results. There were now four corpses of covert Russian government operatives spread around Vladivostok, adding to the stress of the ticking time bomb Magomed had created for himself. If the icebreaker's maiden voyage hadn't been scheduled for the following morning, he might have fled and gone to ground.

Because there were eyes all over this mess.

Thankfully, there wasn't much else that needed to be done.

Except this.

'Wait here,' he said.

The driver nodded.

He stepped out of the car and locked his eyes onto the ground, avoiding the gaze of any passersby who might recognise him from his previous position of power. He stooped his shoulders and hurried for the extravagant marble lobby flooded with artificial warmth. Savouring the heat, he made for the elevators without so much as nodding a greeting at the receptionists and jabbed his finger impatiently against the control panel.

Once, twice, three times.

His urgency was undisguised. Maybe in another life he might have taken his time, assessed how to approach, assured maximum deniability. Or he would have followed through with his plan to use one of his henchmen to do his dirty work, because that made all the sense in the world.

But he had less than twelve hours on this planet.

And he wanted to experience everything before he went out in a blaze of glory.

He reached the sub-penthouse level in half a minute, pacing back and forth across the cable car with his sweaty hands shoved into the pockets of his overcoat. This was the end result of months of deception, of utilising old connections and nodes in the power structure to get his way. Once again, he found himself in disbelief that it had worked.

But it *had* worked.

He stepped out into the same ornately furnished corridor that seemed to populate every luxury hotel under the sun. He'd been gifted enough penthouse suites over the course of his career that the bribes had eventually become an unending blur. It felt freeing to be stepping into such an establishment without having to dangle from the strings of the puppet master that paid the most.

Now he was out of that mad game.

Now he was...

...in control.

He reached the ochre wooden door and rapped on it twice, firm but patient. It opened in a heartbeat. The small unassuming man from the U.S. embassy greeted Magomed with a subtle nod, ushering him into the room as if he had something to hide.

'Great to see you,' the man said. 'About time we got to meet in the flesh. Excited for tomorrow?'

The innocence of following the rule book, Magomed thought.

He almost felt sorry for the man.

'Very,' he said. 'This is an important step in repairing the tension between our countries.'

'I'm sure you understand the need for secrecy. We want this to be a pleasant surprise to the rest of the world. A shock announcement of our renewed peace talks, broadcast across the globe. I think it will be a powerful display of camaraderie. We all do. And it can't come at a better time.'

Magomed gave a sickeningly fake smile. 'I'm glad we share the same sentiments. Our governments have much in common. I think we are both focused on the greater good. This is, of course, a very important step in getting over what happened last year.'

The small man shuddered, as if he wanted to expunge the madness from his memory entirely. Tensions had never been higher. The icebreaker's maiden voyage would help to heal them.

An important first step.

'Now,' the man from the embassy said. 'I have some official letters our President wanted hand delivered to members of your cabinet for press releases. We want this to go as smoothly as possible. I have faith that you will ensure they make their way to the correct parties for the televised press conference tomorrow. Is the location still planned for the Medved Shipbuilding Plant?'

'Yes. Hand delivered?'

'They are signed personally. The President thought it was an important gesture for the cameras. We want to stress peace as much as possible. The alternative is ... not good.'

'Not good at all,' Magomed said.

'I would like to go over logistics, if we could. Just to double check our governments are on the same page.'

'I've got it already,' Magomed said. 'The *Moschnost* icebreaker is complete, and will cast off tomorrow morning at eight a.m. It will lead a convoy of four ships from the United States Navy through the Bering Strait on its maiden voyage as a display of peace between our countries. This gesture will aid in repairing tensions, demonstrating co-operation, and paving the way for a unified future. How does that sound?'

The small man smiled. 'Perfect! A pleasant surprise for the world to watch with optimism. Those words were excellent. Will you be facing the cameras tomorrow as the icebreaker casts off?'

'No,' Magomed said.

The man furrowed his brow. 'Why is that? I thought—'

'Well, in reality, I was disgraced from the government months ago. I have nothing to do with them. You and your country are so fucking stupid that you believed anything I fed you. I'm going to make sure the display of peace goes as horrendously as you could possibly imagine. Then what do you think will happen to tensions between our two countries?'

The small man started to laugh, his voice shaking and his tone wavering.

An awful attempt to nervously dismiss the rant as a bad joke.

Magomed removed the Makarov pistol from the holster at his waist and shot the man between the eyes.

49

The next morning, as pale grey daylight festered at the edges of the horizon, Will Slater stumbled out of the one-storey building with his eyes glazed over and his heart pounding a million miles an hour.

He was still concussed. There was no easy fix to that issue.

But the night's rest had made him functional.

If you could call it that.

His left leg dragged through the muddy gravel as if burdened by ankle weights. He couldn't seem to get control over the limb. There were other lingering problems too. Namely the shocking migraine, and the needles of white hot pain that shot through his head every time he moved his skull in any direction.

He needed rest.

He needed months of rest.

But the encounter with Magomed had put his health on the sidelines.

Because he feared the consequences of walking away from this particular incident were monumental.

The husks of titanic container ships and merchant vessels dotted the sky all around him. This portion of Medved Shipbuilding Plant was a ghost town, wholly deserted. He limped through swathes of no man's land, the deserted stretches of nothingness between construction projects.

Then he saw it.

At the far end of the plant, a colossal industrial zone speared out of the empty land. It was an enormous slab of steel and metalwork, complete with cranes hovering just out of reach of the central point of focus.

The icebreaker.

It was as impressive as Slater had imagined. A gigantic, dark blue hull rising up from the construction site, shined to perfection for its maiden voyage. It rested on gargantuan metal supports, waiting to be lowered into a narrow man-made channel leading into the Sea of Japan. On the open ocean, the swells stirred and frothed and lapped at the edge of the channel, beckoning to accept the icebreaker.

And a few hundred feet away from the ship, activity roared. Hundreds of people. Journalists. Cameras. Men in suits.

A media frenzy.

But the no man's land between the circus and the icebreaker felt shockingly desolate.

Slater froze at the edge of the vast arena, staring back and forth between the small civilisation of media erected around the administrative buildings, and the towering icebreaker perched on its lonesome on the horizon. The bleakness of the morning drenched everything, weighing him down, reminding him how damaged he was.

Something happened here last night, he thought.

But he couldn't quite put it together. His sixth sense was

still there, imperceptible but present, and he noticed the bitter taste of warfare in the air. People had died here last night.

In the plant.

Something was seriously awry.

But the concussion weighed heavy on his brain, clouding his thoughts, delaying his reasoning. He struggled for clarity. Finding none, he dragged his left foot through the gravel and made for the icebreaker.

Because if he had to choose between two paths, he chose the more dangerous one.

Every single time.

Even when his neural pathways disconnected. Even when he couldn't string a cohesive thought together. Even when the world became nothing but a bleak, soulless husk of its former self.

His surroundings pulsed with unnatural vigour, making his vision swim.

His chest felt tight, constricted by a shortness of breath. Suddenly he locked onto that sensation, and it sent him on a downward spiral into a pit of anxiety. A concussion could amplify emotions, skewer discipline, and ruin the confidence that Slater had spent a lifetime building up. Now he could only focus on his heart rate, which only served to amplify the sensation. By the time he made it a hundred feet through the murky pre-dawn light, it seemed as if his heart was about to explode in his chest. It pounded and thrummed and beat hard against his chest wall, swollen to what seemed like bursting point.

What the fuck, he thought.

A full scale panic attack.

He was in no condition to sneak aboard an icebreaker which, as far as he could tell, had been secretly overrun by

Magomed and his forces at some point in the early hours of the morning.

How the hell had they done it?

It didn't matter.

Slater couldn't concentrate on that for more than a couple of seconds. Each time, the terror in his heart roared back to the surface, drowning out the background noise. Sweating in the freezing cold, he crossed to the nearest building, a one-storey administrative complex skewered into the dark gravel, a concrete beacon amidst the barren industrial zone.

He pressed his back to the concrete wall and slid to the ground, out of sight of any curious passersby.

There was no-one.

The workers had been shepherded away from the plant, no doubt to make room for the media frenzy currently unfolding.

But why?

The maiden voyage for the largest nuclear-powered icebreaker in the world was certainly attention-grabbing, but this was something else. There was another level to the media circus, and this had seized it. Even in his inhibited state, Slater had only needed one look at the army of journalists and official-looking representatives to understand there was something else at play here. A surprise announcement, perhaps.

Hence Magomed's secrecy the previous night.

He didn't know. He couldn't concentrate. His heart beat faster and faster, and the more he focused on it the worse it became. But he couldn't focus on anything else. He started hyperventilating, which made the headache compound, his temples throbbing and pulsating and sending nauseating agony through his body.

'You're a mess,' he told himself. 'You're a fucking mess.'

How?

How did this continue to happen?

His body and brain wouldn't hold together much longer if he continued at this pace. He'd taken advantage of a private stem cell clinic to nurse himself back to full health after Yemen, but he couldn't rely on controversial methods forever. Sooner or later he would succumb to it.

Better a fast death than a slow, agonising one.

So he got to his feet. He pointed himself in the direction of the icebreaker and put one foot in front of the other. It was suicide. Utter insanity. He had the scraps of a plan in the back of his mind, but he wouldn't survive anywhere near long enough to pull it off.

He was the scapegoat.

The sacrifice.

And maybe that's all he was ever supposed to be.

Under a swirling, roiling sky full of grey storm clouds, he hobbled between buildings, heading for the icebreaker and the army of rented mercenaries that lay within.

50

In truth, he was never going to succeed.

He'd heard whispers of Magomed's manpower.

Bogdan and Pasha had hinted at it. Slater wondered where they were now. If they were safe. If they'd made it home free. He hoped like all hell they were away from this madness. He hoped they'd stayed true to their word and left it to him.

Because he was so used to the torment that it was worth bearing the burden for everyone else.

He was stumbling blind into an irreparable situation. He had no knowledge of the forces he was up against. He was unfamiliar with the layout of the icebreaker itself. He wasn't even sure how to smuggle himself aboard. He had a gun, and a combat knife tucked into a holster at his waist, but lacked the mental fortitude or the spatial awareness to use either of them effectively. The concussion had ruined his co-ordination and fine motor skills with equal measure.

He was a shell of his former self.

And he wasn't even certain his former self could have triumphed over this particular threat.

So it was with a reserved acceptance of his fate that he stumbled and lurched into the giant industrial zone, moving quietly between larger warehouses and smaller administrative complexes. He didn't run into anyone, and he figured he wouldn't be able to justify his presence if he did.

He passed underneath a towering crane, and for a moment he stared up into the abyss, noticing the dark grey sky through a maze of steel beams.

He paused there, contemplating whether this was the right move.

Yes.

It had to be.

Because last night, everything had changed.

He continued forward. There should be at least a handful of the plant's security milling around, but even in his debilitated state Slater could piece together what had happened. Magomed evidently controlled most of the soldiers of fortune assigned to protect the icebreaker over the course of its construction. When they'd stormed aboard the ship at some point the previous night, the mass confusion and bureaucratic log jams would have been too much to deal with.

And if there was anything the Russian government needed to go swimmingly, it was the maiden voyage.

Because of the media frenzy.

Because of the unknown reason for all the attention.

But they couldn't pull the plug, not this late. Sure, the majority of the shipbuilding plant's workers had mysteriously disappeared, but there was a vast difference between being unable to locate them and knowing they were in the process of something devastating, something unimaginably wrong.

So they'd dismissed it as a communication error and pushed ahead with the voyage.

Unaware that everyone was aboard.

Unaware that they were ready to take control of the ship.

And then what?

Slater didn't know. He couldn't see a purpose for seizing control of an icebreaker out in the Sea of Japan. What purpose would that serve? There was nothing resembling weaponry aboard. The fact that it was nuclear-powered meant nothing. If that was Magomed's intention, he would have been better off constructing a nuclear bomb himself, assembling a team of rogue scientists in some third-world hell hole to build the devastating weapon in secrecy.

No, this was public.

And it was very deliberately public.

Magomed wanted a spectacle.

And, given what Slater suspected was a previous career in politics, he had the experience and the knowledge to pull it off.

Hence the complete lack of security around the ship in preparation for its launch.

He imagined the crew were aboard. Perhaps they didn't suspect a thing. In the brief time Slater had met Magomed, he'd sensed unbridled superiority in the man. Maybe the old man was at the apex of a staggering deception.

Maybe he had everyone dangled from strings.

That was about all the deductive reasoning Slater's brain could compute. The strands of information faded away, his thoughts dissipating, replaced by the reality of what lay in front of him. His mind clouded, and he continued forward.

There was the icebreaker.

It rose out of the supports in front of him, impossibly enormous. Slater stared up at the hull, and a tight ball of nausea twisted his gut into a knot. The slab of steel, coupled with the grim conditions and the overall aura of helplessness, made him sick to his stomach.

But there was nowhere to go but forward.

He implemented what little training he could remember and ghosted across the final portion of the dead shipbuilding plant, keeping to the shadows, searching for non-existent enemies. He might as well have been walking through a graveyard. There was no-one in sight, but the atmosphere was tinged with death. It wasn't something an ordinary civilian could recognise, but Slater knew.

There were dead men hidden nearby.

But he couldn't help the dead.

He spotted movement. Straight ahead. In the lee of the icebreaker's dark blue hull, near the bow of the giant front end, a lone mercenary hunched over against the elements, talking rapidly into a black satellite phone. One hand gripped a rope ladder ascending to a shell door skewered into the side of the hull. He was gesticulating as he spoke, probably screaming commands into the phone, but Slater couldn't hear a thing over the howling wind.

Even if it was dead silent, he might not have heard a thing.

His senses were drastically compromised.

The mercenary seemed blissfully unaware of his surroundings. He stood facing the icebreaker's hull, encapsulated by the phone call, probably dealing with the aftermath of the entire security team breaking away from their predetermined positions. Magomed would have used his leverage, causing diplomatic chaos, and upper management would be scrambling to work out why no-one was at their posts or following their shifts. The mercenary yelled back into the satellite phone, defending himself against a mountain of accusations.

It was a test if Slater had ever seen one.

He could have shot the mercenary in the back of a skull without a second thought. The guy was big and strong, packing the all-weather clothing with enough muscle to fill the uniform out, creating a menacing aura. Slater put him at six foot two and well north of two hundred pounds. Probably ex-military. He had that air about him. Confident, disciplined, hard. He carried himself well. Shoulders back. Chin up. He seemed ready to attack anything at a moment's notice. To a common civilian, this man would epitomise the pinnacle of physicality. He looked like he could destroy anyone in a fight.

Thankfully, Slater had been dealing with ex-military types his entire career. They were usually the first to turn to acquiring blood money. They had certain talents, and a physicality that was imposing to anyone who hadn't seen combat, and that usually meant they could get their way if they turned off their conscience. Which was far more appealing than working odd jobs with their limited resumes.

So he knew what to do.

The only question was whether he could do it.

And he needed to know.

Because if he climbed aboard, facing at least thirty identical soldiers of fortune, it would prove disastrous if he didn't have the physical capacity to engage in a fight. He would get beaten down, and he would die.

You need to find out.

So, despite the combat knife in his left hand and the Makarov in his broken right hand, he strode across the final stretch of concrete and walked right up to the mercenary.

The guy didn't turn around, still hunched over the phone, still entirely unaware of his surroundings. And why should he be? For months he'd been isolated in the Medved Shipbuilding Plant without a threat in sight. The hard work was over. The ship had been seized. All that was left to do was climb aboard.

Or not.

Slater bent his right arm, recognising the uselessness of punching with his swollen hand, and twisted his body into an elbow. The point of his bone whistled through the air, but the wind drowned out the noise. The guy didn't even see it coming.

Bang.

Slater's elbow struck the man's skull, and his entire arm rattled in its socket. The impact speared its way up through his shoulder, his chest, and finally his head. His own skull rattled, and he winced as the headache amplified, warping his sense of reality as he grappled with the pain.

But he stayed on his feet.

And the mercenary didn't.

Knocked out cold by the elbow, he pitched and toppled and sprawled across the concrete, the satellite phone falling free from his hands. It clattered to the dock and spun on its axis.

Slater picked it up, ended the call the mercenary had been on, and dialled a new number.

Someone answered.

'Now,' Slater said, and put one hand on the rope ladder.

51

The fact that he'd physically dominated a hostile in such a debilitated state should have sent confidence surging through Slater.

But it didn't.

If anything, it only reminded him how hurt he truly was.

As he crept inch by inch up the rope ladder, bouncing off the steel hull, buffeted by freezing arctic winds, he should have been experiencing every uncomfortable sensation at once. But they all took a back seat to the headache, roaring between his temples with enough intensity to distract him from any kind of situational awareness. He grimaced as the wind smashed him against the hull again, which only served to compound the migraine.

It got worse.

He didn't even know that was possible.

He had experience with concussions. He knew what they were like. That didn't make them any easier to grapple with. His head seared, and he took a moment to pause halfway up the rope ladder, pressing the forefinger and thumb of his left hand to the bridge of his nose and blinking hard in an attempt to feel something resembling normal. It didn't work. If anything it only made things worse. His right hand had swollen into something unrecognisable, three of the fingers mangled by Ruslan the previous evening. Any kind of hesitation only served to show him how seriously hurt he was.

Keep going.

Never stop.

He made it to the shell door and tumbled in through the steel hull, barely paying attention to the dizzying vertigo. Despite the concussion symptoms, the escape from the wind proved blissful. Unable to feel his right hand because of the broken bones and with his left hand almost frozen from cold, he was largely defenceless against any kind of frontal assault. But one look at the steel corridor revealed it as deserted.

He took a deep breath, got to his knees and then to his feet, and did what little he could to compose himself.

He hadn't released his grip on the Makarov since he'd stepped out of Natasha's final resting place. His hand was turning purple, but one of his two good fingers rested inside the trigger guard, and the rest were wrapped awkwardly around the stock, already ballooning in size.

He used the combat knife to cut the rope ladder free from the lip of the shell door. It twisted and spun away in the breeze, coming to rest in the narrow passage of water between the metal supports and the edge of the dock. Slater surveyed the Medved Shipbuilding Plant one last time, most of its contents quiet and dormant, save for the cluster of movement in the section of the plant reserved for the media.

He set off into the bowels of the ship, without a clue where he was headed, his eyes wide and peeled for any sign of activity. The icebreaker creaked and groaned around him.

He made it thirty feet.

Before he could step foot in the adjoining corridor, he spotted a flash of movement directly ahead. He raised his gun to retaliate, but suddenly his sense of time seemed to leap from one moment to the next. Like a film projector changing reels. The jarring stuttering threw him off, and it took him far longer than necessary to realise the concussion had inhibited his grip on reality. He skipped a patch, and the next moment there was someone right in front of him, thundering a long metal object into his gut.

It hit like a freight train.

He groaned and went down on one knee, searching blindly with the Makarov. A powerful pair of hands seized the gun from his swollen, broken fingers and hurled it into the far wall. The metal object — a crowbar, he realised, as it speared through the air toward him — hit him in the chest and knocked him flat on his back, lashing the back of his skull against the cold steel floor.

That was enough.

He couldn't move. Couldn't sit up. His brain kicked into emergency mode and shut down his motor functions in an attempt to protect him from further harm.

No, he thought. *There's more harm coming. I need to move.*

But he couldn't. The crowbar came down on his stomach again, and he let go of the combat knife. All the fight sapped out of him — not that he had much left in the first place. Flat on his back, he reached his good hand into the air, palm out, trying to swat away the resistance. He couldn't even see who had attacked him.

Magomed?

No.

Too big.

Too powerful.

Through blurry vision he made out another big Russian man with cruel blue eyes and a sociopathic expression on his face. The thug reached down and clamped his meaty fingers around Slater's throat, pinning him in place.

The man needn't have bothered.

Slater wasn't going anywhere.

'Got him,' the big man said through clenched teeth.

His voice rang off the steel walls of the passageway.

On cue, Magomed rushed into view, moving as if he was operating on borrowed time. Slater stared at him through half-closed eyes. The old man stormed up to the pair and seized Slater, dragging him against the wall and shaking him by the jacket.

'You think I'm fucking stupid?' he snarled.

'What?' Slater mumbled.

'You honestly think you could sneak aboard? Like that was ever going to work? I've been trying to contact Ruslan all night. You don't think I could put two and two together?'

'Why ... are you so angry?'

'I don't understand you.'

'What's not to understand?'

'I don't know how the fuck you did it. You must be brilliant. You were chained to the wall, unarmed, heavily concussed. And you somehow overpowered the most dangerous man I have. Ruslan Mikhailov is brutal. I've always known that. So was his brother. That's why I hired him. I wasn't fucking serious when I said I wished you managed to escape. So when I can't get in contact with him, what the hell do you think is running through my head? I spent all night terrified that you'd come and ruin me.'

'Maybe that's ... what I'm here for.'

'Yeah,' Magomed scoffed. 'You're on the verge of death. I

could punch you in the head right now and your brain would never be the same.'

'Do it.'

'Can you put more than a single sentence together?'

'Probably.'

'Good. Because I want answers to this mess before I kill you.'

'Answers to what?'

Magomed slammed Slater against the wall, rage in his eyes. 'Ruslan was half the reason I was able to pull this off. He was meant to be here. He was meant to see it with his own eyes.'

'Sorry.'

'How'd you kill him?'

Slater said nothing. He stared at Magomed through blank, glassy eyes.

The old man snarled and slammed a fist into the wall a few inches above Slater's head. The steel clang resonated through the passageway.

He shot to his feet and turned to the big Russian mercenary. 'Get him up. Take him to the state room.'

'We should kill him,' the big man mumbled.

Magomed just stared. 'There's fifty of us. What the fuck is he going to do? Besides...'

The icebreaker groaned all around them as the supports receded, lowering the enormous ship into the water. A foghorn blared, and far underneath them a massive propellor began to turn. The icebreaker caught momentum and rumbled forward, plunging into the Sea of Japan.

'The crew proved awfully co-operative, didn't they?' Magomed said.

'You threatened to torture and kill their families?'

'I've found that seems to work.'

'The state room?' the big man said, nodding at Slater. 'Are you sure?'

'I'm worried he won't make it. Put him on the bed. But we only need him alive for an hour or so.'

'Why?'

'He almost stopped this. I want him to experience it.'

'Might be a mistake.'

'Look at him.'

Slater knew he didn't paint a pretty picture. At some point he'd been cut — the journey through the icebreaker's passageways had been such a blur that he couldn't pinpoint when it had happened. But blood ran freely down his face, over his swollen eyes, over his puffy cheeks. His right hand would take a couple of months to heal, minimum. Until then it would be useless. And his internals were horrifically, painfully broken.

He closed his eyes and accepted his fate.

He always knew it wouldn't work.

He just had to wait, to hold out, until...

Until what?

Magomed said, 'You really think he'll put up a fight?'

'He got the jump on Ruslan.'

'Yes, and I want to find out how.'

The big mercenary didn't respond.

Magomed raised a furry eyebrow. 'Are you scared?'

'No ... I just...'

'Get him to the state room. And grow up.'

The big man nodded and hauled Slater to his feet.

Slater winced, his eyes still closed, and allowed himself to be dragged deeper and deeper into the abyss.

An abyss from which there was no escape.

52

Through the blood crusted over his eyelids, Slater soaked in the sight of the state room. It was a luxurious first-class cabin, the bed made to perfection and the decorations ornate. Through a broad porthole he stared at the furious ocean outside, the waves stirring and vomiting froth into the swells. They were moving fast. Dejected, stripped of energy, Slater didn't resist as the mercenary dumped him on the king-sized mattress and pointed Slater's own Makarov at his head.

'Don't try anything,' the big man snarled.

Slater coughed and did what little he could to improve his position. He squirmed to the headboard, sat up, and sucked in deep lungfuls of cool artificial air.

Magomed entered a few moments later.

'Did he try anything?' the old man said.

'No.'

'Good.'

Magomed took the Makarov off the mercenary, leant against the dresser on the other side of the state room, and shooed the man away.

'Go back to your post,' Magomed said. 'The patterns we rehearsed. Make sure there's nothing else that can sabotage us.'

'Are you sure?'

'I can handle this.'

The big man said nothing.

Again, Magomed said, 'Look at him.'

'That's not what I'm concerned about.'

'What's the problem?'

'Like you said ... there's fifty of us.'

'Yes.'

'For what?'

'What do you mean?'

'This was all so easy.'

'Because I planned it for months. And it's better to overcompensate than underestimate.'

'We're still going through with ... you know...?'

Magomed eyed Slater, then turned his attention back to the mercenary with a wry smile. 'What? Scared to talk about it in front of our guest?'

'Isn't it better we keep him in the dark?'

'He unnerves you, doesn't he?'

'Somewhat.'

'He's ninety percent dead. You've got nothing to worry about.'

'I know,' the mercenary said, far too confidently, trying to save face.

'Get out of here.'

The man disappeared.

It was just them. The icebreaker rumbled all around them, but Slater barely noticed. He stared into the cold dead eyes of the old man across from him, and certain pieces of the puzzle started to fall into place.

'You were a politician?' he said.

Magomed nodded. 'Got close to the top. And then they threw me out to restructure the new Russia.'

'The new Russia?'

'Can't teach an old dog new tricks. I was a relic. From the old world. From a world that made room for people like Vadim Mikhailov.'

'You knew about that? When you were in office?'

'I fed him most of the contacts that bankrolled it.'

'Ah. And then?'

'And then I was nothing. Cast out. They didn't want to go to war with the U.S., so they rolled over and begged like dogs for peace talks. For tensions to dissipate. I couldn't believe it. It made me sick. They felt like they were responsible for the rogue attack on the supercarrier, even though they'd successfully distanced themselves from that. Pathetic...'

Slater managed a wry smile. 'I was on that supercarrier.'

Magomed froze. 'That's it...'

'What?'

'There was something under the surface. Something that made me want to keep you alive. Even when you killed Ruslan. Even when you made it aboard. It seemed like ... you were supposed to be here. And it all led to this.'

Slater let him talk. He shut his mouth and sagged into the bedspread, barely able to lift his arms. He couldn't put up a fight even if he wanted to.

'You're ... connected to all of this. That's why I want you to see it.'

'Peace talks,' Slater said. 'That's what this maiden voyage is for, isn't it?'

'A diplomatic display between our countries. This

icebreaker will lead U.S. Navy warships through the Bering Strait. Just ... so pathetic...'

'Does anyone know you're aboard?'

'No.'

'You planned this well.'

'I'm a politician.'

'Were.'

Magomed nodded. 'Were. And soon I won't be anything.'

'Going down with the ship?'

'The ship's not going anywhere. But I can't survive.'

'Because?'

'Well, I don't want to live. Not with what I'm about to do to the world.'

'War?'

'There'll be no other option. Things are already unimaginably tense.'

'And what are you going to do?'

Magomed leant forward, edging closer to Slater. He smiled. 'How do you think your country will react when I turn this icebreaker around and ram it straight into one of the warships? It'll kill hundreds.'

'There won't be nuclear war. No-one's that stupid.'

'There'll be no choice.'

'That's it?' Slater said. 'That's all you're doing? Using this thing as a battering ram?'

'What did you expect?'

'Something more nuanced.'

'Then I'll impress you. There's certain ... information I know. From my time in power. I held onto it. I'm leaving it aboard, and then I'm killing myself. The men have been instructed to throw me overboard.'

'So it looks like the orders came straight from the top.'

'Exactly.'

'And no-one knows the details besides yourself. Hence the secrecy. All these men ... all this firepower ... it's not to defend the ship. It's to make it look like a grander conspiracy.'

'You're catching on.'

'They don't know what they're here for.'

'Well, they think they do. They're standing guard. Making sure no-one sabotages the ship.'

'There's not much to do, then.'

'Most are restless.'

'Do they know who you are?'

'No. Most of them don't even know I'm aboard.'

'So if shit were to hypothetically hit the fan, that might prove ... chaotic?'

'You trying to scare me? You can't even get off the bed.'

Magomed levelled the Makarov at Slater's head. The dark barrel stared him in the face. Slater gulped back apprehension and straightened his posture against the headboard.

'I wouldn't do that just yet,' Slater said.

'Why?'

'Because you're going to need me to make sense of what's about to happen.'

Under the harsh artificial lighting, Magomed's left eyelid twitched. An imperceptible gesture, but it rested at odds with the skeptical expression on his face. He couldn't maintain his uncaring aura.

Because, deep down, he knew Slater wasn't displaying everything he knew on the surface. There was something underneath. A subtle understanding of...

Of what?

'You trying to intimidate me?' he said.

But he didn't pull the trigger.

'I know how you got in this position,' Slater said. 'You pirated the largest nuclear-powered icebreaker in the world without anyone understanding what was happening. Because of your political expertise. Because you understand the nuances of human behaviour. Because you know how to manipulate and control and find what motivates people. And you're relentless. You don't stop. You set your mind on something and then barrel toward it. Something that no-one thought would be possible. You're about to try and cause global nuclear conflict, and you're close to doing it. Because no-one told you the odds.'

'You'd better get to the point.'

'I have a friend. He's also relentless.'

'You don't have any friends here.'

'I didn't think I did, either.'

Magomed said nothing. Scrutinised Slater's features. Searched for any hint of deception.

'You were right to question how I overpowered Ruslan,' Slater said. 'Because I didn't.'

Under the lights, Magomed started to pale. 'Your friend?'

'You said this was all connected,' Slater said. 'It is. It's why I came back to the Russian Far East. Because we left a web of monsters behind on the Kamchatka Peninsula. Cut the head off the snake, and two more take its place. So I figured I'd come back here and kill the snake. It didn't take me long to sniff them all out. All the independent contractors who took the hostages, who made sure the mine operation ran fluidly, who offered their services to the highest bidder. I wanted all of them dead. Because I knew they were still here. We killed Vadim Mikhailov, but we didn't kill the rest. And then it turns out you brought them all together. Every piece of shit in the Far East. You brought them to

Vladivostok to protect the icebreaker. So I have to thank you. Because you rounded them up for him.'

'Who?'

The lights went out.

All at once.

Darkness plunged over the state room.

From the passageways below deck, gunfire and screams echoed through the ship.

Slater muttered, 'Hello, old friend.'

53

He thought the fight had left him.

He thought he'd left the past in the past.

He thought he was done with this life forever.

And then Will Slater called from a pay phone in Khabarovsk.

Clad in jet black combat gear, Jason King moved through the darkened passageways below deck, having demolished the main generator seconds earlier. He'd left the prime mover and alternator in ruins. The emergency power system would kick in without much of a delay, but that delay was all he needed.

He sensed unrest in the next passageway. Six or seven men clustered tightly together, caught in an awkward log jam as their visibility disappeared and claustrophobia set in, the icebreaker groaning all around them as it headed further out to sea on its predetermined path. King didn't know when it would intercept the convoy of U.S. Navy warships, but he'd heard every word that Magomed said thanks to an earpiece sitting deep inside Slater's ear canal.

He barrelled into the lip of the passageway and raised his Heckler & Koch HK433 assault rifle, painted black, its shoulder stock folded. He fired a tight cluster of rounds into the unprotected face of the shocked mercenary standing frozen in the centre of the corridor. The guy's facial features disappeared in an explosion of gore and his lifeless body dropped to the metal floor. King vaulted over him on the way down and emptied the rest of the clip into the rest of the bodies, dropping mercenaries left and right, the unsuppressed roar of gunfire resonating off the walls.

When the rifle clicked dry he shouldered aside a bullet-riddled corpse still in the process of falling to the floor and swung the gun like a baseball bat into the throat of the nearest man. The guy was slow to react, inhibited by the darkness and the muzzle flares and the deafening scream of gunfire. King's ungodly power caved in the soft tissue of his throat and he collapsed against the closest wall, suffocating, succumbing to a grisly death.

King snatched hold of the corpse he'd thrown aside and hurled it into the last remaining guy, sending two hundred pounds of deadweight into the centre of his chest. Knocked off his feet by the staggering impact, the guy went down in a tangle of limbs and King leapt on top of him, heaving the corpse aside, its purpose utilised.

He ripped a combat knife from his appendix holster and plunged it into the guy's throat.

He gave a pathetic wheeze, and died horribly.

King reloaded the HK433, slotting a fresh magazine home. He surveyed the devastation behind him as the emergency power system kicked in, illuminating the six corpses, showing the stark reality of what had happened in the dark.

A shudder tore through him.

The Jason King of old was returning.

Piece by piece.

He sensed the anger building, the rage that was necessary to do the things he was capable of. He channelled it toward the men aboard the icebreaker, the remnants of an operation in an abandoned gold mine that had pushed him further than he ever thought he could go. It had tested his limits, showing what a human being was capable of. And he knew the worst of them remained behind, swaying to the highest bidder, which in that case involved an ex-politician with enough smarts to potentially pull it off.

So retirement on an island off the coast of Thailand had to be put on hold.

Because King couldn't sit back and watch nuclear war unfold from a beach.

Supercharged with motivation, he thundered through the below-deck passageways, weaving left and right with no particular agenda or destination in mind.

He was searching for hostiles.

He found two men clutching their weapons like their lives depended on it in a narrow steel tunnel, aiming them in every direction at once. They spotted the hulking silhouette at one end of the passageway far too late. One of them cried out and raised his gun, his lips twisting into a mask of horror.

Because he sensed the calmness with which the intruder approached.

King shot the first guy in the forehead, sending a single lead round burrowing into his brain like a metal beetle. He collapsed into his comrade. The pair were standing far too close together to be tactically efficient. The second guy wheeled on the spot, catching his friend, unaware the man was dead. When the gunshot blared off the walls a few milliseconds later he flinched and tried to raise his weapon toward an unknown presence.

King put a bullet in his throat.

He shoved the corpses aside, slamming them into the wall before they hit the ground, dissipating some of the adrenalin coursing through him.

He hadn't unleashed this side of himself in a long, long time.

As it came out, it was almost too much to tame.

A fresh face tore into view at the other end of the passageway, responding to the altercation with his rifle raised, searching for a target. With King's brain firing on all cylinders, time seemed to slow, and it looked like the newcomer was dragging his limbs through mud, even if he appeared shockingly fast to the untrained eye.

He didn't even draw a beat on King before a cluster of rounds destroyed the lower half of his face, sending him careening back into the metal wall and slumping to the floor.

King sprinted forward, caught hold of the body, and dragged it through the next corridor. A strict powerlifting regime on Koh Tao Island had kept him in serious shape, and now he treated the corpse like it was nothing, even though it weighed close to a buck eighty. When the next two mercenaries materialised at the end of this passageway, they caught their dead comrade square across their chests.

King had heard them coming. He'd noted their footsteps, tapped into the fast twitch muscle fibres crackling across his giant frame, and hurled the dead man double-handed off the floor.

Now, the trio collapsed to the metal floor, one dead, two alive.

King stamped down on the dead man, crushing the two

mercenaries under the deadweight, and fired a well-placed round through each of their skulls.

Eleven dead.

There were more. Countless more. Slinking through the ship all around him, attempting to locate the source of all the chaos. But through the haze of adrenalin King sensed the wind howling against the side of his face. He spun, searching for the source, and noticed an open shell door facing the sea. Sleet and ocean spray tore in, and the wind buffeted down the passageway and lashed at his combat gear.

Slater.

He was close. He retraced the path from memory, remembering the amount of time he'd heard Slater being dragged through the earpiece and extrapolating that to a guide through the icebreaker's underbelly. He sprinted down an endless series of passageways, favouring speed over stealth, and shouldered his way through a giant pair of oak doors into a luxurious state room.

There was Slater.

Sprawled across the bed. Bloody, semi-conscious, concussed.

And there was an unidentified man with a snarl pressing a semi-automatic pistol to the side of Slater's head.

'Whoa,' King said. 'Relax.'

The man stood there, frozen, perplexed, his gun hand shaking. Pumped full of adrenalin.

King pointed the barrel of his HK433 at the floor and raised his other hand high, fingers splayed. 'Relax. You win.'

The guy wasn't used to this. He didn't know how to handle a situation like what was unfolding. He nodded, still staring King dead in the eyes, paying Slater no attention.

'Put the weapon down,' the man grunted.

Gently, Slater lifted a swollen finger and tilted the gun barrel a couple of inches away from his head.

King had the rifle aimed square between the guy's eyes in less than a half a second, and he pulled the trigger.

Blood sprayed and the man dropped limp into the narrow gap between the side of the bed and the far wall.

Slater breathed a sigh of relief. 'You made it in.'

'Told you I would. Did we just win?'

Groggy, eyes half closed, Slater flashed a glance at the corpse in the corner. 'No. That's not him. He left as soon as he heard the gunfire.'

'How are you?'

'Not good.'

That was an understatement.

54

King took up position in the doorway, reloaded HK433 aimed at the other end of the passageway, anticipating resistance at any moment.

'Talk to me,' he said, his voice looping over his shoulder to catch Slater, still sprawled immobile on the bed.

'Did you hear what Magomed said?'

'Most of it. Doesn't sound good.'

'I don't know how long we have. I can't ... focus on anything. I'm in bad shape.'

'You're in better shape than you were last night,' King said.

It was true. King had wrenched Ruslan Mikhailov's head clean off his shoulders with a garrote, and then found Slater curled up in a ball on the other side of the concrete room, on the verge of death. He'd unlocked his cuffs, loaded him with enough pain medication to dull the agony, and let him rest through the night as Magomed's sizeable forces seized the icebreaker under cover of darkness at the other end of Medved.

But King couldn't take them on single-handedly.

He'd needed a decoy.

A distraction.

He'd needed Slater functioning well enough to bear the burden.

And King always knew he would.

'They'll meet up with the Navy fleet soon,' King said. 'Then it's just a matter of catching them off guard. It won't take much effort. Magomed will turn this ship around and tear one of the warships apart. And I heard what you said. About it not being enough. Trust me. It'll be more than enough.'

'You sure?'

'You've been keeping yourself in the dark all these months, haven't you? Ever since we split up in Dubai.'

'Yes. I don't look at the news. I only hear rumours. I don't want to know what almost happened.'

'It's still almost happening. Our government isn't talking to their government. They've gone radio silent on each other. This is the first attempt to repair tensions since the super carrier incident. So it's on shaky ground already. What do you think the mass murder of hundreds of Navy sailors will do to the relationship? It's already patchy enough.'

'No-one's suicidal enough to start nuclear conflict.'

'Maybe not. Not yet. But that's a slippery slope and you know it. Tensions will skyrocket even further. Trade will be affected. Everyone will choose sides. And it's not going to get better. Not anytime soon. It's only going to get worse. What do you think happens then?'

'How many did you kill?'

'Twelve. Including that guy.'

'There's more.'

'I know. There's a hell of a lot more.'

'Are you hurt?'

'No.'

'I'm sorry I pulled you back. I know you found your peace.'

'I found it. That's gone now.'

'What?'

'We'll talk about it later. The old me was gone. I just brought him back.'

'He needs to be back.'

'I might not ever be the same.'

'Later,' Slater hissed. 'Right now everything's on track for Magomed. He'll probably fast track everything. Ram one of the ships as soon as the icebreaker meets up with them. He doesn't need to play along anymore.'

'If we get off this ship,' King said, 'we can reveal the truth. We can tell everyone it wasn't the Russian government.'

Slater said nothing for a long time.

King sighed. 'It won't matter, will it?'

'You really think anyone will care? That's twice in a row. If anything they'll blame the Russians for their own ineptitude.'

'And hundreds of sailors will die,' King said. 'If I do nothing...'

'That's nothing in comparison to who will die in the conflict afterwards. If you're so convinced it'll happen.'

'It'll happen.'

'So you know what you need to do,' Slater said.

'How many more do you think there are?'

'Thirty, maybe.'

'Can you help me?'

'Look at me,' Slater said, mirroring Magomed's words.

King turned and looked. He'd never seen Slater so incapacitated. The man slumped against the headboard, breathing deep and fast, face and hand swollen. Blood covered his features. And there was a fogginess behind his eyes that King had never seen before. He'd lost his lucidity, if only temporarily. He was useless.

'It has to be me,' King said, the inhale rattling in his own chest.

'I can't,' Slater said. 'You know I can't. I wouldn't have needed you if I could do it on my own.'

'Yeah...'

'When did you decide to come?'

'When you called in Khabarovsk. I know who you are, Slater. I know there was a zero percent chance you'd avoid conflict.'

'But the old you wasn't there anymore. You said that yourself.'

'I brought him back. Because I knew you'd get yourself killed otherwise.'

'What's that going to cost?'

'I don't know,' King said, turning back to lock his focus onto the empty hallway. 'My sanity, probably.'

'Klara?' Slater said.

'I told her I was going away. She knew why. But she didn't ask.'

'Will she stay?'

'I don't know.'

'Thank you, King. I'd be dead if you didn't come. And Magomed would get away with this.'

'He still might.'

'Not if you do what you know you need to do.'

'I might not be able to.'

'The world won't be the same if this happens and you know it as well as I do.'

'Yeah.'

'So that's your choice.'

'If I do this,' King said. 'I won't come back the same.'

'That's the choice you have to make,' Slater said.

The silence hung heavy in the air.

Slater said, 'I won't make it for you.'

'You already did.'

'This is your call.'

'It doesn't matter,' King muttered, tightening his grip on the HK433. 'I brought the old guy back as soon as I put that garrote around Mikhailov's neck.'

'Almost poetic,' Slater said. 'You finished off the family.'

'Yeah,' King grumbled, rising off one knee, standing solemnly in the doorway.

'Go finish it,' Slater said.

'And if I fail?'

'When the fuck have you failed?'

King nodded. 'I'll be right back.'

55

They were waiting.

That suited King.

He thrived in tight spaces. He relished the confusion and the darkness and the narrow passageways and the laboured breathing of his enemies as their chests tightened and their heart rates skyrocketed and their palms turned sweaty as they gripped their weapons.

Because all the firepower in the world didn't mean a thing when there were sharp right-angle turns every few dozen feet.

King tore out of the doorway, leaving Slater to his own devices. He didn't need to babysit the man. Will Slater was one of the most dangerous men on the planet. They'd talked as much as they could the night before. Catching up on old times as Slater lay there on the concrete floor, riding out the concussion symptoms, unsure if he would make it to the morning.

They'd spoken of Yemen and Macau, two separate countries that had proved disastrous for Slater's health and long-term wellbeing. But he'd saved a city from a weaponised virus, and he'd saved a young girl from a lifetime of torment.

Both equally noble endeavours.

And sitting there under the weak flickering cage bulbs the night before, a wry smile had crept across King's face. It was the confirmation he needed. Because his own life had become shockingly dormant. He'd started to become accustomed to the relaxation. The itch to hone his body and mind into peak condition had never gone away. He still slaved away at the Muay Thai gyms on Koh Tao. He still pushed himself to near breaking point every day, because he'd never known anything else. But he'd truly never expected to return to the front lines.

That had all changed a few days ago.

Now he barrelled down a claustrophobic passageway, unsure if he would ever escape this life. Perhaps Koh Tao had been his last chance. Fate, telling him to lay low if he wanted to live out the rest of his days undisturbed. The second he'd stepped off that island en route to Vladivostok, all the familiar sensations had returned.

Momentum.

Relentlessness.

Carnage.

Klara knew what was happening. She hadn't pressed the issue. She'd just nodded. Which almost made it worse. He'd wanted her to plead with him to stay, to put that life firmly in the past even if it meant letting the world tear itself apart around him. Because at some point he needed to let go of all this, and he thought he had.

All an illusion.

He approached a T-junction and slowed his pace, gripping the HK433 tight, senses reeling. He was laser focused on the space ahead, listening for any sign of activity. Sure enough, he picked up the unmistakable sound of approaching footsteps.

From both directions.

He stopped dead in his tracks, only half a foot from the T-junction.

Waiting.

There was hesitation. Confusion. He knew what was happening. A man was approaching from each side, and they'd made eye contact. They'd heard something too. They were in the process of silently communicating with their body language, planning some kind of simultaneous assault.

They didn't know King was right there.

The guy on the left stepped into view first and King put him down with three bullets to the centre mass, impossibly loud in juxtaposition with the preceding silence. The second guy flinched hard, moving imperceptibly backward instead of forward. He probably knew confrontation was inevitable, but there was a world of difference between someone mentally prepared for combat and someone who'd lived in the heat of battle every day for ten years. King took advantage of that gap. He didn't hesitate, or flinch, or recoil.

He stormed into the new passageway and unloaded two rounds into the forehead of the second guy.

Stepping over the corpse, he headed right. His intended destination was the wheelhouse — if he could mow through the mercenaries holding the crew hostage, he could bring them back under control. Unless the entire crew were on Magomed's payroll, too. Which would prove difficult. King hadn't the slightest clue how to commandeer an icebreaker of this size. If the crew had gone rogue along with the entire security force, forming a complete army of morally corrupt sociopaths, then the difficulty would amplify tenfold.

But he didn't have to worry about that right now.

He just had to keep moving forward.

He ejected the HK433's magazine to check the number of rounds left in the clip, an automatic process ingrained into his subconscious. But it had been nearly a year since he'd seen combat. His instinctual reactions weren't fine tuned. He was firing on all cylinders, but he didn't have the complete situational awareness yet. That would take time to return.

So he ended up close to another sharp corner as he ejected the magazine.

You idiot, he thought.

Because, as fate would have it, he'd mistimed that particular move.

An enormous Russian brute barrelled into view, throwing all caution to the wind as he rounded the corner. His right hand clasped a massive Desert Eagle pistol, outstretched to aim ahead. His bloodshot eyes were wide and venomous, his pupils dilated, the lids swollen. A drug addict, too. He was three inches taller than King, at least, and probably outweighed him by fifty or sixty pounds. King guessed his previous occupation involved wrenching villagers from their homes and bringing them into the depths of Vadim Mikhailov's lair.

In the back of his mind, King gave thanks to fate for giving him the chance to finish off both murderous brothers in the space of a couple of years.

He didn't slow down.

As soon as he spotted the hulking shape, his natural reflexes kicked in. He was already closing the gap at a lightning pace, reloading at a sprint, so when he recognised the brute in front of him he fired his fast twitch muscle fibres and pulled the empty HK433 up through the air, toward the ceiling. A staggering uppercut with enough adrenalin and speed behind it to generate unimaginable force. The bulk of the gun hit the underside of the big man's wrists, breaking bone and hurling the Desert Eagle off-centre.

The man fired.

Horrific, deafening noise. A blinding muzzle flare. And the nauseating sensation of a bullet tearing past his head, close enough to feel the reverberation between his temples. It took everything in King not to flinch. If he flinched, it stripped valuable time away from his ability to react. Instead he accepted the fact that he was still alive to feel the consequences of the Desert Eagle going off beside his head, and he continued with his mad attack.

The big man had missed.

That was all that mattered.

The uppercut with the high powered assault rifle sent the man's hands flying skyward involuntarily, and before he could correct his aim and fire another shot King kicked him square in the gut, his combat boot akin to a steel whip as it smashed against delicate skin. The guy doubled over — again, involuntarily.

King didn't think twice.

He delivered a colossal headbutt. Forehead to nose. Something cracked. He followed up with a wild manoeuvre, but figured it was suitable against a stunned adversary whilst moving at full speed. He put his left foot forward, unlocked his hips, and twisted one hundred and eighty degrees like a spring uncoiling, spinning a half revolution and building up kinetic energy at the same time. He let loose with a bent arm.

A spinning back elbow.

Now becoming popular in mixed martial arts due to its devastating efficiency.

King had witnessed a knockout blow in a professional bout on a screen in Koh Tao only a couple of months ago.

His own blow struck home.

Bone to jaw.

Another crack.

The big brute collapsed against the side of the passageway, violently stripped of his consciousness.

Flawless execution.

The professionals would have been impressed.

Now that he had a spare couple of seconds, he slipped a fresh magazine from his combat belt and jammed it home. He switched the select fire mode to single-fire, and put a bullet through the side of the unconscious man's head. He figured it was a mercy killing. The guy's brain would have never been the same, had he woken up later.

Breath rasping in his lungs, King sensed nausea in the pit of his stomach. The reality of the situation started to sink in. He'd killed fifteen men since stepping foot aboard the *Mochnost* icebreaker, all combat veterans with enough talent to offer their services to the highest bidder.

There were more. Countless more. He couldn't comprehend the size of the mercenary force leeching through the icebreaker. Last night he'd considered sneaking away from the bunker to observe Magomed and his minions seizing the ship, so that he'd have a sense of what he was coming up against when he stormed aboard the next morning. But that would have meant leaving Slater alone and vulnerable.

Slater was in no position to defend himself.

That also added to the unease — all it would take was a single man to stumble across the state room and find Slater helpless on the bed. King wondered if he would have the composure to put up a fight in any capacity.

He seriously doubted it.

Maybe he would get a shot off. Aim the Makarov, squeeze the trigger, hope for the best. It would probably miss. King was intimately familiar with the myriad symptoms of a severe concussion — he'd experienced a couple of his own in the past on the same level as Slater's.

Sometimes he lay awake at night thinking of the long-term consequences of his brutal career.

Riddled with anxiety, he pressed forward.

Fifteen down.

Probably double that number to go.

Briefly, he wondered how Slater was faring trying to contact someone, anyone. It didn't matter if they were wanted by the government. It didn't matter that they were vigilantes. All that mattered was protecting the lives of hundreds of U.S. Navy sailors. King had no doubt Magomed would expedite the process. As soon as he met up with the convoy, he would destroy one of the warships. It wouldn't be a difficult process — the *Mochnost,* with its reinforced bow designed to cut right through ice, would undoubtedly come out on top against a warship in a head-on collision. It might not split the opposing vessel in half, but it would come close.

And that would cause untold devastation aboard.

In the game of political warfare, two strikes was enough.

There would be no third chance.

There would be war.

With the potential ramifications surging through him, King took off at a sprint down the passageway, heading directly toward the fight, going against all his human survival instincts.

But he was slower.

His steps were laboured.

His breath clogged in his throat.

With a nervous shiver, he recognised the effects of fatigue sinking in. It had been quite some time since he'd been involved in a life or death confrontation. And no matter how aggressively he pushed himself in the gym, no matter his level of physical fitness, no matter how strong his mental resilience, there was always a difference between training and the real thing.

The real thing fired neurons and muscle fibres that King couldn't hope to activate in simulated practice. Besides, he hadn't been training for the real thing. He'd left the real thing in the past, detaching himself from the chaos he'd wreaked across the globe. And now it was all back, tugging at his central nervous system, wearing him down.

Like a three hundred pound deadweight placed on his shoulders.

He continued running, but he was moving through mud. Finally conceding defeat, he drew to a halt at another T-junction and listened hard for any signs of life. There was nothing. The rest of the mercenaries were above deck, coagulating around the wheelhouse and the upper levels. It would be madness up there. A war zone.

One against thirty.

And he didn't think he could do it.

Then he thought of the world that would result from his failure. He thought about surviving the forthcoming battle, stepping off the icebreaker knowing he failed, and watching the nuclear missiles fly. He thought of the hundreds of millions of innocent people who would be caught up in the coming chaos through no fault of their own.

Maybe he was exaggerating.

Maybe there would be no war.

But he knew the current tensions were equal to, if not worse than, the Cuban Missile Crisis. And sending a

Russian government funded icebreaker through the hull of a U.S. Navy warship only a year after a similar incident rocked diplomatic relations to their core would be unforgivable.

So there was an overwhelming possibility.

Find a phone, Slater, King thought.

Find a goddamn phone.

He forced all negative thoughts to the back of his mind, tightened his grip on the Heckler & Koch HK433, felt the cold sweat flowing freely down the back of his neck...

...and leapt onto the nearest ladder, barreling toward the upper deck.

56

With great difficulty, Slater rolled onto his side and patted down the body of the man who had come within half an inch of ending his life. He saw reality through a foggy haze.

The closest sensation he could relate it to was extreme fatigue.

When the lactic acid built up in your limbs after a marathon, and you crossed the finish line and collapsed in a heap, barely able to find a morsel of strength to pick yourself up off the concrete.

It was like that, multiplied by ten.

King's words resonated in his head. Find a phone. Contact someone. Anyone. Slater had sensed the trepidation in King's voice, the hesitancy over getting involved with anyone in the U.S. government, especially after how they'd parted ways.

But King didn't know.

Russell Williams, one of the men responsible for cleaning up the messy aftermath of Black Force's dissolution, had been in contact twice with Slater. First in Yemen, when Slater had desperately called to warn of an impending bioterrorism attack on the streets of London. Then an in-person encounter, deep in the dark heart of Macau. Williams had informed him that the investigation had cleared both King and Slater.

They were in the clear.

They'd done the right thing.

And no-one was hunting them anymore.

But King didn't know that. So he probably wouldn't try to get in touch with any authorities at risk of being ignored. Instead he would focus on shutting down the threat at the source. And if that failed, then everything they'd worked toward would be useless. So it all rested squarely on Slater's shoulders, and in his deteriorated state of consciousness he hadn't realised the burden he was carrying until King was long gone.

He should have said, 'No, King, you can make the call too. They're not looking for you anymore. They'll believe you.'

But he hadn't.

He'd simply stared and nodded with a vacant expression on his face.

Because he couldn't think fast. He couldn't comprehend what was about to happen. He sensed the icebreaker surging through the Sea of Japan underneath him, and the terror caught in his throat. He knew what it symbolised.

The beginning of the end.

To the outside world, everything would appear to be business as usual. The politicians would be in front of the cameras, all smiles, revealing the purpose of the icebreaker's maiden voyage and the pleasant diplomatic nature of the co-operation. The media would lap it up. The headlines would capture worldwide public attention.

And then the icebreaker would destroy one of the warships. Magomed would sink one. Maybe two, if he had the chance. Then he would wipe all evidence of his involvement off the face of the planet with his own death. He would sink to the bottom of the ocean, forever forgotten. And the subsequent investigation would turn up sensitive information aboard, intrinsically connected to the inner workings of the Russian government, an area Magomed was intimately familiar with. Some things would be real, some forged. But no-one would be able to tell the difference.

Christ, Slater thought. *He's thought this through.*

Maybe war wouldn't break out immediately.

Maybe there would be an attempt to remain civilised.

It wouldn't last long.

Slater had spent far too much time dealing with the depths of human depravity.

He knew what panicked people were capable of.

The choices they would make.

The decisions they would reach.

The chaos they would cause.

So, despite the fact that he could barely see a few feet in front of his face, he somehow overrode his body's natural tendencies. He clawed his way through the mud of the concussion.

He reached down, patted the dead man's utility belt, and clenched a small rectangular object with sweaty fingers. He withdrew it from its holster, and ran his thumb over the grimy screen. He breathed a sigh of relief.

A satellite phone.

He dialled. Digit by painful digit. His thumb stabbed down at regular intervals, connecting a long string of numbers, forming a pattern ingrained in his head since he first accepted a position in Black Force's ranks.

He'd used it in Yemen.

He would use it now.

To explain. To justify. To urge his own government not to panic in the event of an actual collision. Because reactions would be swift, and they would be vicious. There would be no time for debate or the quagmire of public opinion. There would just be retaliation.

Slater finished dialling, brought the phone to his ear, and closed his eyes.

Please.

Nothing.

No dial tone.

No response whatsoever from the device.

He checked it was switched on. It was. He spotted the symbol indicating a full battery.

Confirming his deepest fears.

Someone was using a signal jammer to blanket the icebreaker.

Slater realised he shouldn't have doubted Magomed. The man had covered every possible alternative. Of course he had. It was necessary. He was leading a convoy of soulless, relentless, sociopathic ex-combatants, but that didn't mean they unanimously wanted to encourage a third World War. Some of them might baulk in the face of such a revelation. So Magomed had to ensure no-one would speak out, no-one would recoil at the last second and make the requisite calls to the appropriate parties.

Because this was a sensitive situation.

If anyone discovered the true motives before it happened, it would ruin the intended effect.

Slater bowed his head, tossed the phone away, and started to grapple with his helplessness. He wanted to do something, anything, to assist. He couldn't imagine a world in the aftermath of global nuclear conflict.

It scared him to his core.

And he'd been around combat his entire life.

Something happened. Deep inside his brain. An invisible switch, flicked in an instant. It didn't strip him of the concussion symptoms, or the pain, or the nausea, or the heaviness in his limbs. But it cleared his mind — ever so slightly. Just enough to think straight. Just enough to hand him back control of his own body.

He swung his legs over the edge of the bed and planted them on the floor. Knees shaking, he stood.

He could stand.

That was enough.

The pain amplified as he moved, but he could deal with pain. There was superficial agony, and then there was the brain fog that you couldn't fight against. The fog had receded. Not all the way.

Just enough.

He wobbled toward the other end of the state room, heading for the doorway.

What do you think you're going to achieve?

He couldn't fight anyone. He could stumble around the passageways as the weak lights of the emergency system flickered on and off, sending him into an ethereal haze as he tried to navigate below deck.

What did he hope to accomplish?

Then everything went black. He froze in place, heart pounding in his chest, convinced his brain had given up on itself and finally succumbed to a blissful death. But all the pain remained behind, searing his temples and cramping his gut and tickling his nerve endings. So he wasn't dead.

Groaning. All around him. The icebreaker, still moving through the ocean.

The lights had gone out.

The emergency power system, failing for the first time. An untested process, never intended to be utilised on the icebreaker's first trip. King must have destroyed the main generator at the start of the crusade. Now the backups were resting on shaky supports, trying desperately to power this behemoth of a ship as it coughed and spluttered toward the Bering Strait.

The lights flickered back on, blinding Slater momentarily.

Then they plunged into darkness once more.

A strobe-like effect.

And in the shadows, someone crept straight past the open doorway.

Slater flinched.

The lights came back on.

Woozy, on wobbly legs, he stumbled out of the state room in silent pursuit.

Because he'd recognised the faint outline of the silhouette. The stooped posture. The hair swept back. The skinny frame.

An old man.

57

King stepped into the mess hall and heard voices.

Dead ahead.

He froze, then wedged himself into a narrow alcove in the side of the wood panelled wall.

He'd already moved through abandoned passageways on the level above deck, staring out portholes at the churning ocean lashing against the icebreaker's hull. The entire ship bobbed and weaved in the high seas, battling harsh weather. Storm clouds swelled on the horizon. He'd hurried forward and found the mess hall dormant, devoid of life, creaking and groaning as the icebreaker powered through the Sea of Japan. Tables were arranged in a neat grid, bolted into the floor, with room for at least a hundred patrons at once. There were no staff in the kitchen. There were no sailors aboard. Just the barebones crew, and an army of men designed to ensure everything went according to plan.

But all that changed when the panicked voice resonated off the walls in the distance.

Someone had entered the mess hall from the other side.

King stayed deathly quiet, taking the opportunity to recharge his internal batteries, seizing as much energy from the stillness as he could. It didn't help much. The floor still swayed underneath him, and the lactic acid still burned in his arms from throwing strikes with maximum effort.

Not the superficial kind of maximum effort he could dish out in training. That was simulated.

Not real.

Instead, he was now throwing with murderous intent.

It sapped the energy right out of you.

He listened to the voices approaching, getting ever closer, speaking English. One panicked but articulate. One confident but gruff, speaking broken English.

Even without a visual on his target, King worked out what was happening in an instant.

The panicked voice said, 'I don't understand. I don't know why the emergency power's cutting out, okay? I can't help you.'

The firm voice said, 'You figure it out.'

'I'm not an engineer.'

'You are crew.'

'Yes, but my role is—'

'Your role is what we say.'

'I can't fix this. Isn't your boss down there already?'

'Boss make call. He go down there to get better signal. He has device to talk. Down there.'

'To who?'

'Americans.'

'Why? Is he working with them?'

'No. We told you. Everything go to plan. We meet up with convoy. As scheduled.'

'I don't understand what you're planning to do.'

'You don't have to. You fix power.'

'I told you, I can't—'

The panicked voice cut off mid-sentence, and a vicious *thump* resonated through the mess hall, echoing off the walls. King recognised it as the butt of a gun striking bone. He figured the mercenary must have hit the panicked guy on the forehead.

As soon as he heard the sound he burst out of cover.

The mercenary saw him out of the corner of his eye. The guy was small and built like a dump truck, almost cubic in shape. His combat gear was pulled tight over his barrel chest, and his small beady eyes were fixated on the stooped crew member hunched over one of the tables, blood pouring down the side of his head, cowering away from another strike.

King raised the HK433, still switched to select fire, and shot the short stocky mercenary through the forehead before the guy had a chance to wheel his aim around and take care of the new threat.

Sixteen down.

King hurried over to the sailor. He was tall and gangly, dressed neatly in his official uniform. White shirt tucked into black dress pants. From what little conversation he'd overheard, King figured he was Australian. He had the requisite twang in his voice.

King gently sat him down on one of the metal benches and swept the room for any sign of hostiles.

Finding nothing, he bent down and spoke slow and controlled.

'Listen,' he said. 'You're probably in shock. None of this feels real. But I need you to be clear with me for the next minute. I'm not a threat. Can you do that?'

The guy nodded.

'What happened last night?'

'I...' the guy started.

'You don't need to guess. Just tell me exactly what you personally saw. There can be gaps. It doesn't matter.'

'It was late. We were running through the system checks for today. We'd been picked as the crew ages ago. As part of the official government program. We were told what was happening. With the U.S. Navy. So we were all nervous. We knew the world would be watching. We knew how important it was ... you know, for history. So we didn't want to screw anything up. So we were ... probably too focused on our jobs. We weren't paying attention to anything else.'

'And then?'

'I don't know. Chaos. There were men everywhere. I recognised most of them. They'd been guarding the construction for as long as I could remember. As it was nearing completion the crew had been allowed aboard to get familiar with the ship. So we always had to go past these guys to get to the ship. They'd frisk us down. You know. I always thought it was too much. What were they guarding it for? There was never any threat. And then suddenly on the night before the big day they were all aboard, cramming the hallways, threatening people with weapons.'

'Did you make any calls?'

The guy shook his head, eyes wide, throat constricted. 'No. It all happened so fast. They'd planned it. Suddenly they were everywhere, and there was nothing we could do. We all thought it was a joke at first. Guns pointed at us. Didn't seem real. And then ... then it started to sink in. And they kept us up all night at gunpoint. We weren't allowed to move a muscle. And they kept telling us, over and over again, that we were to follow everything exactly according to plan. It's just ... no-one could know they were aboard.'

'So they maximised confusion.'

'Uh ... yeah.'

'Effective. How long until you're scheduled to meet up with the convoy?'

'First contact is in fifteen minutes. There'll be choppers circling above filming. For the news. You know...'

King went pale. 'Fuck. I have to go.'

'What about me?'

'See where I came from, just then?'

'Yeah.'

'Get inside that gap, put your head down, and pretend you're somewhere else.'

'Where are you going?'

King held up the rifle. 'Where do you think?'

'Who the fuck are you, anyway? American?'

'Yeah.'

'How'd you get on board? Is that what all the screaming and gunfire was?'

King muttered, 'That usually happens when I get involved.'

'How many have you killed?'

'Not enough.'

'What—?'

King held up a hand. 'Go hide. You said I've got fifteen minutes?'

'Yeah. Wait ... until what? What are they going to do?'

'Nothing good. Go hide.'

He laid a hand on the man's shoulder for reassurance, gave him a confident nod, and then took off in the direction of the wheelhouse.

Tick.

Tick.

Tick.

58

Slater stumbled through identical passageways with no idea where he was headed. He glimpsed a flash of movement in the far distance, barely perceptible underneath the failing emergency power supply. The lights flashed on and off at random, ruining his sense of direction, only adding to the confusion. All around him the icebreaker rumbled, picking up momentum, moving forward with renewed vigour.

Closing in on something.

Slater knew what was coming.

For some reason, he figured he was instrumental in stopping it. Even though he could barely string a thought together for longer than a few seconds. Even though the dread seeped through him, letting him know the odds were against him. Even though any time he spent lingering on the consequences of Magomed succeeding sent terror through his bones.

Magomed.

It had to be him, up ahead.

But why?

Why was he down here?

Slater pressed forward, dragging one leg behind him, trying to still his rapidly increasing heart rate. He sensed the familiar panic attack rising again, like a fist clenching tighter and tighter around his vital organs, seizing them in place. The concussion. Still there. Heightening emotions. Increasing volatility.

He paused for a beat, staring at the floor, placing his hand against the wall to steady himself. Then he regained his bearings and kept walking, kept hurrying, kept wincing through the agony.

As he passed by an open doorway, completely oblivious to his surroundings, an old man watched him go by.

59

Magomed crouched low in the bowels of the icebreaker, serenely calm despite the carnage unfolding all around him. His men were dying in scores. He heard their screams. He heard the gunshots.

The mercenaries who'd proven fiercely loyal, following his every command, were now falling like dominoes to an unseen force. At first he'd thought they would be hesitant to embrace what he wanted, but as he revealed the depths of his desires their eyes had unanimously lit up with anticipation. He'd screened them well. They were men with broken souls, plucked from the wasteland of the Kamchatka Peninsula in the aftermath of Vadim Mikhailov's grisly demise. With the collapse of the mine operation, the money had dried up.

Magomed had plenty of that.

And no need for it anymore.

Because he was going overboard not long from now.

He'd never wavered on that promise to himself. It had never been up for debate. Getting cast aside from the political system had shattered what little motivation he had left.

He'd already been skating on thin ice at the tail end of his career, flirting with the dangerous dark hole of nihilism. So plunging the U.S. and Russia into an ugly modern war was obviously the logical next step. It would destroy the comfortable, secure positions his disgusting co-workers had forged for themselves, destroying the insulation.

Casting them out into the wilderness.

They'd be torn from their palaces, thrown into the street or murdered for their privileged positions. Magomed considered the utter lawlessness that would ensue. Nuclear fallout. A wasteland. A complete demolition of the existing hierarchy. It stilled his nerves. It steeled his resolve.

So when he sensed someone on his tail, and looped back into a spare room to assess his pursuer, he wasn't surprised when Will Slater stumbled recklessly past the open doorway, heading nowhere in particular.

Completely out of sorts.

Magomed grinned.

Perfect.

Everything was going according to plan, despite the carnage unfolding this very moment above deck. None of that mattered. It was the reason he'd recruited far more mercenaries than necessary. They were expendable. Cannon fodder. All he needed was to intercept the Navy warships and get the crew to set the icebreaker's aim straight.

And once that happened, there was nothing these intruders could do.

Because one of them was barely holding onto consciousness, and the other couldn't possibly pilot an icebreaker on his own.

Not without the crew.

So he let Slater go. Magomed had a gun, but he didn't

know whether the other hostile had doubled back. If he was being stalked, then an unsuppressed gunshot was the last thing he wanted. So he allowed the man to careen left and right, ricocheting off the walls, hurrying down the passageway.

Heading out of sight.

He lifted a modified satellite phone to his ear, designed to bypass the signal jammer he'd implemented the previous night to prevent outside interference, and connected a call he'd been expecting at any moment.

'We see you on our sonar,' an American voice said on the other end of the line. 'Any problems on your end?'

'None,' Magomed said. 'Proceed as planned.'

'You have the co-ordinates?'

'Of course.'

'We'll meet up in five minutes,' the American said.

Someone important in the U.S. Navy.

An admiral, maybe.

Magomed had forgotten the details.

Nothing seemed to matter when he knew he was about to die.

'Perfect,' Magomed said. 'Allow us to lead the way.'

'Of course,' the American said, mirroring Magomed's own words. 'We look forward to it. We can see the *Mochnost* from here. It looks beautiful.'

'It's an amazing ship. I can't wait for you to see it up close.'

In a rare moment of humanity amidst official protocol, the Navy sailor paused and said, 'Do you think this will really help fix the problems?'

'I hope so. It would be a great weight off all our shoulders.'

'Yeah. I've got a wife. And a kid. A baby girl. She's nearly one. I don't want the world going to shit ... you understand? I hope this is the first step, man. We shouldn't be fighting.'

'Of course,' Magomed said, feeling nothing. 'Wait for us to get into position. Then we will lead you through the Bering Strait.'

'Can't wait.'

Magomed ended the call.

Then he made another one.

To one of the mercenaries above deck. The most ruthless of the bunch. He'd selected the guy based on psychological vetting. He'd planned this well in advance. He knew there could be no hesitation when he gave the command. The only option was ruthless action, especially this close to the finish line.

And once this happened, there was no going back.

The final stretch.

The end game.

It went through. A sharp click. Answered with silence.

Magomed said, 'How close?'

The man said, 'A few minutes. There's trouble up here.'

'How many of them?'

'One.'

'You're kidding.'

'He's ... very good.'

'Who is he?'

'Fuck if I know.'

'Are you on course?'

'We see the convoy. They're waiting.'

'The largest warship.'

'In the middle.'

'Aim for it.'

'The crew might not ... comply.'

'You know what to do.'

'And then?'

'Kill every last one of them. Then there's no chance of salvation.'

'Understood. I'll do it now.'

'Hurry.'

'Will I be compensated?'

'As we discussed. I wired two million USD to your account in the Caymans this morning.'

A pause. A deep inhale. A rattling exhale.

Then a laugh. Despite the circumstances. Despite the war aboard.

A true madman.

'Good,' the man said. 'I'll slaughter all of them myself, then.'

'Do it fast.'

'Already on it. The men are making them line up with the warship now.'

'Good,' Magomed said, and ended the call.

When he looked up, Will Slater was there.

With a gun barrel pointing squarely between Magomed's eyes.

60

Slater caught the final snippet of conversation before he barrelled into the room with his Makarov drawn and raised, but that was enough.

He saw what lay in front of him through swimming vision. Reality pitched left and right, tipping his perspective, accompanied by all the unfamiliar woozy sensations of being wrenched off-balance by nothing but the damage in his own mind. He steadied himself against the table — this room below deck was some kind of makeshift office.

Magomed stood on the other side of the cramped space, and watched with a noncommittal expression on his face.

'Cancel that,' Slater hissed through clenched teeth.

His aim wavered, but he didn't need any kind of precision or accuracy from this distance. Even though his condition made the Makarov's barrel droop a few inches in each direction as the room swayed around him, Slater didn't allow himself to get perturbed by it. Magomed had a semi-automatic pistol slotted into the appendix holster at his waist. Even though Slater felt he was skirting a fine line, perilously close to being a walking zombie, he knew he could pull the trigger the second the old man reached for his gun.

So that wasn't an issue.

Their current course, however, was more of a problem.

Slater said, 'Did you hear me?'

'I heard you.'

'And?'

'And you think threatening to shoot me is going to make me call it off?'

'You say you're ready for death,' Slater said. 'But I don't think you are.'

A final attempt. He didn't believe his own words. But maybe there was a hope of cracking through a facade he didn't imagine existed.

And he was right.

It didn't.

Magomed just smiled.

'You don't think so? You think I was bluffing?'

'You're too narcissistic to be a martyr.'

'Sounds like you know an awful lot about me.'

'Cancel the fucking orders.'

'No.'

'I'll kill you, right here.'

'Okay.'

'Three...'

Magomed said nothing.

'Two.'

Magomed said nothing.

'One.'

Magomed said nothing.

The old man crossed his arms over his chest, and raised an eyebrow. Almost bemused. Slater found it wholly unnerving. The Makarov's barrel began to shake. He wasn't in immediate physical danger — if the icebreaker smashed into the warship, he figured he'd live through the impact. But the utter helplessness threw him off, the quiet smugness of the old man standing across from him with nothing behind his eyes.

'You really don't care,' Slater said.

'Shoot me.'

'Not yet.'

'I'm not a narcissist. For once in your life you got something wrong. I couldn't care less what happens to me. Why don't you take a minute to actually think about why I'm doing this?'

But Slater couldn't do that. Because he couldn't concentrate on anything. He could barely maintain the jigsaw of puzzle pieces in his head making up his current consciousness, fitting together poorly, a jumbled mess.

All the pieces rattled and torn apart by Ruslan Mikhailov's boot the previous night.

'Well?' Magomed said.

Slater didn't respond.

'What personal gain will I get from pulling this off? Tell me.'

Slater didn't respond.

'You don't think I've got it in me to be a martyr?'

Slater didn't respond.

Magomed looked into his eyes and said, 'Fuck this world. Fuck everything about it.'

Then he jerked forward.

Slater flinched. Through the distorted goggles of his concussion he bit at everything.

He recognised it was a fake, but he recognised too late.

Magomed lunged off the mark, taking a violent step forward, and Slater pumped the trigger once. The bullet spat out of the barrel like an angry bull and smashed through the old man's delicate forehead. It came out the back of his head a few milliseconds later, creating a gaping exit wound, spraying blood across the far wall. The old man's legs gave out and he slumped to his knees, a perfectly cylindrical hole resting an inch above his eyebrows.

His body, already lifeless, hovered there for a single moment.

Kneeling on the spot.

Back straight.

Hands by his side.

A sick smile plastered across his dead face.

He'd died happy.

Fulfilled.

And that was the worst part.

Because it hadn't been Slater's choice. Magomed had made that decision himself. He'd never intended any harm by the lunge. It was a simple fake designed to elicit an over-reaction. And it achieved what it set out to do. Maybe in a more composed state Slater would have recognised what Magomed was trying to do instantaneously. Maybe he would have held back. Refused to let the old man achieve his voluntary suicide.

The system had broken him. The exact details of what had happened to Magomed in office, and during his subsequent short-lived retirement, had died with the man. But they'd made him vengeful, bitter, wallowing in a pit of his own misery. He'd set to work forging this grand scheme, connecting a myriad of moving parts to align the largest icebreaker in the world with a convoy of U.S. Navy warships, for no ulterior reason whatsoever. He just wanted to spread anarchy. Tear the men from power that had cast him out of the system he'd devoted his life to climbing.

Shit, Slater thought.

Because there was nothing more uncontrollable than someone who didn't give a shit what happened to them. There were no sensitive details to handle. There was no money or power to collect at the end of the rainbow. There was just a blissful death, knowing he'd left the world in as much chaos as he could feasibly manage from a man in his position.

Slater stared down at the corpse in a trance, realising Magomed had accomplished everything he'd set out to accomplish.

It hasn't happened yet.

Those four words pierced through the fog around his brain, and he nodded to himself. He stepped forward. Reached down and scooped up the satellite phone. The call had disconnected. He redialed the last number Magomed had called, figuring the only attempt he had left was to impersonate the old man as best he could.

It dialled.

And rang.

And rang.

And rang.

And then it cut out.

No answer.

The contingency plan. When orders were given, communications ceased. That way there was no room for unnecessary repetition. And it also eliminated the chance of anyone compromising the schedule. Like Slater was trying to do right now.

He gripped the satellite phone in white knuckles, and the reality of the situation sunk in. He stared down at the grimy digital screen, only the size of a thumbprint, displaying a multitude of menu options in Russian. He gulped back apprehension. He couldn't speak the language. Fingers shaking, he tried to navigate through the phone. It proved disastrous. He bogged himself deeper in menus and sub-menus, getting nowhere close to anything productive. The icebreaker shook underneath him, and he gripped the table with a clammy hand.

Standing over Magomed's corpse, he started to realise than any hope of salvaging the situation had died with the old man.

Is this it? he thought.

Is this where it starts?

A third world war. He'd used the buzzwords a couple of times, in conversation with King and others, but it hadn't quite sunk in back then. The sheer scale of what was about to happen. The unimaginable suffering.

He bowed his head, let it drop to the cold surface of the metal table, and fought down the anxiety racing its way up his throat, clogging his airways.

Partly due to the concussion.

Mostly due to the knowledge that he'd failed.

He hoped like hell for a miracle.

61

King stormed onto an exterior walkway, exposing himself to the elements. Wind howled off the surface of the ocean and battered his frame, rattling the metal railing alongside him. He stared down at the weather deck, anticipating rusting machinery and ancient mechanisms but finding everything pristine instead.

Of course.

The icebreaker was brand new.

He squinted against the barrage of Mother Nature and made out the faint outlines of the three U.S. Navy warships in the distance. They floated in the Sea of Japan in a line, end to end, spaced far enough apart to remove any threat of collision. He imagined the plan had been for the trio of ships to fall in line behind the *Mochnost* icebreaker. He thought he could make out a couple of helicopters far in the distance, circling the meeting point like vultures.

Cameras aimed at the fleet, no doubt.

The reality of the situation sunk in.

For the first time.

In all its terrifying glory.

Possessed by an animalistic motivation, King broke into a flat out sprint along the walkway, giving no regard to his personal safety. The wind picked up and threw him against the railing. For a moment, he almost pitched over the side. It would have killed him, either breaking an assortment of bones as he plummeted to the weather deck or tossing him into the ocean itself, to be overwhelmed by fatigue and sink to its murky depths at an undetermined future time.

Instead he snatched at the railing with white knuckles, steadied himself back on course, and tried to fight the urge to stop and vomit.

Partly because of the seasickness.

Mostly because of the consequences of failure.

He kept moving, surging toward the icebreaker's bow, heading for the wheelhouse. He didn't know what to do when he got there.

Halfway along the walkway a door burst open in his face, almost knocking him out cold. A bit more force and the metal door would have caught him clean on the bridge of his nose, probably punching the entire appendage inside his skull. It might even have killed him, if the angle was just right.

Four men spilled out onto the walkway, moving rapidly through the motions, throwing caution to the wind. There was nervous anticipation in their wide eyes. Their skin was all pale and clammy. They also recognised the consequences of failure. This was manic competition. Something primal, reduced to its very essence.

Tactics and carefulness had been hurled out the window.

This was the end game.

King raised the HK433, jabbed the barrel into the stomach of the guy who'd almost bowled him over, and pulled the trigger before any of the four could understand what was happening. A hail of bullets tore through the man's gut, and a handful of them sliced up the two men standing directly behind King's first target.

Three men buckled at the knees and went down in a tangle of limbs, either dead or mortally wounded, the weapons in their hands forgotten.

King tried to aim at the fourth guy, but the angles were all wrong.

The walkway was over capacity, and there'd been five people in a restricted space moving like their life depended on it. Two of the three bodies fell into each other, so there was a delay before they hit the metal floor of the walkway. It restricted King's aim to the fourth guy, and this was a world where a half-second of restriction spelled the difference between life and death.

So King activated Plan B without even consciously registering it.

He didn't think.

He didn't plan.

He just moved like an NFL defensive end.

He shouldered the two bodies that had caught on each other into the railing, hurling them aside as if they weighed nothing, and swept the fourth man off his feet with two beefy arms wrapped around the guy's mid-section. A standard double leg takedown, common on the wrestling mats in colleges and gyms across the globe.

But King simply didn't know whether it would work.

Because the guy had a fearsome looking sidearm in his right hand, and he tilted it downward and jerked the trigger a couple of times as King took him off his feet. One bullet missed, and the other cut a thin line vertically down King's back, slicing straight through his combat gear and tearing flesh away. He sensed the hot fury of pain and understood he'd been hit, but the consequences wouldn't present themselves for another second or two.

So he dropped the mercenary against the railing on the small of his back, probably paralysing him, given the rage behind King's movements. He hit the guy full in the face with an impossibly quick elbow, probably knocking every tooth out of his gums. Then, for good measure, he bent back and hurled a final elbow, connecting so hard he almost took the man's head clean off his shoulders. With a broken skull and a rearranged complexion, the mercenary toppled over the railing and spiralled lifelessly to the weather deck far below.

King straightened up, panting, breathing hard.

He could be a real monster when he needed to be.

The wound was superficial. It hit him with overwhelming relief, because if the bullet had touched his spine he wouldn't have been feeling anything at all. In fact, that would have been his own private version of hell, because it probably wouldn't have killed him instantly. Piece by piece, the feeling would have sapped out of his limbs, rendering him a quadriplegic on the freezing walkway, and he would have been made to watch helplessly as the icebreaker plunged into the warship and destroyed what little goodwill still existed between the U.S. and Russia.

But none of that happened, so he forced it from his mind.

Warm blood ran down his back, but his movement remained uninhibited.

He tested the weight of the rifle in his hand, spotted the wheelhouse directly ahead, and charged straight into the thick of the action without a moment's hesitation.

Because the towering bulk of the warships in the distance grew rapidly closer.

The icebreaker ploughed through the swells.

Full speed ahead.

He had a couple of minutes.

Maybe less.

Heart pounding in his chest, he threw himself into the line of fire.

62

Through the haze, Slater pieced it together.

The phone.

It got through.

Magomed had his own personal device, independent of the signal jammer he'd brought aboard. The satellite phone in his hand was his one hope of contact with the outside world. He wasn't sure what he'd be able to prevent, given the fact that a collision was moments away, but he had to do anything he could to try. He had to exhaust every possible option. Because every second he wasted standing around in agony, wading through a maze of concussion symptoms, was another moment of potential disappearing.

And it would all add up to unimaginable, soul-crushing guilt if he lived to see the world tear itself apart.

Or nothing could happen.

Maybe his concussion was complicating things. Heightened emotions. Panicked reactions. Maybe the world was more civilised than he expected.

No.

He'd seen the look on King's face. And King wasn't concussed.

King figured the ramifications would be like nothing the modern world had ever seen before.

Slater knew human nature better than almost anyone else on the planet. He'd spent a lifetime surrounded by the worst of the worst, the lowest form of human life, and he'd also seen innocent people do horrific things instinctually. When they felt threatened. When they thought there was no other option than all out violence.

He'd seen the bottom of the cesspool.

So he knew how quickly things could escalate if the icebreaker struck the warship.

A rather simple action, all things considered.

Maybe a few hundred deaths aboard the warship. Sailors plummeting to the bottom of the Sea of Japan.

On a planet of seven billion people, nothing too drastic.

But it was what it symbolised. It was the cameras in the helicopters circling above, capturing the incident in all its shocking brutality. It was the transformation of a peaceful meeting into a devastating massacre. And it was the information buried somewhere on board that Magomed had planted, the details that would turn up in a subsequent investigation into exactly what had happened.

Magomed was brilliant. Slater had to concede that point. Most of his adversaries were, or they never would have made it to the level where Black Force had to intervene. So Slater could imagine how intricate the web was that Magomed had crafted. He didn't figure the word of two excommunicated government operatives would change a thing. In fact, he and King would probably be carted off to prison for their acts of vigilante justice, given what the world was about to descend into.

So he wiped sweat off his brow as he continued thumbing through menus on the satellite phone. But he couldn't help the tension twisting his gut tighter, or making him sweat harder, or making the breath catch in his throat. He wished he was outside, so he was able to see the approaching impact before it shattered the rhythmic swaying of the icebreaker and plunged the world into anarchy.

He had no hope of navigating to the weather deck. He couldn't even walk down a corridor without stumbling into walls. He needed rest. Lots of it. But there was no time for rest.

He swore.

Out loud.

His words rang off the walls.

He couldn't figure the phone out. How demoralising that at the most important moment of his life, the language barrier removed any chance of succeeding. In any case, he didn't know what he'd do if he got the phone working.

Who would he call?

How could he stop it this late?

'Hey!' a voice screamed.

Right behind him.

And the barrel of an automatic weapon pressed to the side of his sweaty temple.

He hadn't even heard the hostile approaching. In his peripheral vision he spotted a hulking figure — another faceless mercenary, taking up most of the doorway, both hands outstretched to make room for the giant assault rifle in his hands.

Slater lowered his own Makarov — there was nothing he could do to fight against that kind of firepower at that kind of proximity.

He slumped his shoulders, dejected.

The mercenary reached out, snatched the satellite phone out of Slater's hands, and tossed it away.

Then he snatched Slater's Makarov and hurled it aside.

Then he said, 'Get on your knees. You will beg like a dog before you die.'

Slater had no fight left in him.

He got on his knees.

63

King shouldered the door aside, moving like a man possessed, operating at an incomprehensibly fast pace. His vision narrowed to a tunnel. He tuned out all his surroundings except what lay directly ahead. And he whipped the HK433's barrel onto anything that moved, assessing threats faster than his brain could comprehend.

At this level of the game he ceased to make decisions, instead giving himself over to the unconscious force that carried him through every instinctual reaction beaten into him over a lifetime of training.

He moved fast.

But not fast enough.

By the time he lined the assault rifle up with the only threat in the wheelhouse, the man fired his final bullet. The gunshot was deafening in the confined space, but King didn't retaliate, because the man wasn't firing at him.

With a jolting motion, the last member of the *Mochnost*'s crew took a round to the forehead and slumped across the controls, bleeding profusely, already deceased.

King stared at the bodies.

Eight men in official uniform.

All sprawled across the floor.

All dead.

His stomach sunk into his feet.

The last remaining man smiled. He was tall and carried himself with impeccable posture, not chunky like a body-builder, more lithe like a long distance athlete. His long black hair was swept back off his forehead and held in place with some kind of pomade, revealing his unblemished skin. He was remarkably photogenic for someone involved in life or death combat, surrounded by devastation and blood and suffering. There wasn't a speck of crimson on his combat gear. His jawbone was defined, and his eyes were dark and brooding. He wasn't sweating. He seemed right at home amidst the madness, in direct contrast to the sweat pouring out of King's pores, to the blood drenched across his own gear.

But appearances didn't matter.

Because King had the bead on him.

And the guy seemed to know that. As soon as he executed the last remaining crew member he dropped his weapon, letting the pistol clatter to the floor between his feet. He clasped his hands behind his back, almost standing at attention, and smiled grotesquely at King.

'Seems like you're too late.'

'Seems like it.'

King glanced out the windshield and saw the warship only a mile or so from the icebreaker. He sighed, keeping the HK433 pointed exactly where he needed it.

'I take it you can't control this thing,' he said, gesturing with the gun barrel to the amalgamation of switchboards in front of them.

The man calmly shook his head. 'Afraid not. Even if I could, I wouldn't.'

'If you're holding anything back...'

The man raised an eyebrow in mock enquiry. 'You'll do what?'

'You ready to die here?'

'Would I have dropped my gun if I wasn't?'

'Maybe you thought I'd be merciful.'

'I'm not stupid.'

'Why'd you do it?' King said. 'You know what's about to happen.'

Because if King couldn't prevent the chaos, he could at least try to understand the reasons behind it.

'Same as Magomed,' the man said, adding a shrug as if that explained everything.

'I don't know his motivations.'

'Well ... there's not much to say.'

'Try your best.'

'I'd rather you just kill me.'

'I want to know.'

'Don't want to live anymore,' the guy said. 'Sick of what I do.'

'What do you do?'

'Anything that paid money.'

'Did you work on the Kamchatka Peninsula before this stint in Vladivostok?'

A pause. A sly look. 'I did. How did you know that?'

'Lucky guess. I just don't understand. You're put together well. You're in shape. You seem eloquent. So you have good habits in that regard. You could have put yourself on the right path. At any time. All this potential and ... for fuck's sakes ... I just...'

He knew he was ranting, but the inevitability of the

warship rapidly swelling in size through the windshield sent dread through him. He was in the process of metaphorically ramming his head against a brick wall, trying to understand exactly why this was happening, and he found nothing comprehensible.

He forced himself to accept that humans were wired very differently. Motivations varied in scope, and he would never understand the intricacies of a mind like what lay in front of him.

And now wasn't the time.

So he said, 'One more thing.'

And the man said, 'Yes?'

And King shot him in the face, wiping the inquisitive expression off his features with a single cluster of lead. The guy went down vertically, hitting the floor of the wheelhouse in an ungainly heap, and King found a tiny morsel of satisfaction in the way he'd died. The man hadn't been expecting it.

And right now, King had to take any victory he could.

In the empty wheelhouse, he strode to the bank of digital controls and gave a blank stare.

Nothing he could figure out.

Maybe if he had hours to test the workings of the icebreaker through trial and error.

But he had a couple of minutes.

Maybe less.

He stood at the helm of a thirty thousand tonne behemoth and waited for the impact. It stayed on course, barreling through the seas toward the warship in the centre of the trio. The three Navy ships hovered in place, blissfully unaware of what was about to happen. Above, in the grimy grey sky, the helicopters idled.

King gripped the edges of the control panel.

And bowed his head in abject failure.

64

Slater would never be able to explain what happened. Maybe in future he would liken it to the sheer power of momentum. He would think about the way a million small unnoticeable actions could add up to a massive payoff at the end. Much like the way he'd approached life. He'd honed himself into a human weapon over years of monotonous daily routines, so in the end it was only a condensed version of that concept.

Because everything just fell into place with obscene ease.

First he got angry. Because the sharp edge of the gun barrel against his sweat soaked temple drew blood, and that slight irritation somehow managed to pierce through the fog of the concussion. And that led to a sudden surge in motivation, which made him decide that in truth he really didn't want to give up and die in this cramped, sterile office space in the bowels of an icebreaker.

So as the mercenary leered over him he reached up and plucked the gun right out of the air, moving as if he wasn't inhibited in the slightest.

That sent confidence rippling through him. He got the slightest taste of his old reflexes, the uncanny reaction speed that had seen him defy death for years on end, charging from one objective to the next with little time to stop and consider what an anomaly he truly was.

And somewhere in the recesses of his mind, he told himself he could still find that version of Will Slater.

So he found it.

And the seizure of the gun led to a wrenching motion with all the strength in his system, and he broke the mercenary's finger as he tore the weapon out of the man's grasp. With the fog receding he recognised the gun as an FN FNP-45 semiautomatic pistol with a fourteen round capacity. He made a mental note of his prior history with that particular weapon and corrected his movements in real time, bringing it up to aim at the underside of the mercenary's chin. The guy seemed horrified by how quickly the tables had turned, but Slater didn't give him any time to consider that.

He pumped the trigger twice and the thug tumbled back through the doorway, spilling out into the passageway beyond.

Slater leapt over the corpse and retrieved the phone. His actions were starting to compound. The small things were adding up, and the receding fog made the screen a little clearer, the buttons a little sharper in clarity. He started to recall past menus he'd navigated through and deemed useless. Hunched over the device, he moved faster and faster.

He found some kind of call log.

The first number was useless. Maybe that guy was already dead. King would have ensured that.

Operating on blind instinct, Slater thumbed down to the second last call Magomed had made and dialled.

Hoping for the best.

'Hello?' a voice said, almost instantaneously.

American.

Slightly concerned.

'Are we still on track?' the voice said. 'You're coming in awfully fast. Are you sure—'

Slater digested the words, and they made sense. He couldn't believe it. He didn't need to spend unnecessary time grappling with the implications, connecting the dots as best he could.

He just understood.

There was no time to ascertain which of the three warships the voice at the other end of the line belonged to. There was no time for any real conversation. Not if they were as close to impact as he thought. That was the most nauseating aspect of the whole thing. The absolute unknown. There were no windows, no portholes, no connection to the outside world. Slater was trapped inside a behemoth of steel and machinery.

So he said, 'Listen! We no longer have control of the icebreaker. There's been some huge internal errors. Get your ships out of the way right now.'

'I'm sorry, who are—?'

'*Get out of the way!*' Slater roared.

'Sir...'

'We do not have control.'

'I—'

'We do not have control.'

'Okay. Wait ... oh, Jesus. You're too close!'

'We do not have control.'

'Okay, okay.'

The call ended. From the other end.

Slater seized the table, sweating bullets, and battled down a vicious panic attack.

His throat tightened, closing, painful and searing and...

Is this it?

Is this the end?

65

King figured if he was about to have a front row seat to the incident that would plunge the world into irreparable conflict, he might as well experience it up close. As the icebreaker barrelled incessantly toward the middle warship, he blinked irritation out of his eyes and stared in disbelief through the windshield.

The sea seemed to swell. The waves increased in both height and weight, rising out of the ocean like angry pulses, but they did nothing to deter the icebreaker. Thirty thousand tonnes of steel plunged forward, making a beeline for the side of the warship. Now King could make out the control tower, the aircraft perched aboard the ship. But not much more than that.

He lined up the trajectories. He glanced helplessly at the controls. There was nothing resembling a wheel. This was a modern beast, all electronic, all automated. All locked, set in its ways. There was nothing he could do. He'd never felt more helpless.

The three ships remained in place, perched there. Vessels of this size required dozens of crew members to control, and nothing happened in a hurry. There were no violent changes in direction or anything of the sort.

If a behemoth of a ship was floating in place, it couldn't get out of the way fast.

The icebreaker reached the point where an impact was inevitable, and then it kept barreling in a straight line.

Now King could see how it would unfold. The bow would hit the mass of the warship at full speed, demolishing it where it rested. The icebreaker was three times the size of the warship and reinforced with all the modern marvels of engineering. The warship they were heading toward was a relic of a bygone era, probably outdated in comparison to the technological wonderland underneath King's feet.

He swallowed raw fear.

By now the sailors aboard the warship would understand what was happening. Attention would be drawn to the approaching vessel. Maybe an alarm would sound. It would all prove futile.

Unless...

Heart hammering in his throat, King's eyes widened as he spotted the slightest sliver of movement. It might have been his imagination. He couldn't be sure. There was no way to be certain, considering the surroundings. The icebreaker swayed underneath his feet, and the sea spray pouring off the ocean obscured any hope of a clear view, battering the bow and blasting up onto the weather deck. The storm clouds thickened above the three warships, compounding the dread, adding to the general atmosphere of fear draped over everything. The helicopters continued to circle obliviously, the men and women behind the cameras excited to record a historical unification of the U.S. and Russia in such a turbulent time.

But his eyes weren't deceiving him.

The icebreaker barged forward, and the middle warship started to trundle out of the way.

Too late.

No.

Not too late.

Or maybe it was...

King didn't know. He'd never been so uncertain. The fact that he couldn't control the outcome set him on edge, making the symptoms of stress amplify with each passing second. He fixated on the warship, now scrutinising its every detail, confirming that it *was* moving, slowly but surely. Too slow. It crept through the sea, fighting the waves.

None of this made sense. By the time the sailors aboard the Navy vessel determined the icebreaker was closing the gap with hostile intentions, it would have been too late to manoeuvre out of the way. The distances and speed were too close. There was no room for error. It would have taken a prescient admiral with total unobstructed command of the ship to recognise the intent of the icebreaker and kick the crew into high gear.

And that would have all had to happen well before the *Mochnost* surged into range, well before anyone understood what was truly happening.

Unless Slater had rolled off the bed.

Unless he'd found a way to bypass the signal jammer. Unless he'd somehow navigated the stifling bureaucracy of the American government and managed to get in direct contact with the warship.

All unlikely.

But not impossible.

The bow powered onward.

Two hundred feet.

One hundred feet.

Fifty feet.

The warship inched away from the point of contact. Now the icebreaker would strike the stern, not the centre mass. It would still cause untold destruction. It would probably sink the ship. It would still kill dozens, if not hundreds. Sailors would die.

Not much better.

Then the warship picked up an iota of momentum. It slid through the dark grey waters a little faster. Its stern started to inch out of sight. Moving to the right.

Still, the icebreaker charged.

Then the gargantuan bow of the *Mochnost* swallowed the sight of the warship whole, towering over it, obscuring King's view. He swore. And yelled. Letting out all the adrenalin in his system. He waited with bated breath for the shattering impact, the moment when all his worst fears would be confirmed. The single event that would instigate a political reaction like nothing the world had ever seen before.

It didn't come.

Exploding with nervous energy, he leapt onto the console, perching precariously atop the digital panels. By a stroke of bad luck he twisted his knee unnaturally to the left, too caught up in the terror to focus on planting his feet correctly. Something in the outside of his knee tweaked. A ligament snapping, maybe. It was the straw that broke the camel's back. He'd put his body through the ringer over the course of his time aboard the icebreaker. It was all catching up to him. His limbs felt dead, his muscles heavy, his mind exerted from reacting left and right to combat situations where a moment's hesitation spelled the difference between life and death.

There were physical limits, after all.

He went down on one knee, frustrated by the horrendous timing. He craned his neck as he felt his left leg give out, searching for any sign of the warship on the starboard side of the icebreaker.

He found it.

The warship's bow crept into view, then the bulk of the ship including the control tower, followed swiftly by the stern.

Unblemished.

The icebreaker rolled steadily past.

It had been close.

Horrifically close.

So close that King knew he might pass out from sheer stress if he stopped to think about what might have been. But the sight of the untouched warship rumbling away from the impact zone sent a kind of relief flooding through him that he hadn't known was humanly possible.

He collapsed off the control panel, slumping mercifully to the floor of the wheelhouse. He breathed in a deep lungful of air, his shoulders shaking, his palms sweaty. The compartmentalisation of his emotions dissipated, replaced by the raw reality of how close he'd come to failure.

It must have been Slater.

There was no other explanation.

King gave silent thanks to his brother in arms. In all his time in the field, he'd never seen someone fight through concussion symptoms like Slater had. Anyone with normal human tendencies wouldn't have stepped foot out of that bunker earlier that morning. But Slater hadn't even thought twice about it.

King remembered the conversation.

He'd said, *'I can't go up against them myself.'*

Slater had said, *'You think I can help? In this state?'*

'Maybe you can't fight. But they know about you. You show

your face and that's all they'll focus on. They won't be paying attention to anything else.'

'When?

'In the morning. Rest now.'

'Where do you need me?'

'Wherever you're comfortable going.'

'None of this is comfortable.'

'You know what I mean.'

'You mean the most amount of risk I'm willing to take?'

'Basically.'

'I stopped caring about that a long time ago. I'll go where you need me.'

'It'll be dangerous. I can't guarantee anything.'

Slater had laughed.

66

Slater waited for the world to end.

Moment by moment, the momentum he'd built up started to descend from its peak. First he sensed the fog clouding in again, muddying his thoughts, making him confused and scared and unclear all at once. He stumbled over to the nearest wall and slid down the cool surface, letting his back drag against the metal, dealing with the return of a mammoth headache. It seemed far too familiar. It was almost a return to normalcy. Feeling fine hadn't seemed natural. Ever since Ruslan Mikhailov had stomped down on his head, he'd started acclimatising to his compromised state. Now back in the thick of it, he felt right at home.

He winced, bowed his head, squeezed the satellite phone with all the nervous energy at the forefront of his mind, and waited for the earth-shattering impact.

The giant *crruuunnchhhhhh* as the icebreaker struck the warship, obliterating its hull, slaughtering most of the men aboard and drowning the rest as the Navy ship sunk to a watery grave.

And he kept waiting.

And moment by moment he sensed the danger passing. He started breathing deeper. Less constricted.

With caution, he started getting optimistic.

Something happened. A shuddering groan. The distant muffled sound of a giant object rumbling past in the ocean, perilously close. Fear blasted through Slater's consciousness, and his eyes went wide. He flinched, curled up in a ball, and squeezed his eyes shut.

Here we go.

But the impact didn't follow. The creaking and groaning subsided, replaced by a dark silence. He kept his eyes closed, convinced he was getting hopeful for no reason. His worst nightmare was to open them, reassured that the danger had passed, and then feel the resounding impact that would lead to the deaths of hundreds of sailors and compromise the peace of the free world.

But nothing happened.

Then, after what felt like an eternity, he heard footsteps. He sighed. There was no way King had mown through the entire mercenary army. Even if he'd killed dozens, which Slater seriously doubted, that wouldn't be enough. There were nearly fifty aboard, spread across the floating island. Tucked into the crevasses. Slinking through the shadows. They couldn't hope to come out on top. Not against all of them. If the enemy force was highly motivated, they could flush them out with relatively simple tactics. King had succeeded in the beginning because of his innate ability to take advantage of chaos and confusion, but now that had dissipated.

So Slater opened his eyes and raised the FN pistol, pointing it at the doorway, his hand shaking.

He saw three doorways.

You don't stand a chance, a voice told him.

And he believed it.

Jason King stepped into the doorway. He was armed, the fearsome Heckler & Koch HK433 sweeping the room, but it was only a precaution. He meant no threat. He surveyed the scene, concluding Slater was alone. Then he lowered the rifle and stepped into the room. Blood covered the front of his combat gear, staining his compression shirt. He was pale. His eyes were wide. There were dark bags underneath both lids. It had been a chaotic whirlwind of forward movement ever since he'd left Koh Tao. He'd barely had time to get an hour's sleep.

'You ... killed them all?' Slater said.

King sat down on one of the chairs. He slumped forward. He didn't blink.

He was in shock.

'Not all of them,' he said. 'There'll be a dozen or so floating around. But they won't find us. If they do, it'll be one by one.'

'They could flush us out.'

'They're paid by the hour. They're leaderless. They're stranded on board this thing. The plan didn't work. None of them will have a clue what to do.'

'They've got experience.'

'Not enough.'

'What if—'

'*Will,*' King barked. 'Shut the fuck up.'

Slater froze. 'You okay?'

'I need a minute.'

'What happened? We stopped it, right?'

'Did you make a call?'

'Yeah.'

'How'd you manage that? How are you even awake?'

'I won't be for much longer. The adrenalin's wearing off.'

'You need rest.'

'So do you.'

'I had rest. A year of it.'

'And now?'

'I don't know. Like I said. I need a minute.'

Slater rested the back of his skull against the cold steel, still keeping his ears tuned for any sign of approaching hostiles. But there was nothing. Just the steady groaning of the icebreaker as it continued on its forward trajectory, moving deeper and deeper into the Sea of Japan. Further away from the coastline. Away from Vladivostok. Away from the Navy.

'There'll be an RHIB somewhere on board,' Slater said. 'We can use it to get out of here.'

'I need a minute,' King said.

His voice soft.

His tone weak.

'You can take a minute when we're safe.'

'We're safe.'

'You don't know that.'

King raised his gaze off the steel floor and said, 'Do you understand what just happened?'

'It hasn't properly hit me yet.'

'The concussion's keeping it at bay?'

'Probably. I never stop to think about things anyway. Even when I'm healthy.'

'I think...'

He trailed off.

'What?' Slater said.

King's gaze bored into him. 'Who'd you call? How'd you do it?'

'Stroke of luck. Magomed was in contact with one of the

warships. Impersonating a government official, I imagine. He'd know how to pass himself off as one. That was most of his life, after all. He would have done a good job. Especially with the finer details. Anyway, I just went through his call log and redialled.'

'How'd you recognise the number?'

'I didn't.'

67

King mulled over the words for a long time. He massaged his temples with dirty, bloody fingers. 'Pure luck.'

'About time we caught a lucky break.'

King kept rubbing his forehead, clearly torn apart on the inside, grappling with something deeper than Slater could imagine.

'What?' Slater said again.

'How am I supposed to just walk away again? Knowing what we just prevented.'

'I won't let you get back into this game,' Slater said. 'You deserve your sanity.'

'Don't worry. That was never on the table.'

'But?'

'But how am I supposed to ignore this in the future?'

'What do you mean?'

'You're hurt right now. I can understand that. But you're conscious enough to know if the fire's still there.'

'I guess.'

'Well?'

'It's there,' Slater admitted.

'Has it ever gone out? Even for a moment?'

'No.'

'Are you lying?'

'Why would I lie?'

'Do you think it ever will?'

'I don't know. Why all the questions?'

'Because I don't know what to think about this.'

'About what?'

'You called and I came. Because I was never going to stay on the island. Not after what you told me. Not after I understood the consequences. But there's no spark inside me anymore. I don't want to do this. I'm tired of killing. I'm tired of all of it. I just want to see life without all this suffering in it.'

'How was the year off?' Slater said. 'Run into any drama?'

'None.'

'You enjoyed it?'

'Of course. But am I supposed to?'

'What do you mean?'

'Why does my comfort mean anything? If something like this happens again, and I get asked to help, how am I supposed to say no?'

'You aren't.'

'Then I'm in limbo. I never know whether I'm going to have to bring the old King back.'

'Then that's the best you're ever going to get,' Slater said.

Harsh, but necessary.

King nodded. 'Thought as much.'

'Are you happy?'

'As happy as I can be.'

'It's been a long time,' Slater said. 'We've barely had the chance to talk.'

'We can do that later,' King said. 'You were right before. I don't need a minute. I can take a minute later.'

'I ... can't process all of this. Where do we go from here? What do we do?'

'We run,' King said. 'We lay low. We think about what we just prevented. And we go our separate ways.'

'You don't need to run anymore. You don't need to hide.'

'What? We're still being hunted. Nothing's changed.'

'Not anymore.'

'Who've you been speaking to?'

'The clean up crew. Black Force is done, but we've been given the all clear.'

'By who?'

'Someone I know. Someone in the government.'

'Can you trust him?'

Slater remembered the nine-year-old girl he'd rescued in the dark heart of Macau. He remembered the bond he'd formed with her. He remembered handing her over to Russell Williams with the promise of finding her a new life.

A new family.

A new future.

'Yes,' Slater said. 'With my life.'

'You sure?'

'Yes.'

'And he told you what, exactly?'

'That we've been cleared of any wrongdoing. That no-one's looking for us. That we can go on with our lives without having to look over our shoulders every five seconds.'

'He doesn't want us to come back?'

'He understands what happened. He knows we'll never trust them again.'

'And they're okay with that? Given what we know.'

'I don't think they're thrilled about it. But they ended up accepting that we have our heads in the right place. And, to be frank, we're probably not worth the manpower it would take to eliminate us.'

'True,' King admitted. 'That's bordering on arrogance, though.'

'Just the truth.'

'Only takes one bullet.'

'Oh yeah? How'd that work out for these guys?'

Slater gestured around the room, to the bodies of Magomed and the faceless mercenaries, and he kept sweeping his hand to encompass the entire icebreaker. Including the corpses strewn across the passageways below deck and the walkways above deck and inside the wheelhouse.

'Guess you have a point,' King said.

'Everything's awfully quiet. Where's the rest of them?'

'Probably thinking about what the hell they're going to do next. I imagine they didn't have a Plan B.'

'I doubt they're that stupid.'

'There's dozens of them. And they'd spent months independently contracted to a man who paid them handsomely to stand around and do nothing. So they got complacent. And Magomed knew what he was doing. So he would have exuded authority. And they would have bought into it. They would have thought there was no way they could possibly fail. And they were relying on last-minute orders. There was secrecy around everything. Maybe Magomed had a plan for them after they rammed the warship. But I doubt it. This was always supposed to be his grave. And now they're all starting to realise that. They thought they were important to the plan but now they're standing on an out-of-control floating island with no idea where to go next. They started relying too heavily on Magomed.'

'That's a lot to extrapolate.'

'If I was wrong, then they'd be sweeping the passageways below deck in tight clusters. We'd probably already be dead. You hear anything?'

Slater listened.

The ship groaned.

The engine rumbled.

'There's no fight,' King said. 'If we find any of them on the way out of here, they'll run and hide. No-one's going to care enough. They're not getting paid anymore. It didn't work out.'

'And that plays into our hands, doesn't it?'

King raised an eyebrow.

'It means they're sloppy,' Slater said. 'It means they'll get caught trying to flee. At least some of them. And then it'll all fall apart. No-one will buy that it's the Russian government behind it. Besides, nothing happened.'

'You said we're no longer wanted?'

'Not anymore.'

'As of...?'

'A couple of months ago.'

'Where were you?'

'Macau.'

'How'd that go?'

'I don't want to talk about that.'

'Got it. Well, then, it seems like I can make a few calls. Now that it's safe.'

'I wouldn't push it if I were you,' Slater said. 'We're not on good terms. They just don't want us dead anymore.'

'I don't need to be on good terms. I just need to tell them what happened.'

'And?'

'And then they can digest it. Now that there's no need to overreact. Now that there's no dead sailors. They can understand, instead of reacting impulsively. And they can begin to accept that it wasn't the Russian government.'

'You think it'll work?'

King shrugged. 'Honestly ... we've done enough.'

'We've done enough,' Slater said, and for a moment he dropped his guard, letting relief flood over him.

But only for a moment.

Because footsteps sounded in the passageway outside, sauntering across the floor.

Echoing off the walls.

King sighed, stood up, and picked up the HK433.

68

The man who stepped into the doorway was almost lackadaisical in his movements. He seemed like he would rather be anywhere else. But even the most unmotivated soldier of fortune had a mean streak a mile long, so Slater didn't underestimate the coldness in the guy's eyes.

He was short. Five-eight, five-nine maybe. And thin. There wasn't much of him to aim at. His features were unimpressive — in a crowd, he would be unnoticeable. He had a soft jawline and shockingly styled straight brown hair that fell over his forehead in a bowl cut. But there was that certain level of detachment in his eyes that separated him from ordinary folk. He had a crude Kalashnikov assault rifle in his hands, and he aimed it at King and Slater as if nothing at all was out of the ordinary. As if this was just another day at the office.

King aimed his Heckler & Koch rifle back at the guy.

Slater pointed his FNP-45 at the man's head.

'English?' King said when it became clear they were trapped in a stalemate.

'Of course, mate,' the guy said. He spoke softly. 'I'm British.'

'What are you doing out here?'

'Could ask you the same question.'

'You're the one who bothered us.'

'You two did all this?' he said, flashing a glance down the passageway.

Eyeing the bodies.

'Mostly my friend here,' Slater said.

'You're something else, then. Impressive.'

'How's this going to play out?' King said, wary of the AK-47 barrel aimed at his face. 'I don't like having a weapon pointed at me.'

'And I don't like not getting paid. So it seems we're both pretty pissed off, doesn't it?'

'None of my concern.'

'That's my boss, right there. Isn't it?'

Slater glanced at Magomed's corpse. 'That's your boss.'

'Didn't work out too well for him,' King said.

'And now what am I supposed to do?'

'Want the honest answer?'

'Yeah.'

'I couldn't give a shit.'

'We've got ourselves in a tricky situation, haven't we?'

'Only as tricky as it needs to be.'

'I know what the obvious next step is,' the mercenary said. 'But I don't know if I can trust you.'

'Then it's mutual.'

'I'll put it down if you do.'

'You'll shoot us. We killed your boss.'

'Yeah, well, how is killing you going to change anything? I just want off this fucking ship, mate. Then I can go try and find some other work. Christ, I thought this would be the retirement package.'

'Retirement from what?'

'Same thing you do.'

Out of the corner of his eye, Slater watched King's face. He noted some kind of dark recognition there. Some kind of realisation. But the British mercenary in the doorway didn't notice.

Slater certainly did.

His tone changing, King said, 'Damn. You came here after Vadim's gig?'

The mercenary eyed him warily. 'No idea what you're talking about.'

King waved a hand, almost friendly in nature. 'Of course you do. We go way back, then.'

'What?'

'Vadim Mikhailov,' King said. 'Do I need to spell it out?'

'What did you have to do with him?'

'I was one of the crew that rotated. Snatched idiots out of their beds. Dragged them to Vadim's doorstep. Paid well, didn't it?'

'I never saw you.'

'And I never saw you either. You know how many men he had on the payroll?'

'So why all this? What the hell are you doing now?'

'Working for the Man. Same old news.'

'Which man?'

'Any man. If they pay.'

'You're getting paid for this?'

King shrugged. 'Honest work. Got to put food on the table, don't I?'

'Some of these guys were my friends.'

'I doubt that, buddy. Maybe at surface level. But none of

you are stupid enough to form a brotherhood in a field like this. Tomorrow you could take your last breath. Better not to get attached. At least that's what I've found.'

King's tone was conversational, and even though the two men still had their aims locked onto each other's heads, the threat seemed to have dissipated. It wasn't something easily faked. Slater could sense it in the underlying atmosphere.

You couldn't get rid of it in a hurry.

Unless you were Jason King.

Slater masked a smile.

'How are you getting out of here?' King said, and lowered his gun half an inch.

Barely noticeable.

But the mercenary noticed.

And he bought it.

The British guy lowered his AK-47, his lips starting to form a response.

Then they froze mid-sentence, because the guy recognised that King hadn't lowered his aim any lower than the initial movement. He was now pointing the HK433 at the British guy's throat.

'Well, that was easy,' King noted.

'Fuck you,' the mercenary spat. 'I thought there was honour between us. We're the only two left, in any case.'

'What does that mean?' King said.

The mercenary scoffed, still wrapped up in his fantasy, and waved a hand at the bodies. 'Recognise these guys? I'm sure you worked with them. They're the best, because they came straight from the Kamchatka Peninsula like us. The only troops you left alive on board this fuckin' ship are the ones that panicked and hid. Notice how no-one's around, mate? They're the amateurs. The ragtag group. We're the professionals. From the mine. And you killed all of us.'

King smiled. 'Good.'

'Had a change of heart? Trying to preserve your moral compass? Bit late for that.'

'You're assuming I'm from the Kamchatka Peninsula crew.'

The mercenary froze in place, then a sly smile spread across his lips. He chuckled, his manic scoffing ringing off the walls. He held up a finger and wagged it in King's direction. Then he licked his lips. 'You're good, mate.'

'And why's that?'

'I bought it.'

'I *was* there, though.'

'You just said you weren't.'

'No, I didn't. I said I wasn't part of the crew. Big difference.'

'Then what were you doing out there?'

'Cleaning up.'

The mercenary cocked his head. Scuffed one boot against the ground. Ran a hand through his hair. Jovial in the face of death. A true madman. His lips twisted into a sneer. There was crazed light behind his eyes.

'That was you? The mine?'

'And me,' Slater mumbled, still seated against the wall, his gun still trained on the mercenary.

'You're it,' King said under his breath. 'You're the last one.'

But Slater heard it.

He said, 'Yeah. Last one.'

'I've got cash,' the mercenary said. 'Shitloads of it. Looks like you boys are in need of some. Let me help you out. Just get me the fuck off this ship.'

King pursed his lips. 'I don't know, friend. I'm pretty

much set. Made the most of my day job while it lasted. What about you, Slater? You hurting for cash?'

Slater furrowed his brow. 'You know what, King ... I'm pretty much set, too. Isn't that a shame for our friend here?'

'That's a real downer,' King said. 'Shame you told us you were the only one left, too. Otherwise we might have kept you alive to sniff out the rest.'

'You're the fucking government, aren't you?' the mercenary spat. 'Okay. Arrest me then. Good luck proving anything that happened in international waters.'

'Don't need to prove it,' King said. 'I saw it.'

'Well, then, aren't you an honourable guy? If you're doing all this in the name of justice, or whatever. So give me a fair trial.'

'No,' King said, and tore his forehead apart with three consecutive rounds to the dome.

Slater added one shot from the FNP-45 to the chest. Well after the guy had died. Before he went down in a heap. The added force took him off his feet and he collapsed in a pile on the passageway floor over the threshold.

More symbolic than anything else.

Putting the final nail in the coffin.

Their ears ringing in the confined space, Slater and King turned to each other and exchanged a subtle nod of understanding.

Job finished.

Peninsula cleared.

Game over.

69

Slater couldn't stand on his own, so King looped an arm around his mid-section and hurried him through the dark bowels of the icebreaker. The giant ship continued to trundle through the Sea of Japan, heading nowhere in particular, maintaining the same course that the crew had been forced to set it on before they succumbed to grisly deaths.

Slater didn't think about any of that. If he wanted to, it wouldn't take much effort for his mind to drift to all the horrors he'd seen here. And then he would dwell on them, even though there was nothing he could do to change what had happened, and that would send him down a path he'd taken many times before but had no intention of revisiting.

In truth, nothing on this icebreaker fazed him as much as the lingering memory of Natasha's body hanging from the ceiling.

Thankfully, the concussion had kept the clarity of that sight at bay.

But it wouldn't for much longer.

Because Slater was safe.

He found his mind was no longer occupied by the oppressive thoughts of nuclear war. He wasn't battling for his life at every turn. The threats had dissipated. So more of his brain lay dormant, and that gave him all kinds of room for his mind to descend into madness. He'd always found the most dangerous period was the time directly after an operation. The memories were fresh, and raw, and if he formed negative habits spiralling down into the sadness and pity of his traumatic experiences, he knew he would never be able to crawl out of them. It had been at its worst in Yemen, sending him into cold sweats and feverish nightmares from which he never thought he'd surface.

Then he'd put it behind him.

Finally.

Step by step.

Battling through the darkness in his mind had been one of the hardest challenges of his career. And he thought he'd emerged victorious. But even through the haze of the concussion he could recognise horrific images when he saw them. They floated through the recesses of his consciousness. He glimpsed Natasha's brutalised body. He glimpsed a mental image of the icebreaker's crew strewn across the wheelhouse, shot down where they stood like dogs in the street.

He hadn't even seen it in the flesh.

But he could imagine it all the same.

He sensed King in a similarly silent trance as the pair hobbled down passageway after passageway under the flickering lights.

At one point, he glanced across. 'That guy wasn't lying. There's no-one around. They're all cowering in some corner, I assume.'

'Yeah,' King grunted.

He had his own demons to grapple with.

Now wasn't the time to try and pretend they weren't both going through their own personal versions of hell.

'This is why you got out, huh?' Slater said.

'I feel like you're better at suppressing it than I am. Hence why you've still got the spark.'

'Not really. I'm just better at dealing with being broken, I guess.'

'That's grim.'

'Doesn't have to be. Doesn't matter how I feel. As long as I'm helping people.'

'That's what your spark is?'

'Isn't yours?'

'It was. I don't have it anymore.'

'If I'm sitting around, someone's getting taken advantage of that I'm not trying to stop.'

'Yeah,' King murmured. 'That's why I feel so guilty all the time.'

'You shouldn't. You've done more than enough. I've just got an addictive personality.'

'I have my vices.'

'Not like mine.'

'Drink? Drugs? Women?'

'Keep going.'

'That's perfectly natural given what we do.'

'Given what I do. You're going back to Koh Tao.'

'Am I?' King said, and escorted Slater into a loading dock in the side of the icebreaker's hull.

70

The dock turned out to be sparse and smooth and clean, nothing but sterile surfaces and sterile landings. The multi-level space was arranged in a U-shape around a small bay of open seawater that churned and swelled as the icebreaker powered forward. Exposed to the elements by the ocean flooding in through the archway, Slater braced himself against the ice-cold wind as it howled in, whipping through the railings and lashing at his clothing.

In fact, it almost took him off his feet.

King tightened his grip and kept Slater upright, leading him down a landing. Now sea spray assaulted them, coming off the waves swirling angrily below. In similar fashion to all the electronics aboard the ship, the exterior lights struggled in unison with the rest of the system. The emergency power system battled to keep the icebreaker functioning, and soon it would peter out and plunge the entire interior into darkness.

Like something out of a horror movie.

By then, Slater would be long gone, but it gave him relief to know the *Mochnost* would eventually end up dead in the water somewhere near the Bering Strait instead of incessantly continuing on its path until it ran out of fuel or split another unassuming water vessel clean in two.

King pointed to a vaguely familiar shape hovering by steel cables a storey or two over the docking bay. Slater squinted to make out the object, but the sea spray coupled with his already compromised vision made it impossible. He wiped a hand across his face, only serving to spread blood into his eyes.

He was in bad shape.

King noticed. 'Come on, brother. Let's get you on board.'

'On board what?'

'That's an RHIB. You can't see it?'

'I can't see anything,' Slater grumbled, leaning more weight on King's bulging arm.

He drew the soaked sleeve of his shirt over his eyelids, clearing some of the debris. Now he could see clearer, and he stared up at the rigid hulled inflatable boat as King led him down the final ladder to the bottom level of the landings. Much like the rest of the icebreaker, it was brand new, probably purchased off the plan in anticipation of the *Mochnost*'s launch. No expense had been spared.

King found a control panel and set to work learning the mechanisms. He clearly aimed to lower the RHIB into the waters, and Slater felt that helping would be the honourable thing to do, but he took one step toward King and pitched violently to the left. At first he thought the icebreaker had crested a particularly fearsome wave, but as he stumbled and fell into one of the steel columns, sliding down to his rear in an uncontrollable heap, he spotted King looking awfully concerned, whipping around on the spot, still perfectly balanced.

There was no incident.

Slater was in terrible shape.

'Stay there,' King said. 'Don't move. I'll help you anywhere you need to go.'

'Sure you don't want to leave me aboard?'

'Funny.'

'I'll only slow you down.'

'I only came here to pull you out of this shit,' King said. 'Now stay there. The concussion's talking right now.'

'And you ended up saving the world.'

King paused, bulky detachable control panel in hand, and his gaze wandered over. 'We did, didn't we?'

'Mostly you.'

'I don't think it's sunk in yet.'

'It will. When we're off this ship.'

'Yeah.'

'You think that'll change how you feel about all this?'

'I don't know.'

'It's a lot to grapple with. I know.'

'Now's not the time,' King said, but he turned back to the control panel with his brow furrowed, deep in thought.

'Sorry,' Slater said after a long pause. 'We should talk about this later. You still haven't had your minute.'

'Haven't found the time,' King mumbled.

Footsteps.

On the landing above.

King swore, steadied himself against a particularly violent gust of wind and sea spray, and swung the wet barrel of the HK433 up to aim through the railing above his head.

'Oh, shit,' an accented voice cried out from above.

Slater couldn't see a thing. He started to crane his neck upward but it sent bolts of agony down his spine, so he elected to simply sit with his legs crossed and his gaze locked onto King.

Because he trusted the man with his life.

'Gun down,' King yelled above the din of the churning ocean.

Immediately, something clattered against the metal over Slater's head.

'Good. Now turn and walk away.'

'You mean...?'

'I'm not going to kill you.'

'O-okay...'

'Actually,' King said. 'Make sure you answer this truthfully. The Kamchatka Peninsula. Last year. Were you there?'

'What? I'm Nigerian. I came over for some contract work. Wasn't my fault they put me on board this thing. Where the hell's the Kamchatka Peninsula?'

'Walk away,' King said.

'Uh, thanks, man. Any idea what the hell I should do now?'

'Don't push it. You're fully aware of what happened here.'

'Bits and pieces.'

'So you're not a saint.'

'Ever heard of Stockholm syndrome?'

'I've heard of it. I don't think it applies here.'

'You're probably right.'

'Walk away. And be better.'

'Why haven't you killed me?'

'Because unless you're directly responsible for what I'm going up against then I'm not really in a position to judge.'

'You a mercenary too, then?'

'Used to be.'

'Where'd you work?'

'Everywhere.'

'Just surprised we didn't run into each other at any point, man.'

'You wouldn't have wanted that to happen. Trust me.'

'I—'

'I'm not here to have a conversation. Walk away.'

'Okay, man. You can't help me?'

'Not a chance. And you're lucky I'm retired.'

'You don't look retired.'

'I'll shoot you if you're not out of here in three seconds.'

More footsteps on the landing overhead.

This time rapidly fading into nothingness.

'You should have killed him,' Slater said.

'I'm tired of killing,' King said, turning back to the control panel.

'He deserved it.'

'A lot of people deserve it. But I've reached my threshold.'

'Just because he wasn't on the Kamchatka Peninsula doesn't mean he's innocent.'

'He's far from innocent. That's the nature of the field.'

'So why let him live?'

'You probably expect me to give some philosophical answer, right?'

'No. I just want the truth.'

'Would you have killed him?'

'Yes.'

'Then you're a stronger man than me.'

'What's the reason?'

King looked up with weary eyes and said, 'I'm just tired of it all.'

Then he stabbed down with a single finger and pressed a button on the hefty remote. Something whirred, and the RHIB splashed into the water with a resounding *thud.*

'Let's go,' King said.

71

The RHIB was military grade, with a firm hull and a tough, reinforced windshield that ordinarily deflected most of the howling wind and sea spray. But the conditions were grim, and under a dark grey sky Slater and King ducked their heads to avoid a barrage of the elements. The inflatable craft bounced and jolted on the high seas, tearing away from the looming icebreaker, spearing over the crests of waves with its engine roaring and the throttle lever pushed to maximum.

Slater saw King shiver, one meaty hand wrapped around the lever and the other keeping the Heckler & Koch HK433 stood at attention. But the man's muscles were relaxed. His vision was fixated on the horizon, not on the hulking *Mochnost* icebreaker behind them.

He had no fight left in him.

He'd made that clear.

'What if someone pursues us?' Slater said.

'Then I'll deal with it,' King said, his tone rising to over-power the freezing gale.

'You look like you'd rather do anything else.'

King glanced back at the icebreaker, now just a dark silhouette against the backdrop of the storm clouds, and shivered again.

This time not because of the cold.

He didn't respond.

They shot away from the scene, leaving it far behind, heading back for Vladivostok. Slater adjusted his position resting against one of the hard-backed seats skewered into the deck. He squinted against the sea spray. Pain hung over him in a dark cloud. It took everything he had left in his body to keep himself awake. Because he knew if he fell asleep now, in such close proximity to a severe concussion, he might never wake up again.

Slater said, 'You think it'll keep you up at night?'

'It already did. What's another couple dozen more dead men to add to it?'

'You might feel like you have to do this forever, but you don't.'

'I don't know whether to go back to Koh Tao.'

'Why? You were happy there. Klara's there.'

'She doesn't deserve this.'

'Deserve what?'

'The next time I get a call, my conscience won't let me ignore it. Just like you knew it wouldn't this time. That's why you came to me.'

'I'm sorry I did.'

'No you're not. And you shouldn't be, anyway. Even Koh Tao wouldn't be immune to what we just prevented.'

'So you know it's necessary. When it happens. *If* it happens.'

'It'll happen again. That's the nature of the beast.'

'Go off the grid. Like I did. If no-one can contact you, then you don't have to help.'

'That makes me just as responsible.'

'Does it?'

'She doesn't deserve to have to live with the knowledge that I'll end up getting myself killed one day. She thought I was done with the life. I did, too. But ... things like this...'

'So lie to her.'

'No.'

'Is that one of your rules?'

'I don't have any rules. I just do what I think is right.'

'And it's not right to make her happy?'

'Blissful ignorance doesn't count. Better to know the truth than be wrapped up in fantasy-land.'

'And the truth is...?'

'If I get another call like this, I won't be able to resist.'

'And why is that a burden for her?'

'Because I'll die. One day. My luck will just run out. And that'll be that. And she'll have spent years getting attached to someone who was too dumb to say no to putting their life on the line time and time again.'

'You can't resist responding to trouble,' Slater said. 'But that shouldn't mean you live a miserable life. Think about what you're saying. That means no relationships. No close connections of any kind. That's not a life.'

'Maybe I don't deserve a life.'

'So you'll just keep wandering and wallow in self-pity and get wrapped up in carnage over and over again?'

King paused, thought it through, then shook his head.

'No. Klara would hate me even more if I did that.'

'You care about her.'

'Obviously.'

'It's just ... I didn't know if it was going to last. That's what I thought would bring you back. In the end.'

'It's going to last.'

'Unless you run away.'

'No,' King said. 'I can't.'

'Good. You're realising.'

'But what do I tell her?'

'What you said. The truth. But if I had to guess, I'd say she already knows that.'

'I told her I was done. I believed it.'

'Did she?'

King opened his mouth to respond, but the words didn't follow. He paused mid-thought, mulling, contemplating. Then he shrugged. 'I guess I wasn't paying attention. Maybe she didn't.'

'Seems like I know you better than you know yourself.'

'Yeah, well ... we're the same person, aren't we?'

'Not quite.'

'Don't tell me you've still got the fire inside you. Not after all that. You'll be dealing with concussion symptoms for months. Surely that's a sign to get out.'

'I wouldn't recognise a sign if it was staring me right in the face.'

'Because your brain is scrambled.'

'Even perfectly healthy. Same principle.'

'Slater, I pulled you out of this shit once. I'm not going to do it again.'

'I'm not asking for your help again.'

'What if you run into something else like this?'

'It's done. It's over. The Kamchatka crew are extinguished.'

'There's always more.'

'Always.'

'So what are you going to do?'

'Rest up. Then keep doing the only thing I know.'

'I thought the same thing. Turns out you *can* teach an old dog new tricks. Took me long enough to realise it.'

'Maybe *you* can,' Slater mumbled.

'You could if you tried.'

'I don't want to try.'

'Why not?'

'Because,' Slater said, feeling every iota of the pain in his temples and the agony in his broken hand and the icy chill of the sea spray assaulting his clothing and the uncertainty of how he was going to sneak out of the Russian Far East in the aftermath of an international incident, 'I wouldn't want to be anywhere else right now.'

72

He came back to consciousness, and it mirrored the sensation of fighting through mud.

He sensed internal panic in the pit of his stomach even before his vision returned.

You fell asleep, you moron.

Now you're dead.

But he wasn't dead. He was in a room outfitted in the style of a winter lodge, small and yet spacious at the same time. Every inch of floorspace had been maximised. Slater blinked twice, and realised he recognised the layout of the space.

He'd stayed in an identical room a couple of days previously.

But it felt like a lifetime ago.

He blinked again. His head hurt.

That was an understatement.

His head seared with pain. He figured it would for quite some time. Maybe forever. Even lifting his skull a couple of inches off the pillow seemed like the most difficult burden of his life. So he maintained the exact position he'd woken in. He didn't try moving. Because he sensed the threat had disappeared.

They'd left it behind on the *Mochnost* icebreaker.

Jason King sat with his elbows on his knees in the far corner of the room. A roaring log fireplace separated them. The only illumination in sight, casting flickering shadows off the walls. It was dark outside. Slater tilted the angle of his head and stared up through the grimy window, shut tight. A sea of stars draped the Russian Far East like a sparkling blanket.

Saved from the sub-zero temperatures outside by the warmth of the fireplace, he turned his attention back to King.

The man was watching him.

'How long have I been out?' Slater said.

'Nine or ten hours. Any longer and I would have thought you'd gone into a coma.'

'I probably almost did.'

'The brain's a strange thing. You never know how it's going to react.'

'Mine hasn't reacted well.'

'You should be dead. Or permanently disabled.'

'Maybe I am.'

'You're not. You feel better than before, don't you?'

It was all relative, but as Slater adjusted himself in the bed, he had to concede the point. It was hell, but it wasn't concentrated hell. Not like the disorientation aboard the icebreaker.

'So you'll heal. Eventually. But no-one knows how long it'll take. Not even the specialists.'

'You know that for a fact?'

'They tested me in Black Force. Dozens of times.'

'Me too.'

'Did they find anything?'

'Nothing to worry about.'

'That they mentioned.'

'You ever think about that stuff?' Slater said, his voice low in the silent room. 'How we'll end up in twenty years...'

'Best not to think about it.'

'We've done a lot,' Slater said. 'A hell of a lot.'

'I've done enough.'

'You keep saying that. But you keep coming back.'

'You didn't give me much of a choice.'

'So how do things unfold from here? What if I run into another situation like this?'

'Then you handle it on your own.'

'And if I can't?'

'Then you walk away.'

'And if I can't do either of those things?'

'Then you kill yourself.'

Slater blinked, wondering if he'd heard King correctly. 'What?'

'You've been in and out of unconsciousness for half a day. It's given me a lot of time to think.'

'And...?'

'I'm done. Completely done. I don't want to ever hear from you again.'

'Because you think I'm a bad influence?'

'Not a bad one. You needed me now, and it was noble. You wanted to wipe out the vermin left around the peninsula. I get it. And we ended up pulling off that shit at the shipbuilding plant, too. Imagine if I didn't come. Imagine if you never found this.'

'I was going to find it,' Slater said. 'One way or another.'

'Because you've still got the fire inside you.'

'You keep saying you don't anymore. But how can you do what you did on the icebreaker without the fire? How is it even possible to kill without it? I've always had it.'

'Mine went out. I can't describe it. Neither can you, and I know it. Fire is the closest thing we can think of. But it's that burning desire to never stop. To keep moving forward. To jump from problem to problem. Leave us in one place with nothing to do for too long and we'll go insane.'

'But you were on Koh Tao,' Slater said. 'For almost a year.'

King nodded. 'It's out, Slater. And it didn't come back. I don't think it ever will.'

'What does it mean? Long-term?'

'I don't know. I killed all those men without the motivation to do it. It cost me a lot. In terms of mental capacity. I'm spent. And I don't want to do anything other than go back to that tropical island and live out the rest of my days there. With Klara.'

'But if she knows that there's the possibility—'

'There is no possibility. Not anymore. I'm not doing it anymore, Will.'

'What if I call, and a guy has his finger on the trigger of a dirty bomb that'll kill thousands of people, and the only way I can stop it in time is to—'

'Give me all the hypotheticals you want,' King said. 'I won't pick up the phone.'

Slater nodded. 'I guess I can't understand. Because I don't know what it feels like when the flame goes out.'

'You think it ever will?'

'I'm younger than you, aren't I?'

'Not by much. Not enough for it to matter.'

'And I think that's the difference between you and me.'

King raised an eyebrow.

'I don't think my fire will ever go out.'

'It's hardwired in?'

'I think so.'

'I thought so, too.'

'We're not the same, King. You're done. I'm not. This concussion will put me out for weeks, maybe months. And then I'll jump right back in again.'

'You enjoy it?'

'I can't explain it. You know what I'm talking about better than anyone else.'

'If you stop, you'll start to think about your life.'

'And that's something I *really* don't want to do.'

'The girl. Was she important to you?'

'It was getting there.'

'How long had you known her?'

'Only half a day.'

'Still the ladies man, I see.'

'Less than before.'

'You thought there might have been something there?'

'Maybe. Down the line. I speculated. Turns out it doesn't matter, because she's hanging from the ceiling of a concrete bunker.'

'I'm sorry.'

Slater shrugged. 'It's the life, isn't it?'

'That's why you should take my advice. Follow my example. Get out.'

'Then who's going to stop the next incident?'

'There's always someone else.'

'Not like us.'

'That's bordering on arrogant.'

'Don't you understand what we just did?'

'I'm fully aware of what we just did. I won't forget it for the rest of my life.'

'Because the fire wasn't there? So it made you feel terrible?'

'I feel like a mass murderer.'

'You shouldn't.'

'Thanks for the advice.'

Slater said, 'Fuck advice. Nothing I say to you is going to change how you feel. Nothing you say to me is going to change how I feel. We're two broken minds who happen to be very good at what we do. And we deal with it in different ways. And that's all it's ever going to be. Nothing else to talk about. And I can see the change you're talking about in your eyes. They're different. They're not as intense. You really, truly don't want to do this anymore. So get yourself back to Koh Tao, and stay there. And I'll rest here and hit the road.'

King nodded solemnly. Deep in thought.

Slater said, 'On that note ... where is here? I think I have an idea.'

'I've been following you since you left the bar. Figured I'd bring you back here. Seems like you formed a bond with the barman over something. I didn't push it. Not my job to be nosy...'

'She was taken,' Slater said. 'From here.'

King bowed his head. 'Right.'

'Alexei tried to stop them.'

'He's grateful that you didn't go to the police.'

'Does he know what we did?'

'No. But I paid him fifty thousand dollars for his loyalty.'

'You did *what*?'

'I offered. He didn't ask. It's worth it to be safe. I figured the fastest way to get him on our side was to buy his loyalty. I probably didn't need to. He already spoke fondly of you. He helped me carry you upstairs. So you've got this room for as long as you need. And he promises to hide you and feed you until you're better. No matter what the television says happened in Vladivostok. And then you can carry on your way.'

'And you?'

'I'm leaving.'

'How will you get out of—?'

King held up a hand. 'Maybe it's best we don't talk about specifics. In case one of us runs into trouble. That way we truly don't know where the other person is. If it comes to that.'

'But I'm right here. And you know I'm not moving for a long time.'

'But my mind is bulletproof,' King said. 'So there's no risk of them finding out where you are.'

'And mine isn't?'

'We're close. But I don't know you that well. I don't know you down to your core.'

'Have a guess.'

'I'd guess there's nothing to worry about.'

'Good.'

King said, 'What will you do?'

'After this?'

King nodded.

'Walk around. Put my nose where it doesn't belong. That always leads to something. You know how it is.'

King nodded again.

He said, 'I'd recommend you get out while you still can, but I know you won't listen to me.'

'Would you have listened when you had your own fire?'

'Of course not.'

'Then let me do my thing.'

'Go for your life.'

King got to his feet. There was something final about it. Something symbolic.

'Don't call, Slater,' he said. 'Even if the world's ending. Because my world ends if you call.'

Slater said nothing. Just nodded.

King said, 'Do you think I'm selfish?'

'No,' Slater said. 'I think you're done. For good.'

King nodded, and turned toward the doorway.

Slater said, 'For now.'

King turned back and rolled his eyes. 'Give me a break.'

'I don't know how you'll feel a year from now. And you can say you do, but you really don't. Deep down in your core. You haven't got the faintest clue. Because we're similar in more ways than you think. And I know me. Which means I know you.'

Now, King didn't respond.

Just nodded.

'You're like the reckless younger brother I never had,' he said. 'Always trying to drag me back.'

'If I'm the younger brother, then we have the same blood.'

'Maybe.'

After a long pause, Slater said, 'Be seeing you?'

King just looked at him.

Then he left.

Strode through the doorway and disappeared.

Nothing grandiose about it.

One second there, then gone the next.

Vanishing into the shadows, without a trace.

Slater knew where to find him. He hadn't a clue if King would answer when he called.

But he figured he would need to call. Eventually. Because as he settled back into the pillows in the corner of the empty room and watched the light from the fireside dance across the ceiling, he realised he was destined to seek confrontation until the day he died. Whether that be three weeks, three years, or three decades from now. The warmth of the small wood-panelled room comforted him like a warm blanket.

He would stay here for as long as he needed.

Days.

Weeks.

Months.

Until the headaches disappeared. Until he returned to his normal self. Maybe he would ease back into training when the concussion started to recede. He could probably strike a deal with the owner of the combat gym on the outskirts of Vladivostok. Sneak out in the dead of night and train until his lungs screamed for mercy, concealed by the shadows as all of Russia bristled with conflict.

Because certain details would leak in the coming days. King would make sure of that. A grand conspiracy aboard a nuclear-powered icebreaker. A disgraced politician with a twisted, broken, nihilistic mind. A pair of Mikhailov brothers with profit set to the highest priority and no limits to their depravity.

And a woman.

A worker at the Medved Shipbuilding Plant.

Swallowed up by the evil side of the bear.

There was no justice. Ruslan and Iosif had died grotesquely, painfully, but it didn't bring Natasha back. She'd still suffered the same fate. For no good reason.

Dead at the hands of a sociopathic businessman with more money than he knew what to do with.

The bear had been hungry in Vladivostok.

Slater closed his eyes, trying his hardest to forget. But he never would.

Inside, his own fire raged.

It always would.

MORE WILL SLATER THRILLERS COMING SOON...

Visit amazon.com/author/mattrogers23 and press "**Follow**" to be automatically notified of my future releases.

If you enjoyed the hard-hitting adventure, make sure to leave a review! Your feedback means everything to me, and encourages me to deliver more novels as soon as I can.

Stay tuned.

Join the Reader's Group and get a free 200-page book by Matt Rogers!

Sign up for a free copy of '**HARD IMPACT**'.
Meet Jason King — another member of Black Force.

Experience King's most dangerous mission — action-packed insanity in the heart of the Amazon Rainforest.

No spam guaranteed.

Just click here.

BOOKS BY MATT ROGERS

THE JASON KING SERIES

Isolated (Book 1)

Imprisoned (Book 2)

Reloaded (Book 3)

Betrayed (Book 4)

Corrupted (Book 5)

Hunted (Book 6)

THE JASON KING FILES

Cartel (Book 1)

Warrior (Book 2)

Savages (Book 3)

THE WILL SLATER SERIES

Wolf (Book 1)

Lion (Book 2)

Bear (Book 3)

BLACK FORCE SHORTS

The Victor (Book 1)

The Chimera (Book 2)

The Tribe (Book 3)

The Hidden (Book 4)

The Coast (Book 5)

The Storm (Book 6)

The Wicked (Book 7)

The King (Book 8)

The Joker (Book 9)

ABOUT THE AUTHOR

Matt Rogers grew up in Melbourne, Australia as a voracious reader, relentlessly devouring thrillers and mysteries in his spare time. Now, he writes full-time. His novels are action-packed and fast-paced. Dive into the Jason King Series to get started with his collection.

Visit his website:

www.mattrogersbooks.com

Visit his Amazon page:

amazon.com/author/mattrogers23

Made in United States
North Haven, CT
30 May 2022

19670700R00236